SWEENEY SISTERS SERIES

lowcountry stranger

a novel

ASHLEY FARLEY

Also by Ashley Farley

Breaking the Story
Merry Mary
Her Sister's Shoes
Saving Ben

For my mother, Joanne, my Lovie

One

SAM

A GENTLE BREEZE in the late afternoon of an early June day rustled the Spanish moss draped from the live oak trees, bringing with it the smell of the salty marsh to those gathered on the lawn for the wedding of the youngest of the Sweeney sisters. Women tugged their shawls tighter around their shoulders, thankful they'd remembered to bring a wrap for what promised to be a chilly evening ahead. The sun shimmered off the high tide on the inlet, casting Moss Creek Farm in a pale glow. The white-frame antebellum plantation house—with its green-black shutters, large columns, and wraparound porches—stood like a grand old dame, proud and dignified and handsome. A sailcloth tent with wooden poles and pennant flags waving from its peaks graced the upper lawn, encompassing the terraced area adjacent to the house. Servers dressed in tuxedo shirts and bow ties stood ready to pass trays of hors d'oeuvres and champagne-filled flutes. Their instruments in position, the four-member bluegrass band waited onstage for the minister's signal to begin the recessional music. A picture-perfect evening for Faith and Mike to begin their new lives together.

Samantha Sweeney thought her baby sister had never looked prettier in a simple sundress fashioned out of white eyelet, and a wreath of daisies atop her head, her mahogany locks cascading around her face in soft curls. The only jewelry she wore was a simple gold cross around her neck and pearl studs at her ears.

Sam approved of Faith's new husband, a one hundred percent improvement over her last. Mike's rosy cheeks glowed and his blue eyes sparkled as he stared down at his bride, promising to love and honor and cherish her all the days of their lives. Wearing a dress similar to her mother's, Faith's seven-year-old daughter, Bitsy, peeked out from her hiding place behind her mother's leg—a position the child had not ventured far from in nearly a year. Sam wondered how Faith and Mike managed intimacy with Bitsy a permanent fixture between them.

Sam smiled at her son, Jamie, who was sitting next to her on the right. Emotion suddenly overwhelmed her, as it often did, when she took in the sight of his handsome face, his dark curls, and coal eyes.

Jamie leaned over and whispered, "Bitsy looks terrified."

Sam clasped her hands in her lap. "Poor baby. I'm not sure she'll ever fully recover from her ordeal." She closed her eyes as she thought about the three-week murderous rampage Bitsy's father, Curtis, had gone on the previous summer, traumatizing his daughter and threatening the entire Sweeney family.

Sam caught sight of a doe-eyed beauty with honey-colored hair in the row opposite them on the groom's side. Something about the teenager seemed familiar, although Sam was certain she'd never met her before.

"Do you know her?" Sam asked, dipping her head at the girl across from them.

Jamie cast a quick glance across the aisle, and then did a double take. "Nope. I've never seen her before."

"She's kind of pretty, don't you think?" Sam nudged him with her elbow.

Jamie had come home from his freshman year at the University of South Carolina talking nonstop about a raven-haired beauty he'd met in his Psych 101 class. In that good-natured way moms tease their sons, Sam had tried to tempt him with mention of some of the local girls, his past girlfriends, but so far he'd remained steadfast to Sophia.

"Nice try, Mom," he whispered. "But I prefer girls who bathe."

Sam's eyes followed her son's to the ground where the girl's filthy feet rested in a pair of dollar store rubber flip-flops. On closer inspection, Sam noticed she was wearing denim cutoffs and a red halter top, inappropriate attire no matter how casual the wedding. Her hair was matted and tangled, and her chocolate eyes overpowered her too-thin face.

"She must be a friend of Faith's," Sam said, and Jamie added, "Or one of Mike's coworkers from the hospital."

Mother and son returned their attention to the bride and groom.

The Methodist minister who had baptized all three Sweeney sisters pronounced the couple husband and wife. Mike kissed Faith on the lips, a kiss that lasted longer than their mother would approve of but brought cheers from the congregation. When the band launched into the recessional music, Mike swooped Bitsy up in his arms and the new family retreated down the aisle and across the lawn toward the house.

Seated on her left, Sam's boyfriend of twelve months draped his arm around her shoulder and drew her body close to his. "They look so happy. Aren't you the least bit tempted to take the plunge?" Eli asked, his breath tickling her ear.

She gave him a quick peck on the lips. "We've been through this a thousand times, Eli. You know where I stand on the issue of marriage. We don't need a license to validate our feelings for one another."

She was growing tired of the argument. Eli was the right man for her. Of that, she had little doubt. Problem was, he wanted to take the next step, and she remained terrified of commitment.

The crowd was beginning to disperse when the oldest of the Sweeney sisters joined the minister at the altar. Jackie clapped her hands. "If I could have your attention for just a moment, please."

Why does she always have to be the center of attention? Sam wondered, and then chastised herself at the sudden resurgence of animosity toward her older sister. Much of her bitterness toward Jackie had dissipated during the past year, and their relationship had grown stronger because of it. She would have to work harder to control her feelings.

"I'd like to welcome you to Moss Creek Farm." Jackie opened her arms wide. "The bride and groom will take a few minutes to pose for photographs. In the meantime, please help yourself to refreshments." She gestured toward the tent.

As the band transitioned from the traditional recessional music to James Taylor's "Carolina in My Mind," the crowd began to gather their belongings and make their way up the hill toward the house.

Sam's mother, Lovie, who had been sitting in the row in

front of them, turned around to greet them. "I'm sorry we didn't have a chance to say hello before the ceremony. I was running late, and I noticed you were as well. That was some kind of crazy day we had at the market," she said, referring to Captain Sweeney's Seafood, which she and her husband, Oscar, opened in 1959.

"Tell me about it. I hope that's the kind of business we see for the rest of the summer."

"I've never known Jackie to wear pink, but I must say it suits her," Lovie said.

Jackie had always sworn off all shades of pink, but the fuchsia silk wrap dress was testament to her recent change in personality. Her hairstylist had recently cut layers in her shoulder-length dark hair, which softened her angles, making her face look fuller. Less stark. Less harsh.

Sam leaned over and kissed her mother's cheek. "Yes it does, Mama, as much as this shade of coral suits you."

"Humph, this god-awful suit? Jackie insisted on buying it for me last year when she was convinced I was on my death-bed. Whatever you do, don't let her bury me in it."

"I'll try to remember that." Laughing, Sam turned her attention to the man standing beside her mother. "I hope you realize how much of a blessing you are to us, Mack." She stood on her tiptoes and pressed her lips to the gray bristles on his cheek. "If not for you, she would have shown up in her paja-mas," she said in a low voice her mother couldn't hear.

Lovie's quirky behavior of late had driven many of their close friends to worry about her mental stability. Some thought her a candidate for the funny farm while others feared she was in the early stages of Alzheimer's, despite the recent battery of tests at MUSC in Charleston that proved otherwise.

Regardless of her mental state, the Sweeney sisters were relieved to have Captain Mack Bowman playing an important role in their mother's life. Although none of them dared to speculate about what that role entailed.

"Taking care of your mother is my pleasure," Mack said, giving Lovie's shoulder a gentle squeeze. He removed a bandana from his coat pocket and mopped his brow. "It's hot as daylights out here. Is anybody ready for some refreshments?"

Eli and Mack took drink orders and headed off to the bar, leaving Sam alone with her mother and son. They fell in line behind the throng of wedding attendees and slowly made their way to the tent. They spotted Jackie and her estranged husband, Bill, deep in conversation at the edge of the dance floor near the food tables. From recent conversations with her sister, Sam was under the impression Jackie and Bill were working through their marital problems. But the somber expressions on their faces indicated otherwise.

Sam kissed the air beside her sister's cheek. "You've done it again, Jackie. This is an amazing party."

Lovie wrapped her arm around her oldest daughter's waist, giving her a quick squeeze. "You should wear pink more often. You look ten years younger."

Jackie offered them a stiff smile before returning her attention to whatever, or whoever, was distracting her on the other side of the party.

"Is something wrong?" Sam followed her sister's gaze to the food table where the honey-haired beauty from across the aisle was standing with Jackie's seventeen-year-old sons, Cooper and Sean.

The boys' orange hair emphasized their bright personalities. Nearly every girl under the age of twenty in the town of Prospect had a crush on one, if not both, of the identical twins. Until now, Cooper and Sean had been too preoccupied with outdoor activities like fishing and hunting to express much interest in girls, but based on their lazy grins and the glint in their deep blue eyes, they were both smitten with this doe-eyed creature. The twins were too busy competing for the girl's attention to notice her stuffing her tattered hobo bag with sweet potato ham biscuits.

"Did someone invite that sea urchin to this party, or did she wash ashore with the high tide?" Jackie asked, her lip curled up in distaste.

"Jamie and I were wondering about her earlier," Sam said. "Do you know who she is, Mom?"

Lovie shook her head no. "But I must say my grandsons look so handsome in their blue blazers and my granddaughter as sweet as a little princess in her crown of daisies."

"Never mind about your grandchildren, Mom," Jackie said. "I'm worried about my party. If someone doesn't stop that girl from stealing my biscuits, there won't be any left for the other guests."

Lovie poked her finger in Jamie's ribs. "Go find out who she is. But be sure to come back and fill us in on all the details."

Jamie shook his head in amusement as he ventured across the terrace toward the food tables.

Eli and Mack arrived with their drinks—a cranberry seltzer for Sam and a glass of Chardonnay for Lovie.

"What's wrong?" Eli asked when he noticed their frowns.

"We're at a wedding, not a funeral," Mack said, the ever-present stub of a cigar stuffed between his lips. He raised his hands as if to lift everyone's spirits. "This is supposed to be a happy occasion."

Bill inclined his head toward the honey-haired girl. "It appears as though we have a wedding crasher in our midst."

"And she's stealing all the sweet potato biscuits," Jackie added.

Eli stiffened. A sergeant on the local police force, his responsibility was to protect the innocent citizens of Prospect. He didn't take kindly to theft, even if the loot was perishable.

With rapt attention, they watched the scene unfold. Bitsy tugged on Jamie's coat sleeve and he knelt down beside her, tucking her hair behind her ear and kissing her forehead. He whispered something in her ear and she awarded him with a smile, showing off her two new permanent front teeth.

Despite the difference in their ages, Jamie and Bitsy were closer than most siblings. Less than a year ago, Sam's son had tried to commit suicide after an ATV accident claimed the life of his best friend and left Jamie paralyzed from the waist down. His young cousin was, in part, responsible for him regaining the use of his legs. Jamie, in turn, had comforted Bitsy through the emotional trauma she'd suffered from her father.

Jamie straightened, and, placing his hands on Bitsy's shoulders, presented her to the sea urchin. The girl bent down in order to speak to the little girl at eye level. Bitsy took the wedding crasher's face in her tiny hands, turning her head so she could whisper in her ear. Cupping their hands around their mouths, the girls took turns telling secrets like they were old friends. Never mind that Bitsy hadn't spoken a word to anyone in nearly a year.

Two

FAITH

FAITH AND MIKE stood in the middle of the dance
floor, waiting for the band to play music for their first
dance as husband and wife.

"Happy?" Mike asked, smiling at his bride.

Faith leaned into him. "I didn't know it was possible to be
this happy." She clasped her hands around his neck and kissed
him softly on the lips. "You saved my life, Dr. Neilson."

Mike took her in his arms. "You give me too much credit,
Mrs. Neilson. All I offered was a shoulder to cry on. Your family did the rest."

The band began to play Faith's favorite song, "Crazy"
by Patsy Cline. The country music love ballad brought back
memories of watching her parents slow dance in the living
room of the tiny house adjacent to Moss Creek Farm where
she grew up.

Faith placed her head on her new husband's shoulder,
thinking of her marriage as a Cinderella story come true. She
was now the wife of an emergency room doctor, living in the

house of her dreams, when eleven months ago she'd been married to an abusive man, residing in a trailer in the middle of the woods.

Mike had been the attending physician when Faith sought treatment in the emergency room at Creekside Regional Hospital for the broken bones she'd suffered at the hand of her sadistic husband. Mike had taken a special interest in her. Once Curtis was behind bars, he took her to dinner and their romance began to blossom. In the months since, he'd provided Faith and Bitsy with love and stability.

The song ended and the band launched into a more upbeat tune. A giant of a black man tapped Mike on the shoulder. "Do you mind if I dance with the bride?"

Mike reluctantly handed over his new wife. "Only for you, Moses," he said, slapping the man on the back.

Known to his friends and patients as Big Mo, the black titan was the Georgia linebacker turned adolescent shrink currently counseling the majority of the Sweeney family, old and young. With the exception of Lovie who probably needed therapy the most. Sam had recently joked that their family, alone, was responsible for the down payment on Big Mo's new waterfront condo.

"You look absolutely radiant tonight," Moses said as he swung Faith around the dance floor. "You've changed a lot from the timid woman I met a year ago. You've come a long way, and you deserve this happiness."

Faith beamed. "I couldn't have done it without you."

Moses shook his head. "I can only take credit for the guidance. You did all the hard work."

Her ex-husband's reign of terror had ended in a standoff that had taken place less than twenty-five feet from where she was now dancing with Moses. And Curtis, with a long list of convictions including several counts of attempted murder, was now imprisoned at the Broad River Correctional Institution in Columbia, where he would not be eligible for parole until 2040. Although Faith, for the most part, had come to terms with the havoc he had wreaked on her family, her daughter had not bounced back so quickly. The poor child had seemed fine immediately following her father's arrest, but then woke up from a terrible nightmare and hadn't spoken a word since.

During the past school year, Faith and Bitsy had been living in the guest cottage at Moss Creek Farm, helping Bill out with the twins while Jackie sorted through her midlife crisis in Charleston. Moses had assured Faith that she was doing the right thing by marrying Mike and moving into their new house together.

"Putting your life on hold for your daughter is the absolute wrong thing for both of you," he'd said. "Sending Bitsy the message that her needs come first could cause irrevocable damage in the long run."

While she trusted Moses implicitly, Faith worried she was putting her vulnerable daughter through too many changes at once. A new father *and* a new home. Moss Creek Farm was the one place Bitsy felt safe, where Cooper and Sean showered her with affection and her Uncle Bill's even-tempered personality provided a stable presence.

Moses's body went rigid and he froze in the middle of the dance floor. "Well, I'll be damn. Would you look at that."

"What?" Faith asked, searching the crowd for the object of Moses's interest.

He spun her around ninety degrees until Bitsy was in her direct line of sight. "That, my friend, is your daughter, having what appears to be a meaningful conversation with that waif of a young woman. Do you know who she is, by the way?"

Faith squinted, taking in the teenage girl's unkempt appearance. "I've never seen her before in my life." Her hand flew to her mouth. "I can't believe she's talking. My traumatized daughter has finally come out of her shell. I need to get to her."

When she started off the dance floor, Moses gripped her arm tight. "Not so fast, Faith. This is the wrong time for you to hover. Rushing to her side might make Bitsy angry or scare the waif away."

"But—"

Moses tightened his grip on her arm. "Listen to me. I definitely think you should keep an eye on her, but do it from a distance. Tomorrow, when you have some time alone with your daughter, ask her what she talked about with the girl. My guess is, you'll get more out of her if you try not to make a big deal about it."

"You're right, of course. You always are." Faith threw her arms around the big man. "You did it, Moses. You worked a miracle."

She led Moses off the dance floor, but they were quickly swept up and separated by the crowd. A woman she'd never met before grabbed Faith by the arm. "Best wishes to the bride," the woman said, pressing her cheek against Faith's. "We've never met, but I'm Chloe Morrison, a friend of Mike's from the hospital."

Faith mentally reviewed the invitation list, but she couldn't remember seeing the name Chloe Morrison. "So nice of you to come," Faith managed. She couldn't put her finger on exactly what, but something about the woman made her feel uneasy. Her hair was dyed an unnatural shade of blonde, like wet sand on the beach at low tide, and her blue eyes were so cold they gave Faith the chills.

As Chloe dug her fingers into Faith's arm, she said in a bitter voice, "Aren't you the lucky girl marrying a doctor and working your way up from a rundown trailer in the woods to a beautiful new house on the water."

Faith wrenched her arm free. "If you'll excuse me, I need to tend to my other guests," she said, and hurried away.

Spotting her sisters over near the food tables, laughing and carrying on with Eli, Faith dismissed the strange woman from her mind and navigated her way over to them.

Sam offered Faith a high five. "Isn't it wonderful? Your daughter is finally talking again."

"I can hardly believe it." Faith beamed. "But who's the girl? Who's Bitsy talking to?"

"We have no idea," Sam said. "We were hoping you could shed some light on that little detail, since you're the bride and this is your party."

"I'm telling you," Jackie said. "That girl is an urchin from the sea, washed in with the tide."

They watched as Cooper handed the sea urchin a plate piled high with barbecue and the fixings. She shoveled in the food as if she hadn't eaten in days.

"I'd say we have ourselves a real live wedding crasher," Jackie said.

Sam shot their older sister a look like she'd lost her mind. "Don't be ridiculous. Someone here knows who she is."

Remembering the strange woman she'd just encountered, Faith said, "Mike invited some of his coworkers from the hospital. Maybe she's one of his friends."

"I doubt that," Jackie said. "Cleanliness is a prerequisite for employment at the hospital. That girl hasn't seen the inside of a shower stall in a very long time, judging from her greasy hair and the dirt beneath her nails."

Sam rolled her eyes at Jackie. "Give the girl a break. She's just a kid."

Faith surveyed the crowd for her groom. When she spotted him on the other side of the dance floor with some of his colleagues, she waved him over. "Mike, do you know who that girl is over there with Bitsy and the boys?"

He shot a quick glance in the direction of the Sweeney cousins. "No. Why?"

Faith leaned in closer to her new husband. "Because Bitsy has broken her silence, and it seems that girl is responsible."

Mike shut his eyes tight, then opened them again wide. "Did you just say Bitsy is talking?"

Faith bobbed her head up and down so hard her wreath of daisies came loose.

"Looks like we have double reason to celebrate." Mike signaled for a waiter, who was passing out champagne. When everyone had a flute in hand, Mike offered a toast to his bride, followed by another to his soon-to-be adopted daughter.

Sam held up her cranberry spritzer. "And to the girl who broke Bitsy's silence."

"Hold on a minute," Eli said, interrupting the celebration. "I think maybe your uninvited guest may have overstayed her welcome."

They returned their attention to the sea urchin. They watched, mortified, as the girl lifted a wallet out of the back pocket of the man standing in front of her. Oblivious to her new friend's crime, Bitsy continued to dance around her cousins' legs as they snuck sips of beer from red Solo cups.

When Eli's face grew dark and his body stiffened, Sam grabbed his arm. "Please, Eli," she begged. "Don't burst Bitsy's bubble."

"I'm an officer of the law. I can't ignore the fact that she just pick pocketed that man." Eli pried Sam's fingers off his arm and turned away from them, making swift strides toward the girl. When she saw him coming, she took off across the lawn. She bowled over a waiter bearing a tray of dirty glasses and kept on running. The band stopped playing at the sound of the commotion. The crowd stood motionless, watching Eli chase the girl down the hill and out of their sight.

Three

JACKIE

B Y THE TIME Jackie and Sam caught up with Eli, he was helping the wedding crasher up from where he'd tackled her on the ground. "I need to see some identification," he said, gripping her arm tight.

"Please, Eli. Do we have to do this here, with everyone watching?" Jackie gestured at the dance floor where their guests stood gaping like spectators at the circus.

Eli stole a quick glance at the party of onlookers. "Let's go inside then, where we can talk." He waved at the band. "Everything is fine here. Just a misunderstanding. Please restart the music."

Needing no further encouragement, the band members resumed their play with a song from the Doobie Brothers.

Eli led the girl across the lawn to the house with the Sweeney family on his heels. They surrounded him in Jackie's upstairs living room, ready to pepper his suspect with questions.

Eli held his hand out to the girl. "I'd like to see that identification now, please."

The wedding crasher gnawed on her lower chapped lip. "I don't have any ID. My wallet was stolen."

He nodded at her hobo bag. "What's in there?" She clutched the bag tighter to her chest. "You know… just stuff."

When Eli threatened, "You can either hand it over willingly, or I'll take it from you by force," she gave it to him. He dumped the contents onto the coffee table in front of him, and watched as an assortment of food, mostly sweet potato biscuits, rolled out, along with a man's leather wallet and gold wristwatch.

"Hey! That's my watch." Bill picked it up and slipped it on his wrist. "Why, you little thief. I've been looking for this all afternoon."

"I didn't steal it. You left it by the water hose near the garage." The girl lowered her head, a curtain of stringy hair falling in her face. "You took it off when you washed the dogs earlier. I guess you forgot to put it back on."

A flash of anger crossed Jackie's face. "If that's not stealing, then what do you call it, Finder's Keepers?"

The girl held her chin high. "I'm not a thief. I needed some money for a bus ticket. I just thought… well, since you have plenty to spare. I didn't see any harm."

Jackie glared at the girl. "Have you been spying on us all afternoon?"

The wedding crasher shifted from one filthy foot to the other. "I wouldn't say I was spying, exactly. I was helping the catering people set up for the party."

"I should charge you with trespassing for lurking around on my property," Bill said, the overhead light shining off his balding head.

Everyone began talking at once, the younger Sweeneys

pleading with Bill not to bring charges while the older Swee-neys demanded answers from the intruder. "Who are you and why are you here?"

Eli raised his hands to silence the crowd. "All right, everyone, let's calm down and give this young lady a chance to explain." He turned to the girl. "You can start by telling us your name."

The girl's chin quivered. "Annie."

"Does Annie have a last name?" Eli asked.

Her eyes traveled the room before settling on the water-color above the mantel, a depiction of the sun rising over the inlet. "Um, Dawn. My name is Annie Dawn."

"Annie Dawn?" His eyebrows shot up in question. "Is that first and middle, or first and last?"

Annie avoided his gaze. "First and last."

"Okay, then. We'll go with Annie Dawn for now." Eli didn't believe the girl anymore than Jackie did. "You mentioned needing to buy a bus ticket, but you also said you were working for the catering company. Are you from around here, Annie Dawn? If so, I can call your parents and have them come pick you up."

Annie sighed. "No. I'm not from around here. And I don't work for the catering company either. I was just helping them set up. I'm from Florida. My mom is a maid at a seaside motel and my father works in construction, but he's been out of a job for going on three years. I'm trying to get to New York. I got a gig with a modeling agency up there."

Eli softened his tone. "Prospect is off the beaten track from most major highways. How did you end up here?"

"I hitchhiked most of the way. I got a ride in Georgia with this nice family, the Andersons. They have a real cute baby. Jason was his name. He has the chubbiest pink cheeks."

"What happened to the Andersons?" Eli asked.

Annie shrugged. "I'm not sure. We were on the way to the beach. They were going to take me with them, said they'd give me bus fare to New York if I helped take care of the baby for a week. Then they just ditched me. We stopped at a gas station outside of town. I went in to use the restroom, and when I came back out, they were gone. They took all of my stuff with them, including my wallet."

Eli rubbed his chin. "Sounds like the Andersons weren't such nice people after all. So… you said you were on your way to a job in New York. I find it surprising this modeling agency didn't offer to fly you up. Did you interview with them in person?"

Annie shook her head. "I met them online," she said, her lower lip quivering.

Eli moved closer to Annie. "Hey, now," he said, rubbing her back. "There's nothing to be ashamed of. Lots of kids your age fall for scams like these. I worked on the police force in New York for several years before I moved to Prospect. I met a lot of homeless kids who were out of money and living on the streets. Many of them came to the city under the same pretenses as you. You can't trust anyone you meet online these days."

Annie began to sob, and Lovie removed several wadded tissues from her purse. "We'll just have to figure out a way to get you home to your parents," she said, pressing the tissues in the girl's hand.

Perched astride her mother's hip, Bitsy removed her thumb from her mouth. "Can Annie be my babysitter, Mama?"

When the room broke out into laughter, Bitsy buried her face in her mother's neck.

"That's not a bad idea," Cooper said. "Now that Aunt Faith and Bitsy have moved out of the guest cottage, Annie can live here until she saves enough money to get home."

Jackie drew in an unsteady breath. For the past nine months, she'd commuted to Charleston during the week to manage her fledgling interior design firm. Admittedly, she'd taken a leave of absence from her duties as wife and mother to sort out her personal crisis and jumpstart the career of her dreams. She felt more confident and emotionally stable because of her hiatus. Her life had fallen apart, but she was slowly putting it back together. She'd hired two associates to manage the thriving business in Charleston, and she planned to spend the next three months with her boys, their summer before senior year. Even more important, she needed to find out if the few sparks left in her marriage could be ignited into a flame.

"I don't know, son," Jackie said. "That's asking a lot, not just of us but of Annie."

Annie perked up. "Oh, I don't mind. In fact, I'd be mighty grateful. Just for a while anyway."

Sean cozied up beside his mother. "Please, Mom," he said, and then added in a low whisper, "I think Annie could really use our help."

"We've been swamped at the market lately," Jamie said. "We could hire her to work the afternoons." Sam cast her son a warning glance, and he glared back at her. "What? You know it's true."

Jackie studied Annie more closely, noticing the steely determination in her big brown eyes. Beneath the mop of limp dirty locks, she appeared to be a stunning beauty. This sea creature temptress wasn't the type of girl Jackie would normally choose for her boys. Based on the way they hovered close to Annie, hanging on her every word, they were already gaga over her. Having Annie living in their guest cottage could cause a rift between the twins if they continued to vie for her attention. On the other hand, she couldn't turn her back on the poor child. Jackie felt something for the girl, although she was still confused about what that something was. She sensed a certain spunk, a resilience to tough breaks. And Oscar and Lovie Sweeney had always taught their daughters that to whom much is given much is expected. And Jackie had certainly been given a lot.

"Why don't you kids go back to the party and let the grown-ups talk," Jackie said to their expectant faces. "Tell the caterers we're almost ready to cut the cake."

Oldest to youngest, the Sweeney cousins plus Annie filed out of the room and down the stairs. As soon as the children were gone, Sam said, "I think we might be getting ahead of ourselves by taking in a stranger, regardless of her circumstances. There is still the matter of the stolen watch and wallet." She looked pointedly at Jackie. "Are you sure you're comfortable having a girl who steals things living on your property?"

Faith cleared her throat. "I can't just turn my back on this girl after what she's done for my daughter. I don't need to remind you that Bitsy hasn't spoken to any of us in nearly a year. For some reason she trusts Annie. And that means something to me."

Bill tossed his hands in the air. "Why not just give her the money for a bus ticket?"

"We can't just ship her off to New York," Jackie scoffed. "She'll be bait for the wolves that prey on girls fresh off the farm."

"I agree. New York is no place for girls like Annie. She won't survive the year." Eli paused to consider the situation. "If you decide to let her stay, I'm willing to keep an eye on her for you. I'll make it clear to her that she'll be in serious trouble if she breaks the law again."

Her arms akimbo, Lovie said, "If it's too much for Annie to stay here at the farm, I'm happy to have her stay at my place."

"Mom, please," Sam said. "The last thing you need is a teenage boarder."

Mike stole a glance at his wristwatch. "I've only been a member of this family for two hours and twenty minutes, so my opinion doesn't carry much weight. But I'm sure Bitsy would love for Annie to come and live with us." He blushed from head to toe when Faith kissed his plump cheek in approval.

Jackie turned to Mack next to her. "You're unusually quiet tonight. What do you think?" She'd always valued his opinion, even more so since her father had passed away six years ago.

Mack's face reddened and a bead of sweat appeared along his brow. "This girl has already proven her worthiness to the family by getting Bitsy to talk again. I think she at least deserves a chance."

"That leaves you, Moses," Sam said. "Where do you stand in all this?"

He chuckled. "I didn't realize I had a say in Sweeney family business."

"Don't be ridiculous," Sam snorted. "None of us is capable of making a decision without your input."

Moses smiled. "In that case, as long as everyone understands the boundaries, I say give it a shot. If we're lucky, Annie might help facilitate the breakthrough we've been hoping for in Bitsy."

Jackie raised an eyebrow in question at her husband across the room. He responded with a why-not shrug. "Sounds like we're all in agreement, except for you, Sam."

"Me? What about you?" Sam jabbed a finger in Jackie's direction. "*You're* the one who called her a sea urchin and a wedding crasher earlier."

"True, but I think maybe I was too hard on her," Jackie said. "Like you said earlier, she's just a kid."

"I'm fine with letting her stay as long as we proceed with caution," Sam said. "Jamie is right. We could use an extra set of hands at the market."

"And I'll hire her to babysit for Bitsy during the mornings while I'm at work," Faith said.

"Then it's settled," Jackie said. "For the time being, Annie will stay here at the farm, in the guest house."

Four

SAM

FRIENDS AND FAMILY gathered on the dock to throw handfuls of rose petals and blow bubbles at the bride, groom, and Bitsy as they made their getaway. The party wound down quickly after that. Despite the rejoicing that had transpired that evening, Sam departed Moss Creek Farm with a heavy heart. Preoccupied with the mounting concerns about her relationship with Eli, she hadn't felt like herself in weeks.

She stared out the car window on the way home, lost in thoughts, her mind replaying the events of the evening, while Eli and Jamie carried on about the local man who had broken the state flounder record earlier that day.

Eli squeezed her thigh. "You're awfully quiet. Is something bothering you?"

"I can't stop thinking about this Annie Dawn character. I can't put my finger on it, but something about her gives me the willies." Shivering, Sam wrapped her pashmina tighter around her shoulders.

"No kidding." Jamie reached over from the backseat and

ruffled his mother's short hair. "I'd say you already made your feelings about Annie Dawn pretty clear."

Sam shifted in the passenger seat to face him. "I wasn't rude to her, if that's what you're implying. I just wasn't as quick to forgive her crimes as the rest of you."

Jamie shrugged. "I'm surprised you're so down on her, when you're usually the first to help others in need. That's all I'm saying."

Perhaps she *was* taking her frustrations with her personal life out on Annie.

Sam turned to Eli. "What about you, Mr. Policeman? She stole Bill's watch, for crying out loud. You, yourself, saw her pick pocket that man. Which is something I'd expect to happen on a crowded street in a big city, not at a private wedding at someone's home."

"There's some truth to that. But, as we all agreed earlier, she's just a kid who deserves a break." Eli waited for traffic to clear before turning left at the main intersection in the center of town. "Don't worry. I fully intend to honor my promise by keeping a close eye on her."

"You'll change your mind about Annie, once you get to know her," Jamie said. "She's smart. She's only sixteen, but she acts like she's thirty. And she knows a lot about guy stuff. I'm glad she's staying. She'll be fun to hang out with this summer."

Eli sought out Jamie in the rearview mirror. "Do I detect more than a platonic interest in Annie?"

"You know I'm in a relationship with Sophia," Jamie said with a wide grin. "Now Cooper and Sean, they're a different story."

Sam chuckled. "I noticed. Funny thing is, Annie seems more interested in Bitsy than either of the twins."

Eli pulled into the driveway of the yellow Cape Cod cottage and parked in front of the detached garage. Jamie reached for the door handle. "I'll leave you two lovebirds to do whatever it is you do when you're alone. But don't stay up too late now, you hear?"

They watched Jamie disappear around the back of the house. "He seems like he is in a good place," Eli said. "I know it hasn't been easy for you raising him alone, but you have done a great job with him."

"Thanks, Eli. I am proud of the young man he's become. But the truth is, Jamie and I would never have survived without my family's help."

Eli ran his finger down her cheek, and then traced her lips. "Have I told you how hot you look tonight?"

She smiled. "About a million times."

Placing his hand on her neck, he pulled Sam to him, kissing her gently on the lips, and then with more urgency. "Can I interest you in a make out session on the front porch swing?"

"Perhaps," she said, her voice throaty with desire.

He rubbed the silky fabric of her ice-blue sheath between his fingers. "This dress looks amazing on you, but I'd rather see it lying on the floor while your naked body lies next to me in bed." He ran his hand across her breast."

Her breath caught. "I thought we were going to make out in the swing."

He pressed his lips against her neck. "I changed my mind. I can't grope your breast on the front porch."

She rubbed her body against his. "That's never stopped you before."

Eli fell back against the driver's seat. "Because Jamie has been away at college for most of the year." He raked his hands through his dark wavy hair. "I feel like I'm making out in the driveway in the family station wagon while your father is inside pacing the floors waiting for you to come in."

Sam laughed. "I can assure you Jamie has no interest in what we're doing out here. If he's not already asleep, he's texting with one of his friends or talking to Sophia on the phone." She opened the door and got out of the car. "Come on. Let's sit on the porch for a while and talk."

Sam and Eli walked hand and hand around to the front of the house. They settled in on the bench swing and sat in silence for a while, listening to the crickets chirp. The sweet smell of confederate jasmine, growing in the flower bed that bordered the porch at their feet, filled the air. Sam tilted her head back against the swing and closed her eyes. "That breeze feels nice. It won't be long before it's too hot and humid to sit out here."

"Only a few days if the weather forecast is accurate." Eli snuggled up close to Sam. "I wonder what Faith and Mike are doing right now—certainly not making out on the front porch swing."

"I doubt they are making out at all with Bitsy around." Sam cracked one eyelid. "I'm sorry. I didn't mean that the way it sounded. My poor niece has been through so much for someone so young. How great was it to hear her talking again tonight?"

"Pretty terrific. I've missed hearing her call Faith 'Mama' in her sweet Southern drawl."

"Hopefully the worst is behind Bitsy, but I doubt she's completely cured," Sam said.

"She may never be completely cured. But they'll work through their issues together, as a family." Eli placed his arm around Sam, and pulled her close, giving her a gentle squeeze. "We could be a family too, you know? Just the three of us—you, me, and Jamie."

Sam drew away from him. "Do we have to talk about this tonight?"

"Yes, Sam, as a matter of fact we *do* have to talk about this tonight." Retracting his arm, Eli sat up straight. "I've been trying to have this conversation with you for months. We aren't teenagers, you know. We're middle-aged adults who have been dating for nearly a year. Marriage is the next logical step for us, and I, for one, am ready to take the plunge. You owe it to me to at least tell me how you feel."

"You already know how I feel."

Eli's mouth fell open. "How could I possibly know how you feel when you shut me down every time I mention our future?"

Sam jumped up. "You want to know how I feel, then I'll tell you how I feel," she said, her voice a loud whisper. "I love you, Eli Marshall. You and I respect one another, which is a rare thing these days. At least with most couples I know. We have fun together. And the sex is mind-boggling. I don't see how a marriage license could possibly make our relationship any better."

He stood to face her. "For starters, we wouldn't be sitting out here on a swing. We'd be lying in our bed together, in *our* bedroom, in *our* house, exploring each other's body parts."

"I see. This is all about sex," she said, her voice a soft hiss. "You're upset because I won't make love to you while my son is under the same roof. If it means that much to you, Eli, we can go to your apartment."

"This is not about sex and you know it. Sit back down

and let's talk about this rationally." He dropped down to the swing, pulling her with him. "I have enough money saved to buy a small house on the inlet, nothing as fancy as Moss Creek Farm but something we could be proud of. I want to grow old with you, watching the sun rise and set every day over the water." He lifted her chin. "I love you, Sam. And I love Jamie, every bit as much as if he were my own son. I'm pretty sure he sees me more as a friend than a father, but our relationship is strong. Marriage is the next natural step. I, for one, don't see what the problem is."

"The problem is marriage in general. Too many of them end in divorce. Look at Faith and Curtis."

"You can't compare us to them. Curtis is a sadistic asshole who deserves to spend the rest of his life in prison for putting his wife and child through hell."

Sam crossed her arms over her chest. "What about Bill and Jackie? He cheated on her for crying out loud."

"Their problems stem deeper than his infidelity, as you well know." Eli stared out into the dark night. "I actually admire them for admitting their mistakes and trying to work through their problems."

"But Jamie needs me—"

"That's a cop out, and we both know it. No doubt your son needed you this time last year when he was confined to a wheelchair, struggling with depression, but all that is behind him. He doesn't need you now. He got his baseball scholarship back. He's making solid grades. And he can't stop talking about the redhead named Sophia."

"You don't understand, Eli. Jamie and I are a family, the two of us against the world. That's all we've ever known."

"Are you saying there's no room for one more?"

"I'm saying there's no reason to upset the apple cart," she said, her chin set in defiance.

Eli slid over on the swing, putting distance between them. "I hate to tell you, my friend, but the apple cart is losing a wheel whether you want it to or not. Jamie is already in college. He lives in Columbia for the majority of the year. The coach redshirted him this year, but he'll be playing, maybe even starting, from now on. He'll be lucky to get a month off next summer. He'll get married one day, and I can't see him bringing his bride home to live with his mama." He softened his tone. "You'll make it that much harder for Jamie to fly the coop if he is worried about you being alone. Your son wants you to be happy."

An awkward silence settled between them. Sam tried to imagine her life without Eli. Her love for him was not in question. But she worried it wasn't enough.

Finally able to put voice to the concerns she'd had for the past few weeks, she said, "You're younger than I am, Eli. You need to find someone you can start a family with. You'll make a good father. Being a parent is the greatest joy in life. I don't want to be the one who deprives you of that opportunity."

"I can have all that with Jamie."

"Jamie will be twenty years old in December. Going fishing with a young man his age is a far cry from holding a newborn in your arms." Sam stood and pulled Eli to his feet. "I have loved you with every fiber of my being these past months, but I can't hold you back from finding the woman you're meant to be with."

"*You* are the woman I'm meant to be with. There has never been any doubt for me." He took her by the arms and looked so deep into her eyes she was sure he could see her heart breaking into pieces. "You forget how well I know you. And I sense there's more you're not saying. Talk to me, Sam. Tell me what's really bothering you."

"I'm sorry, Eli. I just can't give you what you need."

He raked his hands through his wavy hair. "You've had an emotional night, with the excitement of the wedding, Bitsy breaking her silence, and the drama with Annie. Please, don't make this decision until you've had a chance to think about it." His voice was full of desperation. "Get a good night's sleep, and we'll talk again in the morning."

"There's nothing left to say. Thank you for all you've done for my family and me." She kissed him on the cheek. "But I have to say goodbye." She turned her back on him and went inside.

Through the window, she watched him, head lowered and shoulders slumped, make his way to his police cruiser parked on the curb. Although Sam sensed that she was making the biggest mistake of her life, she was convinced that breaking up with Eli was the right thing for both of them.

When his taillights disappeared down the street, Sam turned off the porch lights and locked the front door. Careful not to wake Jamie, she tiptoed through the house to the kitchen, switching off lamps along the way. She opened one cabinet, then another. She'd long since removed every drop of alcohol from her house, but that didn't stop her from searching anyway.

She'd never been much of a drinker until the previous summer when Curtis had threatened their family and nearly destroyed Sam's house, when she'd sought solace in a glass of wine, which had quickly become an addiction. As the officer assigned to her case, Eli had been there for Sam both in a professional capacity and then on a more personal level once their mutual attraction began to grow. A recovering alcoholic himself, Eli helped Sam understand that she couldn't blame her alcoholism on Curtis. The addiction had been there all along, lying dormant, waiting for a spark to fly and light the flame. Eli nurtured Sam through those dark days and set her on the twelve-step plan to a clean life.

Who would chase the ghosts from her closet, if not Eli? She opened another cabinet. He deserved so much better than her.

Jamie appeared in the doorway. "What are you looking for?"

"A drink." She slammed the cabinet door and turned to face him. "You don't happen to have any beer hidden in your closet, do you?"

He scrunched his face up in confusion. "Since when do I hide beer in my *closet*?"

"Isn't that what teenagers do? I've heard other mothers talk about it."

"Not this teenager." When she reached for another cabinet, he grabbed her hand. "Why do you need a drink, Mom?" He took her by the shoulders, forcing her to look at him. "Tell me what's wrong."

Unable to hold back the tears any longer, she said, "Eli and I broke up."

A pained expression crossed her son's face. "But that doesn't make any sense. The two of you love each other."

"That's the problem. Sometimes love just isn't enough."

Five

FAITH

FAITH WOKE THE following morning to find her
daughter sleeping peacefully, sucking her thumb, wedged
between her body and Mike's. She noticed her new husband
staring at her. "Not the most romantic way to begin our life
together," she whispered. "I should have taken Jackie up on
her offer to let Bitsy stay at the farm last night. At least we
would've had our wedding night to ourselves."

He smiled, his adoration for Faith written all over his
face. "You made the right decision about last night. We'll
have plenty of time for romance later, once she settles into her
new home."

Mike and Faith had talked about it at length before the
wedding. They wanted to send the right message to their
daughter, that the marriage was the beginning of their lives
together as a family. With Bitsy in silent mode, Faith had no
way of knowing how her daughter felt about Mike, aside from
her actions. Bitsy appeared to enjoy his company. Faith often
found her curled up in Mike's lap with a book or helping him

with one of his many weekend projects. In the end, they'd agreed to tread carefully, at least during these first few weeks while Bitsy transitioned to their new circumstances.

Faith tried to pry the thumb from the child's mouth, which only made her suck harder. "Her front teeth are coming in crooked, just like the dentist said they would if she didn't stop sucking her thumb."

Mike pressed his lips to the top of Bitsy's head. "Lucky for us, the best orthodontist in town is a friend of mine."

"One of the things I most love about you is how quick you are to offer a solution instead of deliberating the problem ad nauseam." Faith slid further under the covers. "I'm sorry, Mike. I hope you aren't having doubts about marrying me. I know how anxious you are to start our own family."

"Hey." Mike searched under the covers for her hand. "I came into this marriage with my eyes wide open. You told me about the complications with Bitsy's delivery, so I'm well aware that any additions to this family will happen by unconventional methods. We'll pursue those means when we are both ready, when Bitsy is on solid ground." He brought Faith's hand to his lips and kissed her fingertips. "Besides, if we never have more children, it won't be the end of the world. Making sure Bitsy develops into a mentally stable adult is the most important thing."

She leaned across her daughter to kiss him. "Thank you, Dr. Neilson, for taking such good care of Bitsy and me. This house, you, our family—it's all a dream come true for me." Her gaze drifted to the bank of windows that looked out over the inlet creek. "I will never get tired of the view."

"Nor will I," he said, staring at his new wife and not the inlet. "Do you feel safe?"

"How can I not with all this souped-up security?" She frowned. "I hope I can figure out how to use the features. Lord knows, I'll never remember the passwords."

"We'll start with the features we're comfortable with, and go from there. In case you need it, I have a file stored on my laptop with all the pertinent information, including the passwords."

"It just occurred to me how the nanny cams might come in handy now that I've hired Annie to babysit for Bitsy. Are they easy to use?"

"Very." Rolling over on his back, he took his iPhone off the nightstand. His fingers flew across the screen. "We can watch the nanny cams live from any mobile device." He held the phone up to show Faith the camera view of the three of them lying in bed together.

She scrambled to sit up. "Hold on a minute. Where is that camera hidden?" she asked, her eyes darting around the room.

"It's attached to the top of that frame." He pointed to a pastel of water lilies hanging on the wall in front of them.

"I'm not sure I like the idea of being on camera while we're... well, you know..."

He chuckled. "I haven't thought about it like that, but I know what you mean. Might give a guy stage fright. I'll dismantle it this afternoon."

"Good." She slid back down again beneath the covers. "What if I'm at work and can't watch the camera live? Does the system record it?"

"Yep." He returned his phone to the bedside table. "It's set up to record all detected motion on a hard drive that's installed in the utility room."

Bitsy stirred between them. Plucking her thumb from her mouth, she asked, "Can Annie babysit for me today?"

Laughing, Faith and Mike exchanged a look of relief that their daughter hadn't reset to silent mode during the night.

"I'm hurt," Mike said, placing his hand over his heart, wounded. "Here, I've been trying to get you to talk to me for months, and you go and open up to a total stranger. What is it you like about Annie more than me?"

Bitsy giggled. "She's a lot prettier." She placed her tiny palm on the top of Mike's balding head. "And she has hair."

"Funny, haha." Wrapping his arms around her, Mike snuggled closer to Bitsy, settling his chin on the top of her head. "Let's be serious for a minute. Your mom and I really want to know what Annie said that got you to open up to her?"

"She told me she was new in town and asked me if I wanted to be her friend. She seemed sad and lonely. I felt sorry for her. Did you see her feet? They were really dirty. She doesn't have a mommy to make her take a bath."

The situation suddenly made perfect sense to Faith. Despite the difference in their ages, the girls had something in common, something tragic no child should have to experience. Neither of them had any friends. Faith had told her daughter time and again, "You can't expect to be invited for playdates when you don't talk to your classmates."

"What else did you and Annie talk about?" Faith asked.

The little girl bit down on her lower lip. "She told me that friends don't keep secrets from one another."

Faith's eyebrows shot up. "Is that why you haven't been talking to us, because you've been keeping a secret? You can tell us anything, honey. We're your family. We love you."

Mike held his ear close to her lips. "Tell me your secret?"

Thumb in mouth, she buried her face in his chest. "I'm scared."

Mike rocked her gently. "Everyone gets scared sometimes."

"What are you afraid of, sweetheart?" Faith asked.

Thumb still in mouth, Bitsy said, "That daddy will break out of jail and come back to hurt us."

"Look at me," Faith said, lifting her daughter's chin. "That's not going to happen. Your daddy is in prison. He can't hurt us anymore."

Bitsy nodded. "That's what Annie told me. She said I needed to be tough, that the police will keep Daddy locked up. She also said that I'm lucky to have such a nice family with three big strong cousins to protect me."

Mike kissed the top of her head. "And a stepdaddy who loves you very much."

Bitsy tilted her head back so she could see Mike's face. "Does this mean Annie can come over?"

Faith blew a raspberry on the back of her daughter's neck. "Today is Sunday, kiddo. Mike is going to work while you and I get settled in our new house."

"When are we going on our honeymoon? Annie says that's what newlyweds are supposed to do."

Faith blushed. "We're already on our honeymoon, sweetheart. Right here in our brand-new house."

Mike's face filled with mischief. "Actually, Bitsy, I was thinking of taking you and your mama to Disney World in a few weeks."

"Disney World!" Bitsy looked at him wide-eyed and he nodded. She kicked back the covers and sprang to her feet. "We are going to Disney World," she sang, jumping up and down on the bed. She stopped suddenly. "Do you mean it, really?"

"Yes, I mean it, really. Come here, you little rascal." Mike reached for Bitsy, pulling her back down and tickling her until she begged him to stop.

Bitsy rolled over to face her mama. "Can we have pancakes for breakfast? Puh-lease."

Faith dragged her fingers through her daughter's unkempt hair. "Of course. But go find your robe first. I think it's on the foot of your bed."

Once Bitsy had left the room, Faith snuggled close to her new husband. "Disney World? Seriously, Mike. You are too good to us."

"I can't think of anyone more deserving," he said, nuzzling her neck.

She stretched out her legs. "Mmm... I could stay like this all day."

"Wouldn't that be nice?" He nibbled at her earlobe. "What's on your agenda for your first day as Mrs. Neilson?"

"Well, let's see." She folded her arms across her midriff. "After I finish unpacking, I plan to make my new husband a spectacular dinner. Any special requests?"

He paused for a minute to think. "Well, the market is closed today, so seafood is out of the question. Why don't you surprise me? Everything you cook is good."

A decent cook at best, Faith knew her culinary skills failed in comparison to Lovie's, who was known as the authority on seafood in the Lowcountry. "Liar!" She tossed back the covers and threw her legs over the side of the bed. "Maybe I'll stop by Mama's on the way to the grocery store. With any luck, she's trying out one of her new recipes." She slipped on her robe. "I want to check on Mack, anyway. He didn't seem like himself last night."

Mike propped himself up on one elbow. "Now that you mention it, Mack was quieter than usual last night. And he looked pale and drawn. He's probably overdue for a checkup."

"Like eighty-five years overdue," Faith said, running a hairbrush through her tangled locks.

"Tell him to give me a call," Mike said. "I'll make it as painless as possible for him."

She set the brush down and turned to face him. "Whatever you do, don't suggest he give up the bourbon and cigars unless you want it to be his first and last visit to the doctor."

Six

FAITH

BITSY CHATTERED NONSTOP about Annie Dawn during the ten-minute trip through town, past Sweeney's Seafood Market and the Inlet View Marina, to her grand-mother's townhouse in the Dolphin Run subdivision.

"Puh-lease, Mama," she begged. "Can we go see Annie today?"

"We'll see, honey," Faith said, parking her bucket-of-rust truck in front of Lovie's corner unit. "I promised Mike we'd make dinner for him. If we have time, we'll stop by the farm after the grocery store. But only for a few minutes."

"Yay." Bitsy bounced up and down in her car seat behind Faith.

Faith was not at all surprised when Mack answered the door, his white hair sticking up straight on the left side of his head. She knew he spent most nights at the townhouse. Whether he slept on the sofa in the sunroom or in Lovie's bed was none of Faith's business. She preferred not to think about the intimacy, if any, that took place between her mother and her boyfriend. Logistically, it made more sense for Mack to stay in town rather than drive all the way out to the property where he kept his houseboat. Especially if they'd been out to dinner or at a party like the previous evening.

"Good morning, Mack. Is Mama here?"

His face went blank and he stared at her with a puzzled look, making her wonder if he'd forgotten who she was. "Oh, Faith," he said, shaking his head as if to clear the cobwebs. "Yes, of course, come in." Opening the door wider, he stepped out of the way. "Your mom is in the bath. She should be out in a minute." He left them standing there and returned to the fishing show he was watching on the TV in the sunroom.

"What's wrong with Captain Mack, Mama?" Bitsy said, her lip trembling. "He didn't even speak to me."

In fact, he'd barely glanced at the little girl he considered his granddaughter.

"I think Mack is tired after the big party last night, sweet-heart. But that's nothing for you to worry about," Faith said, scooping Bitsy up and carrying her to the kitchen. She set her daughter down in a chair at the square pine table and poured her a glass of freshly squeezed orange juice. While Bitsy slurped on her juice, Faith surveyed the contents of the refrigerator to make certain nothing was growing legs, before moving on to the stack of mail on the counter beside the telephone, checking for any past due bills.

Despite the doctor's report that their mother was the picture of perfect health, both physically and mentally, the Sweeney sisters had agreed to keep close tabs on her. Which included making sure she kept her home neat and paid her bills on time.

When her mother entered the room a few minutes later

and found Faith studying her credit card bill, Lovie took the stack of mail away from her, including the bills, and placed it in a nearby drawer. "What a pleasant surprise to see two of my favorite girls," she said.

"Mack is being mean to me," Bitsy complained to her grandmother.

"Aw, honey." Lovie kissed the top of Bitsy's head. "Did Mean Mack refuse to give you a cookie so close to lunchtime?"

"I wouldn't necessarily say he's being mean," Faith said. "But he is acting a little strange. If you want to know the truth, I don't think he even recognized us."

Lovie waved off her daughter's concern. "There you go again, making plans to ship us off to the old folks' home. You girls need to stop getting your knickers in a bundle every time one of us has a lapse in memory or behaves out of the ordinary."

Faith noticed for the first time that her mother was still wearing her robe and the hair on the back of her head was splayed out from the pillow. "Why aren't you dressed? Mack said you were taking a bath."

A worried look crossed Lovie's face, but she quickly tried to hide it. "Believe it or not, I just woke up. I was worn out after your lovely wedding. Why don't you girls help your-selves to some cantaloupe salad—it's in a container on the top shelf—while I go say good morning to Mack."

Cantaloupe salad? Faith located the container and sat down at the table with Bitsy. She took a bite, and then fed her daughter a forkful. They were devouring the salad when Lovie returned. "This is really good, Mama," Faith said, jabbing the fork at the container. "What's in it?"

"Hmm, let's see," Lovie said, tapping her chin. "A little

bit of ginger, some lime juice, a few sprigs of mint, and cantaloupe, obviously."

Faith rolled her eyes. Only Lovie Sweeney could toss
together such an unlikely mix of ingredients and yield such
outstanding results. "It's refreshing in a tropical kind of way.
Something I might expect to be served at a five-star resort
on Tahiti."

Bitsy smacked her lips, eager for more. "I like it, Lovie!"

"And I like hearing your sweet voice again." Lovie grimaced
as she lowered herself to the chair next to her grandchild.

"Is your hip bothering you again, Mom?" Faith asked.

Lovie shot her a warning look. "Nothing I can't live with,"
she said, reaching for the container of cantaloupe salad.

They heard a knock on the door, but before they could get
up to answer it, Jamie strolled into the kitchen. Bitsy stood up
on her chair and dove on top of Jamie. Caught off guard by
her surprise attack, he stumbled under her weight.

"Good grief, squirt," he said, catching her and righting
himself. "Are you trying to put me back in the wheelchair?
You need to warn me before you jump on me like that." He sat
down at the table with his young cousin on his lap. "Say something." He held his ear close to her lips.

She looked up at him, her hazel eyes sparkling. "Will you
take me to see Annie Dawn today?"

He snickered. "You really like her, don't you?"

Bitsy bobbed her head up and down. "Don't you?"

"I guess she's pretty cool. For a girl." Jamie pinched Bitsy's
nose between two fingers, wiggling it back and forth. "And I'm
thankful to her for getting you to talk again."

Bitsy's face lit up. "Does this mean you'll take me to
see her?"

Faith brushed a lock of hair out of Bitsy's face. "We'll get by there at some point this afternoon. I promise."

Lovie turned to Jamie. "What brings you out here so early on a Sunday morning? Not that I mind having my wonderful family visit me, especially since we're all playing hooky from church."

"I came over to check on Mack," Jamie said. "He didn't seem like himself last night."

"Mack is fine." Lovie gestured toward the sunroom. "He's in there watching some old fishing show. You should go in and say hi."

"I will before I leave," Jamie said.

"Where's your mom?" Faith asked. "Working herself to an early grave as usual?"

"Pretty much. She's already cut the grass and blown the driveway. When I left a few minutes ago, she was cleaning the house."

"Sounds like she's got a bee buzzing around her bonnet today," Lovie said.

"You know my mom. Keeping busy is her coping mechanism. She's trying to forget she just made the worst mistake of her life."

Lovie went still. "Uh-oh. What'd she do?"

"She broke up with Eli last night."

Lovie gasped, and Faith's hand flew to her lips. "I thought the two of them were next in line for the altar."

"I'm so sorry," Lovie said, stroking her grandson's arm. "I know how much you like Eli. Did your mother tell you why they broke up?"

"Not really. She made some lame excuse about love not

being enough. If you ask me, I think Eli was pressuring her into getting married, and it freaked her out."

"What a shame," Lovie said, with a solemn shake of her head. "After all these years, the idea of marriage still terrifies her."

"What was my father like, Gran?" When Lovie hesitated, Jamie added, "Don't hold out on me. I'm old enough to hear the truth. He's a dirtbag. I know that much. Good guys don't walk out on their pregnant girlfriends the way he walked out on Mom."

Lovie looked at her granddaughter, who was playing with the buttons on Jamie's polo shirt, oblivious to the grown-up talk. "I think it's time you heard the truth." She straightened her shoulders. "Your grandfather and I didn't necessarily dislike Allen. He was always polite when he came to the house. We just thought he was ordinary, not good enough for Samantha. We wanted more for our daughter than to be married to a fisherman."

Jamie's mouth fell open. "That's kind of hypocritical, don't you think? Considering Big Pops was also a fisherman."

"It was different with your father. He seemed so restless. And we worried that he lacked the drive to ever be more than a deckhand. We never questioned his love for your mother. That much was obvious. But we got the sense he wasn't ready to put down roots."

"Why do you think he took off the way he did when he found out Mom was pregnant?"

"I can't answer that, son. Your father always had a dark side. I guess maybe he felt like he was in over his head, and he let that get the best of him. His leaving took us all by surprise. Allen had already asked Oscar for Sam's hand in marriage, and we were planning the wedding." Lovie paused, lost in thought. "Your mother was never the same after Allen left. He destroyed her confidence and spoiled her fun-loving nature. All she knows how to do now is work."

"That definitely explains why she's so opposed to getting married," Jamie said.

Lovie squeezed his arm. "Sometimes your mother has a hard time seeing what is right in front of her. Which means it's our job to show her the way."

Seven

JACKIE

EAGER TO GET on with their day, Cooper and Sean
excused themselves and their new friend Annie Dawn
from the lunch table, leaving Jackie and Bill alone on the
porch overlooking the creek.

"I left a stack of clothes on the sofa in the living room
for you," Jackie called after Annie. "One of the bathing suits
should work." Earlier that morning, she'd gone through her
closet and found an assortment of clothes that she'd aged out
of. "Poor girl has one pair of ratty jean shorts to her name," she
said under her breath to Bill once the kids were out of earshot.

"Why don't you take her shopping?" he asked, and stuffed
the crust of his grilled pimento cheese sandwich in his mouth.

"You know the shopping is terrible in this town." Jackie
sipped her sweet tea. "I'll pick up some things for her when I
go to Charleston tomorrow."

"What bathing suit did you give her? I hope it's not my
favorite black-and-white striped bikini."

"I gave that old thing away years ago." She walked her

fingers up his arm. "I bought a new one for the summer. Maybe I'll show it to you later."

Excitement crossed his face. "Can I see it now?"

She sat back in her chair. "Sorry. But you'll have to wait."

Annie and the twins crossed the lawn below them, weighted down with nets, fishing rods, and bait buckets. Jackie got up and walked to the railing. "I thought y'all were going tubing," she hollered down to them. "I seriously doubt Annie wants to go fishing."

The three of them stopped walking and lifted their faces to her. "Whose idea do you think it was?" Sean said.

Annie nodded enthusiastically, her honey-colored ponytail bouncing around her head. "It's true, Miss Jackie. I challenged Cooper and Sean to a fishing tournament."

"You do realize my boys are veteran watermen, don't you?"

"Yes, ma'am. I'll try not to show them up too much."

Jackie covered her mouth to hide her smile. She had to admit, she admired the girl's spunk.

Not so long ago, Jackie had tried to control her sons' extracurricular activities. But she'd recently come to appreciate their love of the water. This summer, instead of insisting that Cooper and Sean work as counselors in the mountain camp in North Carolina they'd attended every year since they were boys, Jackie had agreed to let them work for her family by supplying seafood of all sorts to the market. Whether they made money or not was immaterial. She wanted them close to home. She had a lot of making up for lost time to do.

Bill joined her at the railing. He shielded his eyes from the sun as he stared out across the water. "The tide is about right for flounder, if you go out near the shoals—"

Cooper dismissed his father with a flick of his hand. "We

know, Dad." And they headed off again, down the hill to the dock.

"I'm not sure what to think about a girl who likes to fish," Bill said. "Especially one so pretty."

Jackie propped her elbows on the railing and watched the kids load the boat. "She certainly cleans up well. She's quite stunning." Annie had showered off several layers of dirt and grime, revealing a wholesome beauty with a dazzling smile.

"Careful Jackie," Bill warned. "Annie Dawn isn't one of your renovation projects."

"I know that. She's a girl down on her luck. Where's the harm in showing her a little compassion?"

"There's no harm in it, as long as we keep the situation in perspective. Cooper and Sean are both infatuated with her, in case you haven't noticed. I'm not sure the relationship between the three of them is a healthy one."

"In case *you* haven't noticed, Annie is completely oblivious to their charms."

Bill chuckled. "You're right. And I admire that about her. I can't wait to see what comes of this tournament. Something tells me she knows a lot more about fishing than we think."

Jackie straightened, leaning back against the railing. "Something tells me she knows a lot more about a lot of things than we think."

Bill closed his eyes and tilted his face to the sun. "What's on the agenda for the afternoon?"

"Rest and relaxation. I need it after all the celebrating we did last night. I figured you'd be headed to the golf course."

"I'd rather spend the afternoon with you." He cracked an eyelid, and watched for her response.

"You would, would you? Choosing me over golf is a first."

She batted her long eyelashes at him. "But I'm flattered. What did you have in mind to occupy our time since the kids have taken the boat?"

"Imagine this." He waved his hands in front of them as he painted a picture for her. "You, wearing your new swimsuit. Us, lounging on the dock in the sun with tall tumblers of mojitos in hand."

An hour later, Bill and Jackie were lounging on the dock, soaking up the sun, sipping their way through a pitcher of blueberry mojitos toward an afternoon buzz.

Jackie held up her glass. "One more of these and I'm going to need a nap."

"I like the sound of that," Bill said with a naughty smirk playing on his lips. "Maybe I'll join you." He dragged his fingers across the silver lamé fabric of her one-piece suit. "Your sexy new suit is turning me on, but I'd rather see what's underneath."

"That's not such a good idea with the kids due back soon. In case you haven't noticed, Cooper and Sean are watching us like private investigators on a stakeout. They are hoping you'll move out of your study and back into our bedroom with me."

"Then what are we waiting for?" He sat up in his lounge chair, raring to go.

"We can't afford to get it wrong this time, Bill. My emotional well-being can't take it. And it's not fair to the boys. This time it has to be for keeps. I'm willing to admit that our relationship got into trouble because of me, because of my midlife crisis, for lack of a more sophisticated way of describing my career mental breakdown. But I'm having a hard time coming to terms with your affair."

"I understand." He rolled his head to the side to look at her. "But, just so you know, I'm willing to wait as long as it takes. I'm all the way in, Jack. You let me know when you're ready, and I'll book a second honeymoon for us to Nantucket or Sea Island or Tahiti, if that's where you want to go. When the time is right, we'll send a clear message to Cooper and Sean that their parents are back and better than ever."

Jackie pulled her oversized sunglasses off her nose and peered at her husband. "You sound awfully sure of yourself."

He puffed out his chest. "That's because I'm confident you'll eventually succumb to my charms. If I were a betting man, I'd play the odds that it happens this summer."

She fished a lime out of her drink and threw it at him. "You're incorrigible."

"Damn straight. That's why you love me so much," he said as he tossed the lime wedge in the water.

She settled deep in her lounge chair. "A long weekend at the Cloister *does* sound nice right about now." She sipped her mojito thinking about candlelit dinners and long nights of making love—until reality brought her fantasy to a screeching halt. "On second thought, I don't see how we can leave our three teenagers here alone."

"We can get Eli to house-sit," Bill suggested. "The boys wouldn't dare misbehave with a police officer on duty."

The vision of Big Mo breaking up a teenage beer bash popped into Jackie's mind—the nearly three-hundred-pound former college football player tossing one boy over his left shoulder and wrestling another to the ground. "Better yet, we could hire Moses. I'd feel safe having a linebacker around."

Jackie and Bill waved to friends cruising by in front of their dock, towing their two young daughters on a tube behind the boat. "Seems like just yesterday we were pulling Cooper and Sean on skis and tubes, nearly anything that floats," Bill said.

"Where did all the years go?" The girls' toothless grins reminded Jackie of her own freckle-faced little boys, their eyes so full of wonder at every new discovery.

They watched the boat round the bend out of sight. "It's hard to believe our boys are entering their senior year of high school," Bill said. "I'd hoped we could spend some quality family time together this summer, that you might cut back on your schedule like we talked about."

"That's the plan." Jackie removed her sunglasses and closed her eyes against the bright sun. "If I work Monday through Wednesday, I'll be away from home only two nights during the week. With your Fridays free, we will have long weekends together."

While she wanted to spend time with her boys before they flew the coop for good, Jackie had mixed emotions about not working 24/7 at this crucial stage in her company's development. How much did her sons really need her anyway? As twins, they'd always counted on each other for support. She provided food, clean clothes, and spending money. They were self-sufficient beyond that. Besides, they were so absorbed in their own goings-on they barely even acknowledged her presence. At least most of the time. And she was fine with that. It set her free to pursue her own goals.

"I'm sure the two designers I hired, Lexie and Cecilia, can handle most of the work in my absence. But I have two new clients who will need kid-glove treatment. When I'm finished, their homes will be worthy of a magazine. I'm counting on those two projects to launch my career into the next decade."

"I take it things are going well for JSH Designs."

"So far so good," Jackie said with crossed fingers. "The biggest challenge we face right now is finding office space. We've outgrown the carriage house."

"Sounds to me like a good problem to have."

"It is. And honestly, I'm not sure how Clara feels about having my clients traipsing all over her property. You wouldn't believe how nosy some of these women are. I've seen them walk right up on Clara's side porch and peek in the window of her dining room. I don't blame my clients for being tempted by her gorgeous home, but they should show some respect. Poor woman's not getting any younger."

"How is Clara, by the way? Has she taken anymore falls?" Bill had only met Clara once, when he was helping Jackie move some of her things into the carriage house, but they'd hit it off immediately.

"Yes, two more that I know about. Luckily she didn't break any bones. I'm scared to death I'm going to find her splayed out at the bottom of the stairs one morning. She's considering moving to a retirement community. I would miss her, but I think it's probably time." Jackie chewed on the earpiece of her sunglasses as she envisioned the improvements she would make to Clara's house, a Georgian that dated back to before the Civil War. "I would love to get my hands on that house. Talk about a renovation project. I could really showcase my work."

"What would you do with the house once the renovations were complete?"

"That's a good question. I hadn't really thought that far ahead. Sell it, I guess."

"Or we could keep it for ourselves."

Her eyebrows shot up. "Are you serious?"

"Sure, why not? I'm thinking about cutting back on my hours after the boys leave for college. I would love to spend the time in Charleston with you."

"Oh, Bill, really? That sounds like a wonderful idea."

"If you'll give me a chance, I'm full of good ideas on ways we can spend our golden years together."

She winked at him. "If you keep this up, you'll win me back before the week is over."

Pouring another round, they sipped mojitos while day-dreaming about the future. They'd drifted off to sleep when the kids returned sometime later. Cooper maneuvered the boat into the slip while Sean prepared the lines. Annie sat on the bow like their hood ornament, waving as though riding on a float in a parade.

Once the boat was tied up, Sean dropped a large cooler on the dock and opened the lid. "Check this out," he said to his parents. The cooler was filled to the top with doormat-sized flounder.

"Wow." Jackie got off the lounge chair and walked over to the cooler. "Looks like Sam will be offering a flounder special this week at Sweeney's."

Bill joined her beside the cooler. There is some serious meat on this sucker," he said, lifting the top fish. "I say we fry him up for dinner." He lay the fish back down. "So, who won the tournament?"

Sean, the more competitive of the twins, said, "We haven't

decided whether to judge based on combined weight or number of fish caught per fisherman."

Annie stepped off the boat and play-punched Sean in the
arm. "He refuses to admit that his brother caught the most
and the biggest."

Judging from the way the twins squirmed, Jackie got the
impression Annie had out-fished both of them.

Sean closed the lid to the cooler. "I don't know about y'all,
but I'm hot as hell. I'm declaring it family swim time." Before
she could protest, he scooped his mother up and dropped her
off the side of the dock into the water.

Jackie disappeared for a few seconds, and then popped
back out of the water, coming to rest on her back. "I would
punish you for that, young man, if the water didn't feel so
good. Why don't y'all get the tubes out of the garage and
join me?"

The three teenagers dashed up to the house and returned
with inner tubes, floats, and a paddleboard. They all claimed
their rig of choice, and for the next hour, they floated down-
stream and then paddled back up. Annie ruled the paddleboard when the kids played King of the Mountain. No matter
how hard Cooper and Sean fought, they couldn't dethrone her.

Jackie sensed Annie Dawn was the type of girl who accomplished everything well and with ease—an observation that
fascinated her as much as it scared the hell out of her.

Eight

SAM

POURING RAIN DROVE vacationers off the beach on Monday. They came to town for what limited shopping Prospect offered. Typically their slowest day, Sweeney's Seafood Market was mobbed with customers from the moment they opened at ten o'clock that morning. Stretching their resources even further, Sweeney's cook Roberto and his right-hand gal Sabrina had come down with a horrible case of the stomach flu. Jamie readily volunteered for kitchen detail, anxious to be away from his mother whom he'd been avoiding since her breakup with Eli. He'd been preparing Sweeney's signature shrimp salad since they arrived at the market at eight. Containers were flying out of the door as quickly as they could restock the shelves.

All hands on deck were needed in the showroom. Sam hated to see Faith go, but her sister needed to leave by noon in order to pick Bitsy up at the farm, drop Annie back by the market, and still make it to her standing appointment with Moses by one o'clock.

"I hate to leave you and Mama alone," Faith said, casting a nervous glance around the crowded showroom. "Why don't I call Mike and see if he is free to take Bitsy to her appointment?"

"You should be the one to take Bitsy," Sam said. "Just be sure to drop Annie off on your way. Surely she'll be of some use around here."

"You can put her to work in the kitchen with Jamie," Faith said, slipping on her raincoat. "Anybody can cut up shrimp."

Sam noticed the floor by the front door was slippery again from the customers' wet feet. "If nothing else, she can mop the floor." When the lights blinked, Sam cast her eyes to the ceiling. "The last thing we need is for the power to go out. I can't remember hearing the generator run its weekly test recently."

"Now that I think about it, neither can I. I'll call the electrician in the morning, and get them to come check it out." Faith pushed the front door open a crack. "Of course that won't do you any good if the power goes out this afternoon."

"Stop worrying about us, and go pick up your daughter." Sam gave her sister a gentle shove. "I'll call the electrician if we need him."

Annie arrived thirty minutes later, and Sam was relieved to see the girl had not only cleaned herself up but was wearing khaki shorts like she'd ask her to.

"Here." Sam tossed her a green polo shirt with the Sweeney's logo on the front. "Put this on. There's a bathroom in the kitchen. Come back once you've changed and we'll find something for you to do." When fifteen minutes passed and the girl hadn't returned, Sam went to the kitchen to check on her. She stopped short at the sight of Annie wrestling live crabs to a steamer pot on the stove.

"Shame on you boys for letting a woman do a man's job,"

Sam said to the twins and Jamie who stood by watching Annie do all the work.

Sean shook his head in amazement. "I hate to say it, but she's doing a much better job than we could ever do."

Sam inspected the buckets of crabs lined up beside the back door. "That's quite a haul." She gave a thumbs-up to Cooper and Sean. "And none too soon considering we are down to our last dozen. I'm sorry you had to go out in this weather to bring them in."

Cooper shook the rain from his copper hair like a wet dog. "A little rain never hurt anyone."

"Check this out, Aunt Sam." Sean opened the lid on a large Yeti cooler. "All cleaned and ready for you."

Sam gaped. "There's enough flounder in there to feed the whole Lowcountry." She grinned up at the twins. "I'm giving the two of you a raise."

When a fresh crop of customers entered the market, Sam gave instructions to Annie and Jamie on the tasks that needed completing before she returned to the front to help her mother. The Sweeney's crew worked nonstop for the next several hours. Much to Sam's satisfaction, Annie jumped right in, seeming to know by instinct what needed to be done without being told. Sam and Lovie filled orders and provided cooking tips while Jamie and Annie kept the shelves stocked with the food they prepared. Even Cooper and Sean pitched in to help by slicing and dicing vegetables for the white gazpacho that had become increasingly popular with their customers in recent years.

A thunderstorm moved through the area around three o'clock, producing the first lull in business they'd had all day. Sam and Lovie used the time to straighten up the showroom.

"Please tell me Mack isn't out in the ocean in this weather," Sam said when lightning lit up the dark sky and a rumble of thunder vibrated the building.

"Goodness, no." Lovie sprayed Windex on the glass of the raw seafood display unit. "He's lying on the sofa at my house watching television. I'm worried about him. He won't admit it, but he's been feeling kinda poorly lately."

Sam wrung her mop out and looked up at her mother. "I noticed he seemed out of sorts at the wedding the other night. Do you think he should see a doctor?"

"Yes, I do. But that old man is as stubborn as your father was when it comes to doctors and hospitals."

"If he's not better in a few days, Faith can ask Mike to talk to him about the importance of routine checkups."

The streets outside the market suddenly came to life with flashing lights and blaring sirens. Sam and Lovie moved to the front window to watch the police cars, fire trucks, and rescue vehicles flying by.

"I wonder what on earth is going on," Lovie said.

"With this storm, I imagine a house got struck by lightning. I hope it wasn't mine."

During the next half hour, when the storm died down and customers began to trickle back in, Sam overheard snippets of conversation, enough to piece together that a hostage situation was taking place at an area business down the street. A few minutes before four, when she noticed Mack come through the front door, she knew something was terribly wrong by his pursed lips and the deep lines etched in his forehead. He removed his Inlet View Marina cap from his head and stood off to the side, out of the way of the customers.

Her stomach twisting in knots, Sam finished wrapping up

eight pounds of flounder for an older couple who was planning a fish fry for their children and grandchildren the following day. Once she'd completed the sale, she crossed the showroom to him. "What's wrong?"

Mack stared down at the cap he held tight in his hands. "Uh… I don't really know how to say this."

Jamie came out of the back to greet Mack, who seemed relieved at the interruption.

Sam tugged on Mack's T-shirt. "You're scaring me. Tell me what's wrong."

"I received a call from a buddy of mine who works as a security guard at the bank. He's not on duty today, but he received a report from a coworker that two men bungled a robbery attempt and are holding a hostage in the vault. According to my friend, that hostage is Eli."

Nine

SAM

SAM FELT HER blood run cold as she collapsed against her son. "Please, God, no. Not Eli."

Jamie wrapped his arm around her for support. "He's gonna be fine, Mom. Eli is smart. He'll know how to handle the situation."

Sam's heart began to race. "I need to get over there, to that bank."

Jamie held out his hand. "Give me your car keys? And I'll drive you."

"Who's going to close up if we both leave?" Sam asked.

Lovie rushed to her side. "Don't worry about a thing, honey. You and Jamie need to go see about Eli. Annie and the twins are still here. The four of us will manage just fine," she said, nudging Sam toward the door.

With Jamie at the wheel, they flew through the slippery streets of downtown Prospect, arriving in less than five minutes at the shopping center where the Bank of Prospect was located. They hopped out of the Wrangler and worked their way to the front of the crowd that was gathered around the outparcel building.

Eli's partner, Brad Swanson, approached them. "Sam, I'm glad you're here. I've been trying to call you."

"We've been swamped all day at the market and I haven't checked my cell phone in hours. Are the rumors true, Brad? Is it Eli? Has he been taken hostage?"

Brad hung his head. "Unfortunately, the rumors are true."

Sam raised her hand to her throat and fingered the silver heart pendant Eli had given her for her birthday a week ago. "I don't understand. Why were you not with him? Oh, sorry. That didn't come out right. Considering the circumstances, I'm glad you're not with him. But you're his partner. Why were the two of you not together?"

"We went off duty at three. When I saw Eli leaving the station in plainclothes, I asked him where he was going. He told me he had a meeting with a loan officer on personal business, but he didn't offer specifics. He must have been in that meeting when the bank got robbed. According to our sources, around three-thirty, two scraggly Caucasian men in their midthirties entered the bank and held a teller at gunpoint. They ordered all the customers to lie flat on the floor while the security guard sealed off the building. I don't have all the details, but somewhere along the line, one of the robbers handcuffed a briefcase to Eli's wrist."

"What's in the briefcase, Brad?" Jamie asked, the color draining from his face.

"We've yet to confirm the reports, but the gunmen are apparently claiming there's a bomb in the briefcase."

Sam gulped back a sob. "What are you doing to get him out of there?"

"Our local hostage negotiator has attempted, unsuccessfully, to make contact with the gunmen. We are waiting for FBI reinforcements from Charleston. They should be here any minute." Brad stopped talking and held his finger to the headset in his ear. "Okay listen. I need to clear these pedestrians out of the way. Why don't you two come with me?" He walked them over to his squad car, and opened the back door for them. "You'll be safe in here, but whatever you do, don't get out of this car until I come back. You can listen to the radio while you wait."

Sam climbed into the backseat and Jamie slid in beside her. She burst into tears and he wrapped his arms around her, pulling her close. She couldn't bear the thought of Eli in danger. And to have a bomb handcuffed to his wrist. He must be terrified out of his mind.

"Eli might not be the biggest or the strongest person, Mom, but he's the most intelligent guy I've ever met. He will outsmart his captors. I trust him, and you need to trust him too."

"Of course I trust him," Sam said. "How could I not after everything he helped us through last summer? But he's alone in that bank, Jamie. With none of his officers to back him up."

"His backup is here." Jamie pointed at the police officers lined up in front of the squad car. "Just because they're not inside the building doesn't mean they aren't supporting him."

Sam's cell phone vibrated with incoming text messages and calls from her family. "I can't deal with this right now." She shoved the phone at Jamie. "Will you please respond to them?"

He took the phone from her. "I'll create a group text," he said, his thumbs navigating the screen.

If he survived the ordeal, Eli would need his loved ones around to support him. Sam didn't think she should be, or could be, the one. "I need to call Kyle." Snatching her phone away from Jamie, she punched in a number and briefly explained the situation to Eli's older brother.

"I'm on my way," Kyle said before ending the call.

Kyle and his wife, Shay, owned and operated a sushi restaurant in downtown Charleston. Considering the weather and late afternoon traffic, it would take them at least an hour to get there if they left right away.

Since breaking up with Eli on Saturday night, Sam had done her best not to think about him. But she missed him. She longed to feel his arms around her, to see his gray eyes darken with lust for her. What if Eli didn't make it out of the bank alive?

Sam put her phone on the seat and sat with Jamie in silence, neither of them knowing what to say to the other. Aside from discussions regarding market business, Jamie had barely spoken to her since Saturday night. She knew what her son was thinking. Because she was wondering it as well. *Is this life-and-death situation enough to bring us back together?*

The world would be a lesser place without Officer Eli Marshall. He showed kindness and compassion to everyone he met both professionally and personally. She didn't need him to be taken hostage in order to prove how much she loved him. Her love for him was never in question. Eli knew that. Didn't he?

The holidays had always been difficult for Sam and Jamie. Sure, they'd had plenty of family around for Easter brunches and Christmas Eve dinners, most of which were held out at the farm. But the unaccounted for member of the family—Sam's husband, Jamie's father—was the elephant everyone danced around and no one dared to mention. Because of Eli, this past Thanksgiving had been the happiest in her life.

With plans for an early morning duck hunt with Jamie on Thanksgiving Day, Eli had spent Wednesday night in her guest room, respecting Sam's wishes that no hanky-panky occur under her roof while Jamie was home from school. She'd slept in, a rare luxury for Sam, then spent the morning puttering around the kitchen in her robe and slippers, working on her contributions to the potluck Thanksgiving dinner they would attend later that day.

After the past few days, Sam needed downtime to regain her composure. Her testimony as a key witness in the trial of Faith's soon-to-be-ex-husband had helped send him to prison for a long time. But in the process, the prosecution and defense attorneys had forced her to relive the painful events of the previous summer, which had made her crave a drink worse than ever.

Now—with Curtis locked away and Faith racing toward a speedy divorce—the Sweeney family had plenty to be grateful for. Mack invited the entire Sweeney family to his property on the outskirts of town for a picnic celebration, an oyster roast and turkey fry. The weather was unseasonably warm, not unusual for late November in the Lowcountry. Mack and Lovie supplied the oysters and the turkeys, and everyone else contributed the fixings. While the adults prepared the meal, Jamie and the twins fished off the dock and Bitsy swung in the rope swing Mack had hung from the branch of a sprawling live oak down by the water.

They all gathered later around the farm table Jackie had

rented and helped themselves to the casserole dishes and trays of oysters and turkey. Mack offered the blessing, and then everyone took a turn sharing what they were especially thankful for that year. Mack nudged Eli to go first.

"At the risk of stating the obvious… I think I speak for everyone here when I say how thankful I am that Curtis is behind bars."

"Here, here," Mike said, and they all clinked glasses of tea and wine and bottles of beer.

They continued to circle the table with each of the remaining family members expressing their gratitude for friends, family, love, and health.

Jamie was the last to speak. Looking up from his plate, he stared directly at Eli. "I am most thankful for you. I never knew what it was like to have a father, until you came into our lives."

Voices chirped from the radio as the local officers discussed the FBI's progress in making contact with the bank robbers and setting up the SWAT team. From the sound of the conversation, Sam and Eli were in for a long wait. The only thing she knew to do was pray.

Minutes dragged into hours. The clock on the cruiser's dash was approaching six when Brad came to them with an update. "The negotiators have reached an agreement with the gunmen. The crisis should be over soon."

Sam fell back against the seat, relieved. "What happens now?"

"The gunmen claim that the briefcase is a prop, that the bomb inside isn't live. But we can't take any chances with it handcuffed to Eli's wrist. The bomb squad is standing by. They'll go in as soon as they get the signal."

"That's great news, Brad," Sam said. "Thanks for keeping us informed."

"I'll see if I can get word to Eli, to let him know you're here."

When Jamie shot Sam an expectant look, she turned away from him. "I'm not sure that's such a good idea. Eli and I... Well, we're not together anymore. He probably mentioned it to you."

"Actually, he didn't." Brad looked away, toward the bank where his partner was fighting for his life. "But that explains a lot about his bad mood today."

"We should probably go." Sam made a move to get out of the car. "Eli's brother, Kyle, should be here somewhere. He's the one you should be communicating with."

Sam climbed out of the car and, with Jamie on her heels, dodged the crowd on her way back to the Jeep.

"What the fuck was that about, Mom? Are you crazy?"

Sam put the key in the ignition and started the Jeep. "Watch your language, son."

He raked his hands through his dark curls. "Are you kidding me? The man who is like a father to me could have died today, and you are telling me to watch my language. Didn't you learn anything from this ordeal?"

"If you're asking me whether I suddenly changed my mind about breaking up with Eli, the answer is no."

"Stop the car!" He slammed his hands against the dash. "I want to get out." He reached for the door handle. "You may be a heartless bitch, but I'm not leaving here until I see Eli."

He slammed the door behind him, and Sam spun out of the parking lot.

Jamie was too young to understand that she was doing him a favor. Eli made it through this crisis, but who's to say he would survive the next. Better to end the relationship with her emotions intact than risk having her life destroyed later down the line. When their relationship was more complicated. When they were married.

Ten

FAITH

FAITH WAS ON her way to take Bitsy for her one o'clock appointment, her bucket of rust stalling out at every stop along the way, when Moses's receptionist called. "Dr. Ingram had to go to the hospital on an emergency call for one of his patients. He asked if he could see Bitsy later this afternoon, around five."

Faith jumped at the opportunity. Postponing the appointment would allow for a rainy afternoon cozied up to her daughter in their new home. She called the market to see if she was needed there, but her mother was adamant they had plenty of help.

Bitsy and Faith settled in with ham and swiss sandwiches at the banquette in the breakfast room. They watched through the bank of windows as the rain poured in sheets, the heavy droplets bouncing off the creek and beating the annuals in the window boxes until the plants lay limp and lifeless. She couldn't believe this new beautiful house belonged to her—with its stainless steel appliances and granite countertops, reclaimed pine floors and ten-foot ceilings—when less than a year ago she lived in a run-down trailer in the woods.

Barely touching her food, Bitsy babbled on about the morning she'd spent with Annie. While she was encouraged by her daughter's enthusiasm for her new friend, Faith found some of Bitsy's chatter disturbing. In the case of Annie Dawn, two and two did not add up to four. She dismissed her daughter's talk as best she could, reminding herself that these disclosures were coming from the perspective of a seven-year-old. Besides, Faith hadn't heard her daughter talk in months. She couldn't be sure what ran through her little mind anymore.

As Bitsy washed the last bites of her sandwich down with lemonade Faith was relieved to see her daughter's eyelids becoming heavy.

"I think someone needs a little quiet time," Faith said, stacking their plates on top of one another. "Do you want to go curl up in your bed with some of your books?"

Nodding, Bitsy stuck her thumb in her mouth.

She brushed Bitsy's hair out of her face. "The dentist says your pretty new permanent teeth will grow in crooked if you don't stop sucking your thumb."

Removing her thumb from her mouth, Bitsy examined it from all angles before sucking it back in.

"Have it your way," Faith said with a scowl. Lifting her daughter from the banquette bench, she carried her to her room and lay her down on the antique cannonball bed Mike had painstakingly stripped and pickled white.

With her Aunt Jackie's help, Bitsy had chosen the flowery bedspread, yellow-green shag carpet, and pale-pink striped wallpaper. Faith and Mike wanted their daughter to think of her bedroom as a safe haven and not the prison her father had turned her room into when they lived in the trailer in the woods in the middle of nowhere. After her divorce was final, Faith had tried to sell their property just outside of town. It'd come as no surprise when no one wanted to buy it.

Faith and Bitsy had moved to Moss Creek Farm and shared the master bedroom in the guest cottage. It was only now that Faith understood what a mistake that had been. She couldn't expect Mike's patience to last forever.

Faith selected three books from the built-in rack on the wall opposite the bed and handed them to Bitsy. "I'm going to stretch out on the sofa and read for a while, if you need me." She pulled the covers over her daughter and tucked in beside her the cloth doll Mike had given her. With brown-colored yarn hair and green button eyes, Dolly reminded Mike of his new daughter. And Bitsy never went anywhere without her.

The steady pounding of rain on the roof lulled mother and daughter to sleep. A few minutes after four, the sound of mail dropping through the slot in the front door woke Faith—just in time to rouse Bitsy from her nap, brush their teeth, and get over to Dr. Ingram's office for their five o'clock appointment.

As she did every week, Faith sat in the waiting room, skimming through magazines and chatting with the receptionist while Bitsy met with the doctor in his office. Fifty minutes later, Mo's office door opened and Bitsy skipped out.

"Alice, will you please take Bitsy down to the vending machines and buy her a juice?" Mo said to his receptionist. "Unless her mother thinks it'll spoil her dinner."

"Not at all." Faith removed a five-dollar bill from her wallet and handed it to Alice. "Juice only, though. No soda and no snacks this close to dinner." Bitsy had eaten half a bag of parmesan-flavored Goldfish on the way over.

Moses showed Faith into his office, and she took her usual seat on the end of the sofa nearest the window in anticipation of Moses's briefing on his session with Bitsy.

"I must say marriage agrees with you, Mrs. Neilson," Moses said, sitting down in the club chair opposite her. "You look wonderful."

Her face blushed pink. "I didn't know it was possible to be this happy. If only I could get my baby girl straightened out." Faith settled back against the sofa cushions. "Don't get me wrong. I'm thrilled my daughter has regained the use of her speech. But I'm not sure if the underlying reason for her not talking all those months has been sorted out." Faith told Moses about Bitsy's confession, about her fear of Curtis breaking out of jail and coming back to hurt her. "Why would Bitsy open up to Annie, a total stranger, and not her family?"

"Because she sensed the stranger wouldn't judge her. Sometimes when people meet, they experience an immediate connection. That seems to be the case between Bitsy and Annie." He laced his fingers together and rested them in his lap. "I agree with you. I don't think your daughter's sudden willingness to speak means she's any less vulnerable But admitting her fears is an enormous breakthrough.

"Our session today was productive for a change. It helps when Bitsy is a willing participant. But she seemed tired, and I didn't want to push her. I only touched on the subject of Annie. Your daughter is quite enamored with her new friend. I'm curious what *you* think about this newcomer?"

Faith crossed her legs. "I haven't been around Annie enough to have an opinion about her one way or another. Although Bitsy told me several things about the time they spent together today that didn't sit well with me."

"Such as?"

"According to Bitsy, Annie was asking a lot of questions about our family. She told Bitsy they would one day be cousins."

Moses wrinkled his brow. "I'm not sure how that's going to happen unless Annie marries Cooper, Sean, or Jamie. Perhaps that's wishful thinking on Bitsy's part. What else concerned you?"

"Without asking permission, Bitsy and Annie played dress up in Jackie's closet," Faith said. "It struck me as being presumptuous. But maybe that's because I know how fussy my sister is about her clothes."

"No, I agree. It was a bold move on her part. I'm afraid to ask how Jackie reacted when she found out."

"I haven't told her yet. She's in Charleston, working. I need to establish some ground rules with Annie, declaring Jackie's house strictly off limits."

Moses leaned in, propping his elbows on his knees. "If you don't mind me asking, why is Annie babysitting for Bitsy at the farm?"

"Jackie suggested it, and I agreed. With the twins coming and going, since Bitsy knows them so well and Annie is a stranger to us, it seemed to make sense. Besides, we both thought it might help Bitsy adjust to the move to the new house."

"Adjust, or is it dragging out the inevitable?" Mo asked. "Why not take advantage of your daughter's comfortable relationship with Annie by having them spend time together at your new home?"

Faith stared at the ceiling as she contemplated the idea. "I like knowing Cooper and Sean are around if Bitsy should need them. But you make a good point. We'll give it a couple of days before we make the change."

"That sounds like the logical plan. In the meantime, I would keep a close eye on the situation. If anything comes up that you think I should know about, do not hesitate to email or text me." Moses stood and Faith followed his lead.

"A big part of me wants to approve of this kid, while a much smaller part is warning me to be wary of her. I can't put my finger on it. I guess time will tell."

Moses was reaching for the doorknob, when Alice burst in. "I just received a message from Jamie," she said, waving a pink slip of paper. "He needs you to call him right away. There's been some kind of hostage situation down at the bank."

Moses took the slip from his receptionist. "Thank you, Alice." He glanced at his watch. "I know it's almost time for you to go home. We'll be out in a minute, if you don't mind keeping an eye on our little friend."

"Of course," she said, and closed the door behind her on the way out.

Faith rummaged in her bag for her phone, which she'd kept on silent during their meeting. She skimmed the stream of texts from Jamie, and with alarm mounting in her voice reported the crisis to Moses. "Gunmen are holding Eli hostage in the vault at the Bank of Prospect. He has a briefcase with a bomb in it handcuffed to his wrist. Jamie and Sam are on the scene, in Brad's patrol car waiting for an update. The FBI agents have negotiated his release. The bomb squad determined the bomb to be a fake."

Moses went to his desk and removed his cell phone from the top drawer. "I've got a voice message here from Jamie," he said, pressing the phone to his ear.

"What did he say?" Faith asked when he hung up.

"Jamie and Sam got into a terrible fight." Placing his hand on the small of Faith's back, he walked her to the door. "Jamie asked me to meet him at their house." Moses flipped a switch and turned out the lights in his office.

"I'm going with you." Faith swooped her daughter up off the waiting room sofa where she'd been drinking her apple juice and reading a book to Dolly.

They bypassed the elevator and raced down three flights of stairs to the lobby and out the front door to the parking lot. Moses followed Faith on the short drive through downtown, his supersize body crammed into his tiny sports car. When she turned right onto Dogwood Lane, she spotted Jamie walking down the street, his wet clothes plastered to his body. She pulled up beside him and rolled down the window. "You're soaking wet. You're gonna catch pneumonia. Get in."

He climbed in the front seat. "Mom has lost her mind," he said, and slammed the heavy truck door shut.

Eyeing her daughter through the rearview mirror, Faith was relieved to see Bitsy deep in conversation with her doll, oblivious to the drama taking place around her. She was usually beyond herself with excitement in Jamie's presence, but she was exhausted after spending the morning with Annie and her session with Moses.

Holding her finger to her lips, Faith whispered to Jamie, "How is Eli?"

Jamie nodded and lowered his voice. "He's alive—that's the most important thing. He asked me about Mom, and I couldn't lie to him. I told him she'd been there, but that she'd left when we found out he was safe. I could tell he was crushed that she didn't stay around long enough to congratulate him on not getting killed. He had a briefcase containing what he thought was a live bomb attached to his wrist, for crying out loud. What the heck is wrong with her?"

Sam's Jeep was in the driveway, but she wasn't in the back part of the house, at least not in the kitchen or sitting room. "She's probably in her bedroom," Jamie said, and went to the front of the house to check. He returned almost immediately. "Yep. She's in there with the door locked. She told me to go away, which is fine by me because I have nothing to say to her anyway."

Moses shot Jamie a warning look. "I know this is hard on you, Jamie, but remember that she's your mother. She's hurting, and we all need to support her."

"I'm sorry, Mo. But I'm so angry with her, I can't even be in the same room with her right now."

Moses squeezed Jamie's shoulder. "She got pretty angry with you at times last summer, when you were going through your crisis, but she never gave up on you."

Jamie hung his head, and shuffled his feet. "I know. You're right."

Bitsy tugged on Faith's skirt. "I'm hungry, Mama. Can I have something to eat?"

"Sure, baby." She hoisted her daughter onto a bar stool. "Maybe Jamie will fix you a peanut butter sandwich while I go talk to Aunt Sam." She winked at Jamie who was already reaching for the jar of peanut butter.

Faith knocked lightly on her sister's door. "Sam, honey. It's Faith. Can I come in? I want to hear about what happened today at the bank."

"Go away, Faith. Jamie can tell you whatever you want to know." Sam's voice sounded muffled and hoarse, like she'd been crying.

"I can't imagine what you went through, waiting in the patrol car like you did. You must have been scared out of your mind." Faith twisted the doorknob, but of course it was locked. "Please let me in so we can talk about it."

"In case you haven't heard, Eli and I broke up." Sam sounded clearer and closer, as though she'd moved from the bed across the room and was now standing on the other side of the door. "His safety is no longer my concern."

"Whether you and Eli are still together or not, you cared about him a great deal. The two of you were together for almost a year. You can't just turn your feelings off with the flip of a switch."

"Go home, Faith!" Sam said, her voice now hostile. "To your perfect husband and beautiful new house."

Faith hesitated, unsure of whether she should push her sister or leave her be. "Fine, I'll give you your space. But I hope you know you can call me anytime day or night if you need to talk."

When she returned to the kitchen, she saw Jamie and Moses rummaging through the trash can. "What are y'all looking for?"

"This," Jamie said, holding up a brown paper bag.

Faith eyed the bag. "Looks to me like an ordinary brown paper bag like the ones we use at the market."

Jamie pulled a white slip of paper from the bag. "This particular bag contains a receipt from the ABC store." He placed the receipt on the kitchen counter and pointed at the printing. "Says right here, one pint of Absolut Vodka."

Faith dropped to the bar stool beside her daughter. "So that's why she won't let anyone in her room."

Moses rubbed his temples. "However strange this may sound, I'm encouraged she only bought a pint."

"I don't understand my mom at all." Jamie crumpled up the bag and tossed it back into the trash can. "She and Eli are perfect for one another. She's told me so herself more than once. If she knows he's the right one, why won't she just marry him? What purpose does breaking up with him serve?"

Moses sat down at the island next to Bitsy. "My gut tells me there is something else going on here, aside from her fear of commitment. I'll talk to her, but not until she calms down."

"She'll be drunk by then," Jamie said under his breath.

"I've got to get this kiddo home," Faith said when she noticed Bitsy fighting off sleep. She lifted the child off the bar stool, and Bitsy wrapped her arms and legs around her mother. "Mike should be home from the hospital soon. I can come back once I get this little one settled."

Moses waved her on. "Go home to your family. I'll stay here as long as it takes."

Eleven

SAM

SAM BLINKED HER eyes open, then quickly shut them again against the bright morning light streaming through her window. Her head ached and her tongue was stuck to the roof of her mouth. As the events of the previous day came flooding back, a wave of nausea overcame her and she ran to the bathroom, emptying her stomach of its meager contents. She lay down beside the toilet, relishing the feel of the cold tile against her face.

If I'm so sure that breaking up with Eli is the right thing to do, why does it hurt so much?

She allowed herself a few minutes of remorse before forcing herself to get up. Not only did she need to be at work on time, she couldn't let anyone in her family suspect her of having a hangover. Unable to look at herself, she avoided the mirror as she brushed her teeth and splashed water on her face. Removing her robe from the back of the door, she returned to her room where she slipped the evidence of last night's pity party into her pocket to dispose of in the kitchen trash can.

She was taking a shortcut through the sitting room on the way to the kitchen when she stumbled over Moses's ginormous stockinged feet, hanging off the end of the sofa. He bolted upright and she stumbled backward.

"Good grief, Moses, you scared me to death," she said, her heart pounding her ribcage. "Did you sleep here all night?"

Dazed, he looked around the room. "It appears so, yes. I must have drifted off to sleep."

"What on earth are you doing here? Did something happen to Jamie?"

"Jamie's fine. I'm here because of you." He sat back against the sofa cushions, his giant paw rubbing his face. "You shut us all out. We were worried about you."

Dread settled over Sam like a dense fog. "Who is *we*?" She remembered Jamie and Faith coming to her door, begging to come in. But everything after that was blurry. Understandably so considering the amount of vodka she'd consumed. Jamie must have called Moses. Did he call Lovie and Jackie as well? The image of Eli pounding on her door made her stomach lurch, and she worried she might vomit again.

"Jamie, Faith, and me."

Her body relaxed with relief. "I don't know what to say."

"You can start by talking to me about what's troubling you."

"Can I have some coffee first?" she asked, already moving toward the kitchen.

"Of course. I could use some caffeine myself." Moses heaved himself up off the sofa.

He removed the cream from the refrigerator and located the sugar while Sam brewed the coffee. They sat down side by side at the kitchen island.

"I believe we've done this a time or two before," he said, referring to the early mornings they'd spent together last summer, sick with worry over Jamie's depression.

"And not so long ago." She blew on her coffee. "You're too good to us, Big Mo. And you don't charge enough for house calls."

"I don't charge anything for house calls." He cocked his head to the side. "I reserve that VIP treatment for my special patients."

She cast him a sideways glance. "That's not true, and you know it. You're known for your dedication to each and every one of your patients."

"Regardless, today you have my undivided attention."

She removed the vodka bottle from her pocket and placed it on the island in front of him. "I'm sure you know by now that Eli and I broke up. Looks like I'm going to need a new sponsor."

Moses held the bottle up close to his face, inspecting the inch or so of vodka that remained. "You sure put a hurting on this pint." He set the bottle back down. "Considering the circumstances, I agree with you. We need to find a sponsor for you right away. Like today. I have a couple of folks in mind. Would you prefer male or female?"

"Female."

"Done. I'll have someone call you by the end of the day. Do you want to talk about what's going on between you and Eli?"

Sam took a noisy slurp of her coffee, and then set her mug back down. "There's not much to talk about. Eli was pressuring me into marrying him. I broke up with him, because I'm not ready to be joined at the hip with someone for the rest of my life. End of story."

"Just like that." Moses snapped his fingers. "Did you even bother to negotiate?"

"You make it sound like we were business partners instead of lovers."

"Which is sometimes a fine line. Every type of relationship requires give and take, hence negotiations."

"But there's nothing to negotiate. I don't want to get married. Not now, maybe never."

"You could try living together first."

"I'm surprised that you would suggest such a thing. What kind of message would that send my son?"

"Come on, Sam. Jamie is nineteen years old. Next year he'll be a sophomore in college. Believe me, he knows where babies come from. It has become the norm for people to live together for a few years before they get married. In fact, premarital cohabitation is having a positive impact on the divorce rate.

"There are two different ways of looking at the situation, and in my book neither is wrong. You can continue to set a good example for your son by maintaining propriety in your relationship with Eli. Or, if you and Eli decide to try living together, you would send the message to Jamie that you're a modern woman, making the most of your life in a not-so-perfect world." Moses sat back on his bar stool and crossed his long legs. "You know as well as I do that Jamie would be thrilled if Eli moved in with you."

"Oh, so now Eli is moving in with me?" The coffee made her stomach churn, and she pushed her mug away. "This is my house, Moses. Mine and Jamie's. It wouldn't feel right for another man to live here."

Moses propped his elbows on the counter and planted his face in his hands. "You are one stubborn woman, Samantha Sweeney. I only suggested that Eli move in here because I've been to his apartment. He doesn't have enough room for you to fit all your shoes."

"Humph. I think you have me confused with my sister. I have only four pairs of shoes, two of which are Top-Siders."

"And that's exactly my point about the size of his apartment." They sat in silence for a few minutes. "So maybe you look for somewhere new together. Would that be so bad? You've always wanted to live on the water."

"Look." Sam placed her hands, palms down and fingers spread, on the counter. "This is not just about logistics. I've already talked about this with Eli. He can do better than me. I'm too old for him. He needs to find someone younger so he can start a family. Parenting your wife's nineteen-year-old son is not the same as having your own child."

Moses's intent gaze made Sam squirm. "Better, or younger? Sounds to me like you are saying two different things."

Sam shrugged.

"Okay, first of all, let's discuss the age difference. Eli is what, two years younger than you?"

Sam looked away from him. "Something like that."

"Okay, so he's forty-sevenish, which is not that much younger than you. Has he ever mentioned wanting to start a family?"

Sam shook her head. "I just know he would make a good father."

Moses let out a sigh of frustration. "We've talked about this time and again. You can't assume things are a certain way just because you believe them to be so. You are not in control of other peoples' emotions. If Eli wanted to start a family, he would have gotten married and had a litter of kids by now."

"Maybe not, if he hasn't found the right person."

"He found the right person, all right. He chose you, didn't he?" Moses drained the last of his coffee. "As far as I'm concerned, there isn't a better person for Eli. You are a good mother, provider, sister, friend. You are kind, caring, and loving. And you're not too bad on the eyes either."

Sam's cheeks burned.

"I've counseled a lot of couples in my day, but I've rarely come across two people better suited for one another than you and Eli." Moses got up and walked his empty mug to the sink. "Enough preaching for one day." He went to Sam and pulled her to her feet. "You know I don't normally talk so frank to my patients. But doggone it, Sam, someone needs to talk some sense into you before you make the biggest mistake of your life."

She stood on her tiptoes and kissed his cheek. "I appreciate your concern, Moses. I honestly do. And I promise I will think about everything you said."

Twelve

SAM

S AM DREADED FACING her sister as much as she hated
the awkward silence in the car on the way to work that
morning. Jamie was so angry with her, he couldn't bring himself to even look at her during the short drive. She resented
the intrusion in her personal life, but they were her family and
they loved her, just as she loved them. While she wanted to
crawl under a boulder and block everything and everybody
out, she knew her family wouldn't leave her alone until they
had some answers. She'd give them some answers. Just maybe
not the ones they wanted.

She walked into the market ready to face the firing squad.
She'd prepared her defense, with supportive arguments ready
for action. She only hoped Faith wouldn't give her the one-
eyebrow-cocked,   I-know-you're-not-telling-me-the-whole-
story glare. Her sisters were one thing. Her mother another.
Sam's fish was fried if Lovie had somehow found out about her
breakup with Eli and her subsequent relapse with the bottle.

Sam went about her chores in the showroom—scrubbing

and straightening and stocking—in preparation for the day ahead while Jamie retreated to the kitchen to help Roberto.

Lovie arrived shortly before nine. "The story has been all over the news this morning—in the state paper and on national TV. Thank heavens the bomb was fake, but I can't imagine what was going through that adorable man's mind. You all must have been scared out of your wits. Lucky for you he came out of that bank in one piece. What kind of horrible people would do such a thing to such an innocent officer of the law? I hope they lock those men up and never let them out."

Faith came through the door a few minutes later. "We need to talk," she said, and dragged Sam right back out into the parking lot.

Sam leaned against the side of the building, the brick warm from the morning sun. "Look, Faith. Whatever you're going to say, I've already heard it from Moses. And Jamie's cold shoulder is almost more than I can bear. I get it. Y'all are not happy about my breakup with Eli. But this is not your decision to make. It's mine."

"Sam, honey, you have always taken such good care of us. Now it's our turn to look after you. Don't shut us out. Something is obviously bothering you. This whole breakup thing with Eli makes no sense. I know how much he means to you. Talk to me." Faith tried to hug her, but Sam pushed her away.

"Nothing is bothering me. I don't want to get married. It's that simple. I'm not like you, Faith. I've been alone all my life. I'm the giver, not the taker. And that scenario works for me."

"Really?" Faith cocked her eyebrow and gave her *the* look. "Because it doesn't seem like it was working so well for you last night."

"I'm going to pretend you didn't say that." Sam pushed off the wall and began pacing back and forth in the parking lot. "I'm willing to admit I screwed up last night. Everyone is entitled to a slipup every now and then, especially after what I went through yesterday at the bank. It won't happen again."

"I'm certainly not one to judge you." Faith stepped in line beside Sam as she paced. "Lord knows, I've made more mistakes in my lifetime than most. What I'm trying to say is, I love you. And I'm here for you. I don't want you to suffer alone."

"That's exactly what I'm trying to tell you. I *am* a loner. I don't like burdening people with my problems, even if those people are my family. I can handle it."

"If you're such a loner, explain why you've been so happy with Eli these past months?"

"Eli was a fling. But Jamie is my life. He has always been my primary focus. I can't let anything interfere with that." Head bowed and shoulders slumped, Sam increased her pace, trying to shake off her sister.

"That's the most ridiculous thing I've ever heard." Faith grabbed Sam by the arm so she couldn't move. "Jamie has a girlfriend. You are no longer the center of his universe. Don't get me wrong. He still adores you. But Jamie is your past. Eli is your future."

She eyed Faith's hand, her fingers pressed into Sam's forearm. Her sister's strength surprised her. "Let go of my arm," she said with vehemence.

Faith released her grip. "You're misunderstanding what I'm trying to say to you. Whether Jamie comes back to Prospect after college or not, he will have a life of his own. You say you like being alone, but you've never known it any other way. Sharing your life with someone else can be pretty amazing."

"Spare me," Sam said, throwing her hands up in the air. "I don't want to hear your newlywed hogwash. You don't need to remind me how great your new life is. It's written all over your glowing face." When her sister's chin began to quiver, Sam knew she'd gone too far. "I appreciate your concern, Faith. I really do. But nothing anyone says is going to change my mind. You're wasting your time. I've made my decision."

"Did Jamie tell you he went to see Mama on Sunday morning?"

Sam paused, trying to recall if her son had mentioned a visit to Lovie's. She'd been so distracted the past two days. "I don't think so. Why? Is something wrong I should know about?"

"I meant to tell you about it yesterday, but we were so busy I never got a chance. I happened to be at Mom's on Sunday when Jamie got there. He was real down in the dumps about your breakup. I don't have to tell you that your son sees Eli as the father he never had."

So her mother knew she'd broken things off with Eli. Funny, she hadn't mentioned it. Yet. "Great," Sam said. "So now I have to hear about all this again from Mom."

"I wouldn't worry about that. You know Mama. She'll take your side no matter what."

Sam stared at her sister as though an alien had landed on her head and sucked out her brain. "We must have two different mothers. Because my mom likes to tell me every time I do something wrong."

Faith cracked the first smile of the morning. "Now that

you mention it, when *I* do something wrong, *my* mom makes me suffer by giving me the silent treatment."

Recognition crossed Sam's face. "Ah, yes. The silent treatment. I know it well."

"You can always talk to me about anything. If this breakup is really what you want, then I'll support you." Faith looped her arm through Sam's and they reentered the market together.

Thirteen
FAITH

FAITH HAD BEEN involved in a mental tug of war with her daughter since breakfast when she'd broken the news that Annie and Bitsy would be spending the morning together at their new house instead of the farm.

"Puh-lease, Mama," Bitsy begged in the truck on the way to pick Annie up. "Our house is boring. There's nothing to do there. It's more fun at the farm with Cooper and Sean."

The throbbing behind Faith's left eye intensified. She couldn't stand this torture another second. "All right, fine. You can stay out at the farm today, but starting tomorrow, Annie will babysit for you at *home*."

"Yay," Bitsy said, kicking her feet in glee.

Faith had kowtowed to Bitsy's every want for the past year in an effort to help her recover from the ordeal with her father. Problem was, she'd lost her authority over her daughter in the process. She needed to reestablish some parental boundaries. Time to show the kid who's boss. If only she knew where to start.

"Y'all are not allowed to play in Jackie's house," Faith said to Annie a few minutes later when she dropped Bitsy off. "You may go inside to get a snack or make a sandwich. But bring your food out here to eat." She looked up at the cloudless periwinkle sky. Yesterday's storm system had moved out, leaving plenty of sunshine and low humidity. "It's a beautiful day. I'm sure you can find plenty to do outside. You need to enjoy this fresh air. But stay away from the water."

Bitsy stomped her foot. "But Mama, Jackie's house is so much fun."

"Come on, Bitsy." Annie motioned for the little girl to follow her. "I saw some sidewalk chalk in the garage. We can play hopscotch and tic-tac-toe, or draw pictures of houses with trees and flowers and butterflies."

Bitsy beamed up at Annie as she skipped alongside her to the garage.

Faith climbed into her truck, satisfied that she'd established the necessary ground rules. But when she returned a few minutes before noon, prior to the designated twelve-thirty, she found the girls inside Jackie's house eating bologna sandwiches at the breakfast room table.

Faith's face flushed with anger. "I thought I told you to eat outside!"

Bitsy and Annie looked up from their sandwiches, surprised to see her back so early. Their pretty faces were caked in makeup so thick they looked like little girls pretending to be prostitutes.

Faith's temper soared. She hadn't felt anything but pity and sorrow for her daughter in so long these new emotions scared her. Blood pulsed at her temples. She wouldn't be able to fight off the migraine much longer.

She snatched Bitsy's napkin from her and smeared the makeup off her pouting face.

"I'm sorry, Miss Faith." Annie jumped up from the table and went in search of more napkins. "Sean invited us in. I thought it would be okay, since this is his house."

Faith stared at her, mouth agape. By taking a teenage boy's word over hers, Annie had completely undermined Faith's authority over her child. "Sean isn't the one paying you to babysit, now is he? Are the twins even here?"

Both girls cringed at the anger in Faith's voice. "No ma'am," Annie said. "They went out in the boat a little while ago."

Faith balled up the soiled napkins and tossed them onto Bitsy's empty plate. "Listen, Annie. I want this relationship to work for both our sakes. But you have to do as I ask."

Lip trembling, Annie turned her head away. "I understand. I'm sorry, and I won't let it happen again."

"All right." Faith picked her daughter up and took the empty plate to the dishwasher in the kitchen. "I'm going to give you one more chance. But tomorrow, the two of you are spending the morning at our house."

As she showed Annie around her home the following morning, Faith was once again careful to establish boundaries. "Don't go in here." She closed the door to the master bedroom. "I haven't finished unpacking and the room is a mess. You won't find any fun clothes to dress up in anyway. My wardrobe is nothing like my sister's."

"What're we supposed to do, then?" Bitsy asked.

"We could build a fort under the dining room table and

read books with a flashlight." Annie cast a sheepish look at Faith. "I mean, if that's okay with your mom."

"I think that's a wonderful idea," Faith said. "You'll find some blankets in the closet down the hall, and you can use the pillows off the sofa or the ones on Bitsy's bed."

Faith walked Annie to the kitchen. "There's ham in the refrigerator, and chicken nuggets in the freezer."

"I'll be sure to give Bitsy a big glass of milk to go with her lunch," Annie said, winking at her little friend.

Bitsy slapped at Annie playfully. "Stop! You know I don't like milk, silly."

Faith smiled at the easy camaraderie between the two girls. Perhaps she'd been wrong to get so angry with Annie the previous day. "It's fine if you want to go outside for a picnic, but I don't want you anywhere near the dock."

"I didn't bring my bathing suit today, but I'm a good swimmer," Annie said, the tone in her voice full of hope.

Faith smiled. "And we'd love for you to come over sometime for a swim, as long as a grown-up is around."

Unable to dispel the vision of Annie and Bitsy performing cannonballs off the dock, Faith called home several times throughout the morning to check on them. Each time, Annie answered promptly, assuring her that she and Bitsy were in their fort playing games. Faith had finally convinced herself that she'd been overreacting, until she got home and discovered her bedroom door ajar. She and Bitsy had just returned from dropping Annie off at the market for her afternoon shift.

"Bitsy, I thought I told you not to go in my room."

Her daughter looked up at her with fear in her hazel eyes. "We didn't, Mama, I promise. You can call Annie and ask her."

"Bitsy," Faith said, a warning tone in her voice. "Don't lie to me."

The little girl burst into tears. "You told us not to go in your room and we didn't. We played in our fort the whole time. Come see." Taking her mother by the hand, Bitsy led her down the hall to the dining room. She peeled back one of the blankets to reveal a cozy den illuminated by the dim light from Mike's battery-operated lanterns. A mountain of pillows was piled in the center, surrounded by stacks of books and games. "We even ate our lunch in here."

Guilt from being so hard on the girls bore down on Faith. "This is a seriously cool clubhouse. May I go in?"

Nodding, Bitsy stepped out of the way so her mom could crawl in. Faith leaned back on the pile of pillows and patted the empty space beside her. "Come here, you."

Bitsy crawled in and curled up next to her, resting her head on Faith's chest.

"I'm sorry if I scared you," she said, kissing her hair.

"I can hear your heart beating—thump, thump, pitter, pitter, patter." Bitsy fingered her mother's collarbone. "Where's your necklace?"

Faith's hand flew to her neck. "I don't know, honey. I guess I forgot to put it on." Retracing her steps from that morning, she couldn't remember one way or another whether she'd put on her necklace when she was getting dressed.

Bitsy rubbed her eyes. "I'm tired, Mama."

Faith was beyond tired. She was exhausted from the morning spent worrying about her daughter and the babysitter. Maybe it made more sense for Bitsy to come to work with her after all.

"You know what?" Faith said. "I'm tired too. How about let's you and I take a little nap?"

After getting Bitsy settled in her room, with Dolly tucked beneath the covers beside her, Faith made herself a pimento cheese sandwich and took it back to her room. She stopped dead in her tracks when she saw the imprint of an adult-size body in the duvet cover on Mike's side of the bed. Further inspection of the room revealed her favorite framed photograph of Bitsy and Mike face down on the dresser beside the empty pottery dish where she kept her jewelry.

Annie.

Faith's appetite vanished. She returned to the kitchen and stuffed her sandwich down the disposal. She poured a glass of iced tea and took it outside to the porch to debate her dilemma. If she knew how to work their fancy security system, she could pull the surveillance tapes from earlier. But did she really need the video as proof? Annie and Bitsy had been the only two people in the house while she was gone. Annie's behavior didn't surprise her as much as Bitsy's. It was a teenager's job to disobey and lie about it. But her own sweet seven-year-old child? She knew she should confide in Mike, but she hated to burden him after everything he'd already done for them.

She picked up her cell phone and called Jackie. Her sister answered on the second ring. "When are you coming home from Charleston?" Faith asked.

"I'm on my way now. I should be there in half an hour. Is something wrong?"

Faith sighed. "Maybe. But I'm not sure. Do you mind stopping by my house on your way into town?"

A short time later, Faith went outside to head her sister off in the driveway, so as not to wake Bitsy from her nap.

Jackie drove up and rolled down her window. "What's up?"

"I need to talk to you about Annie, and I don't want Bitsy to hear. Can I get in?"

"Sure." Jackie unlocked the doors and Faith climbed into the air-conditioned car.

She explained to her sister about the dress-up incident and the makeup and the missing necklace. "I don't know what to make of it. I want to believe Annie is innocent, but her behavior suggests otherwise. Truth is, we know very little about this kid whom I've entrusted with my daughter's care."

"I'm sure there's a logical explanation about the missing necklace," Jackie said. "Maybe you snagged it on something this morning at work."

"That occurred to me too, and I hope you're right. I'll retrace my steps to see if I can find it."

"I'm disappointed in Annie for going against your wishes," Jackie said. "But I'm not surprised. She's a teenager. Her prefrontal cortex is far from being fully developed. And, in Annie's case, I get the impression she wasn't brought up with our kind of values. She probably doesn't know any better. But if it'll give you peace of mind, why don't you call Eli and get him to run a background check on her?"

"Good idea. We should have done that in the beginning. A background check would at least tell us if she has a police record."

96

Fourteen

JACKIE

O N THE WAY out to the farm, Jackie convinced herself that Faith was blowing this business with Annie out
of proportion, but when she arrived home to find the twins
fighting in the backyard, she suspected that the honey-haired
waif currently occupying her guest house had something to do
with it. Cooper and Sean weren't engaged in their usual rolling
around on the ground, trying out their wrestling moves in various contorted positions. They were swinging fists and throwing punches. She left her SUV running and raced across the
yard to them as fast as her three-inch spiked heels would allow.

"What is wrong with the two of you?" she hollered. She
grabbed one of them by the arm, but couldn't tell which one
with blood covering their faces and their red hair standing
straight. The twin turned on her, his fist poised to strike.

"That's Mom, you idiot," the other twin screamed, tackling his brother full on. The boys tumbled to the ground, their
gangly limbs thrashing about as one struggled to gain control
of the other.

Jackie clapped her hands loudly. "Stop it this instant!" When they ignored her, she placed her thumb and index fingers between her lips and let out an ear-shattering whistle the way she'd learned from her father. Cooper and Sean immediately stopped fighting and scrambled to their feet.

"Get inside." Jackie pointed at the house. She didn't want the neighbors or boaters on the creek to hear her giving the boys a piece of her mind.

As Jackie was turning off her car engine, she caught a glimpse of Annie watching her from the window of the guest cottage. She couldn't see the girl's face to gauge her reaction to the fight, but the idea of Annie spying on them from behind the curtain made her skin break out in goose bumps.

She found the boys upstairs in the kitchen tending to their wounds. Cooper held an ice pack to his swollen left eye while Sean pressed a towel to the bloody gash on his upper lip. Both of them had fingernail scratches on their arms and necks.

Jackie placed her hands on her hips. "I'm disappointed in the two of you. Come in here and sit down." She led them to the sofa in the adjoining family room and waited for them to get situated. "I have never known the two of you to fight. Not even when you were little boys. Tell me what this is all about."

Their eyes bounced around the room, landing everywhere but on her or each other.

"Fine, since you won't tell me, I will assume your fight,"— she waved her hand in the air as she searched for a word she could stomach—"let's call it a disagreement, has something to do with Annie." The boys remained silent. "I hate to tell you, but that girl is more interested in your cousin Bitsy than she is in either of you."

Lowering their heads, they remained silent. Cooper

repositioned the ice pack on his eye, while Sean fingered a scratch on his knee.

"I'll admit she's an interesting girl, and fun to have around. But if this behavior continues, I'll have no choice but to ask her to leave. Do I make myself clear?"

"Yes, ma'am," they mumbled in unison.

"Good. Now… I could use some help unloading the car. I bought some things for Annie while I was in Charleston."

Both boys perked up at the prospect of seeing Annie.

"On second thought, I'll get Annie to help me while the two of you clean yourselves up."

Annie swung open the front door of the cottage before Jackie had a chance to knock. "Are Cooper and Sean okay? I saw them fighting."

"Nothing a little ice and Neosporin won't take care of. They were fighting about you. You know that, don't you?"

A look of genuine sadness crossed the girl's face. "I thought maybe they were, but I wasn't sure."

"I hope you're not encouraging them."

"No, ma'am. We're just friends. I've told them both that separately."

Which, in Jackie's mind, meant both Cooper and Sean had made unsuccessful passes at Annie and she'd turned them both down. "Does this mean you're interested in my nephew, Jamie?" The thought had occurred to Jackie before. A relationship between Annie and Jamie would undoubtedly cause a rift between the twins and their cousin. "It's really none of my business, but since you're living in my guest house and my sons are infatuated with you, I guess maybe I have a right to know."

Annie's shocked expression assured Jackie that the thought had never crossed her mind. "I'm not gay or anything like that, Miss Jackie. I'm too busy trying to get by to think about boys."

Jackie softened her tone. "Of course you are. How insensitive of me to suggest such a thing when you already have so much on your plate."

"Jamie has a girlfriend anyway," Annie said. "Sophia is all he talks about."

"Now that you mention it, I believe I have heard Jamie mention Sophia." Relief washed over Jackie. Best for the Sweeney cousins to keep their relationship with Annie platonic until they learned more about her.

Jackie gestured at the open tailgate on her Escalade. "I picked up some things for you while I was in Charleston."

Annie's jaw dropped when she caught sight of the vast assortment of shopping bags. "All that's for me?"

Jackie smiled. "Aside from two or three bags of groceries. I might have gotten a little carried away. I've always wanted a daughter to shop for."

Annie walked over to the car and peeked inside one of the shopping bags. "I usually buy my clothes at yard sales and the Goodwill store. I've never owned anything that came with a tag on it."

They loaded their arms with shopping bags and carried them inside the cottage. "I just hope everything fits." She held out a small shopping bag from the Verizon store. "And one last surprise."

Annie's mouth fell open. "You bought me a cell phone?"

"A pretty girl like you needs a cell phone, for safety reasons if nothing else."

"I've never owned a phone, Miss Jackie." Removing the

iPhone box from the bag, she cradled it in her hands as if it might break. "I have no idea how to use it."

"I'm sure you can find someone to help you. Although it won't be me. I'm somewhat challenged when it comes to electronics. The phone is already activated and ready for use." Jackie handed Annie a slip of paper with the number written on it.

"I don't know what to say." Annie gave Jackie a quick hug. "Thank you so much!"

Jackie noticed a can of Vienna sausages and a piece of string cheese on the coffee table. "I hope that's not your dinner."

Annie's face blushed pink. "I haven't had a chance to go to the grocery store yet."

Of course she hadn't. The girl had no way of getting around, except on foot, unless someone drove her.

Jackie squeezed Annie's arm. "I'll be here through the weekend. I'm happy to take you anywhere you need to go."

"Actually..." Annie stared down at her feet. "I noticed a couple of old bicycles in the garage. I was going to ask if maybe I could use one of them."

Jackie couldn't remember the last time anyone in her family had ridden a bike. She doubted any of the ones in the garage were fit to ride. "Can you carry groceries home on a bicycle?"

"I could if I had a backpack."

"In that case, I'm sure we have plenty of old backpacks lying around that you can use." Jackie took Annie by the arm. "Let's go out to the garage and see what we can find." They walked arm in arm across the driveway. Jackie punched the button and the garage door opened. "This place is a mess. I haven't been in here in ages."

"The bikes are over here." Annie led Jackie to the far corner of the garage where several old bicycles were lined up against the wall.

"I'd totally forgotten about this," Jackie said, wheeling a baby-blue Schwinn bicycle out from behind a riding lawnmower. "My fellas gave me this several years ago for Mother's Day. I would love to see it get some use." She handed the Schwinn over to Annie.

"Are you serious?" Annie asked, excitement dancing across her face.

"Of course. You'll need to put some air in the tires. There's a pump around here somewhere. And here." Jackie retrieved a bike lock from the workbench. "Use this so no one steals it. I'll find the combination for you. It's written down somewhere inside."

"This is too much, Miss Jackie. No one has ever been this kind to me. I don't know how to thank you."

"You can start by helping me with dinner. Don't tell Sam, but I bought three pounds of shrimp from the Harris Teeter."

Annie helped Jackie carry the grocery bags to the kitchen and unload them.

"How do you want to cook the shrimp?" Annie asked.

"I thought we'd steam them," Jackie said. "Do you know how to do that?"

"Of course," she said, and ripped the plastic wrap off the package of shrimp.

Jackie kept an eye on Annie while she mixed together the ingredients for pan cornbread. She found it surprising when the girl knew where to locate the things she needed. She went straight for the steamer pot, which Jackie kept in an out-of-the-way cabinet above the refrigerator, and the utensil drawer for a pair of scissors.

Has Annie been snooping around my house while I was in Charleston?

"What're you going to do with those?" Jackie asked, pointing a wooden spoon at the scissors.

Annie carried the shrimp over to the sink. "Cut the vein out. It makes them easier to peel."

"Did your mother teach you how to cook?"

"My mother?" Annie questioned, furrowing her brow. "Oh yeah, my mother. No, she works most of the time. My dad and I do all the cooking."

Jackie felt a shiver crawl up her spine. She thought back to the night of Faith's wedding. Annie had mentioned a mother, hadn't she? If memory served Jackie correctly, this mother worked as a maid in a seaside motel. Strange that Annie seemed to have forgotten all about her.

Jackie slid the pan of cornbread in the oven. "How are things going with your two jobs?"

"Things are going great. At least I think so. I don't have to work tomorrow, though. Sam and Faith have decided that Thursdays and Sundays will be my days off." The girl chattered on while she expertly cut the vein from the shrimp. "Lovie is like the grandma I never had. We came up with a new slaw recipe. Do you want me to make some for tonight?"

"I'm not sure I have the ingredients." Jackie went to the refrigerator. "What do you put in it?"

"Cabbage mostly. As long as you have olive oil and vinegar, you can add whatever other vegetables you want. Cucumbers are good. And green onions, maybe some carrots."

Jackie removed the items from the refrigerator and set them on the counter beside Annie. "Why don't I finish deveining the shrimp while you mix up the slaw?" She butted Annie out of the way of the sink. "What're you planning to do tomorrow on your day off? If you want, we could go out to lunch, maybe do a little shopping afterward."

"Maybe. I'll probably just sleep all day." The less-than-eager tone in Annie's voice left little doubt in Jackie's mind. Shopping was the last thing this girl wanted to do on her day off.

Jackie cut the vein from the last shrimp, then ran hot water in the pot and set it on the stove to boil. "What do you know about Eli and this hostage situation I keep hearing about? It's all over the news."

Annie shrugged. "Not much really. Everyone at Sweeney's is afraid to mention Eli's name since he and Sam broke up."

Jackie peered at Annie over her readers. "Did you just say that Sam and Eli broke up?"

"You didn't hear? They broke up Saturday night after the wedding."

Four whole days and nobody bothered to share this bit of news. "Poor Sam. She must be devastated. I thought for sure they would get married."

Sean entered the kitchen, and headed for the stove. "I'm starving. Are we going to eat soon?" He lifted the lid on the pot. "These shrimp do not look like creek shrimp. Please tell me you didn't buy them."

Annie placed her hand over her mouth to hide her smile.

"She did, didn't she?" Sean waved the lid at Annie. "She bought these shrimp at the Harris Teeter."

Annie lifted her shoulders in an I'll-never-tell shrug.

Jackie held her finger to her lips. "Don't tell Sam." She took the lid out of his hand and placed it back on the pot. She saw that his lip had swollen and the cut was still oozing. When she tried to clean it with a piece of paper towel, he smacked her hand away. "At least put some ice on it."

"Ice, hell. I know what will make it feel better." He went to the refrigerator and removed one of his father's craft beers. He unscrewed the cap and guzzled a third of it before Jackie could snatch it away.

"Are you crazy? You can't drink that. You're underage." Jackie poured the rest of the beer down the drain.

"Being underage doesn't prevent me from drinking, Mom. Duh."

"That may be so, but underage drinking is forbidden while you're living in *my* house." She dropped the empty bottle in the recycling bin. "Here." She opened the silverware drawer. "Make yourself useful by setting the table."

Sean went to the drawer and began counting out forks, spoons, and knives.

Jackie opened the drawer beside him and removed a stack of placemats. "Annie and I were just talking about Sam and Eli. I can't believe you didn't tell me they'd broken up?"

"Since when am I the gossip net?" He set the silverware on the counter and reached for the cabinet where Jackie kept the plates. "You have sisters. I figured you and Faith would be all over that noise like stink on shit."

Jackie stiffened. "Watch the language, son. I don't know what's gotten into you today, but whatever it is, you need to adjust your attitude unless you want to spend the rest of the evening in your room."

So far, compared to some of the other boys in their grade, the twins had been angels. Jackie and Bill thought they'd somehow managed to escape teenage rebellion, but maybe Sean was a late bloomer. Or maybe a certain young lady in the room was bringing out the worst in him.

Fifteen

SAM

COOPER AND SEAN showed up at the back door of the market late in the day on Thursday, their Yeti cooler parked on the ground between them. "What on earth happened to y'all?" Sam asked when she saw their battered and bruised faces.

"Cooper ran into my fist," Sean said, and Cooper added, "And vice versa."

"I hope she was worth it." As soon as the words departed her lips, Sam realized who the girl was they'd been fighting over. "I'd be careful if I were you. The jury is still out on Annie."

The twins exchanged a bewildered shrug. "I don't know why everyone keeps telling us that," Cooper said. "We think she's awesome."

Each of the twins lifted one end of the cooler and carried it inside, setting it down on the floor in the kitchen.

"Speaking of Annie, have you seen her today?" Sean asked.

"Her bicycle is over at the marina, but she's not answering her cell phone. We've been trying to reach her all day?"

Jamie was standing at the stainless steel counter slicing a sushi roll. He looked up from his work, his knife poised to make another slice. "Wait, what? Since when did Annie get a bicycle?"

"Forget about the bicycle," Sam said. "Since when did Annie get a cell phone?"

"Mom is letting Annie use her Schwinn," Cooper said. "The one we gave her for Mother's Day two years ago that she never bothers to ride."

"And she brought her home a brand-new iPhone 6 from Charleston." Sean flashed his iPhone 5. "Meanwhile Cooper and I are still using these old things."

"And I'm still using the model before that, if it makes you feel any better." Sam lifted the lid on the cooler. "Good grief. I'm gonna have to give you boys a raise. Did you stay out in the creek all day?"

"Pretty much, yeah," Cooper said.

Sean scooped up a handful of medium-sized gray shrimp. "These are real shrimp, fresh from the inlet, not those farm-raised fakes Mom brought home from the Harris Teeter last night."

Sam dropped the lid on the cooler and stood to face the twins. "You mean to tell me your mother actually paid for shrimp, when she has strong, healthy sons who will go out and catch them for her?"

Sean nodded. "And a sister who will sell them to her for wholesale."

Cooper's expression grew serious. "But don't tell her we told you, Aunt Sam. She doesn't want you to know."

"Already forgotten." Sam waved her hand above her head, signaling that the knowledge about the store-bought shrimp had left her brain and disappeared into thin air. "Let's get these on ice. We should probably divide them." She removed three smaller coolers from the storage closet. "Any chance the two of you can hang around for a while to help peel and devein a few dozen? We can charge more for them without the shell."

"Sure," Cooper said, and Sean added, "We're waiting around anyway to see if Annie shows up."

Sam returned to the front to help her mother begin the process of closing shop for the day. Business had dropped off after lunch. With eighty-degree temperatures and cloudless skies, most vacationers had spent the day on the beach. But they needed to stock up for Friday and Saturday, which were always their busiest days.

"I'm curious, Mom. What do you think of Annie?" Sam asked Lovie as she circled the showroom, making a mental list of tasks that needed completing.

Her mother looked up from the cash register where she was running a summary of the day's activities. "For the most part, I find her delightful. She's easy to be around, willing to help in any way, and creative when it comes to cooking."

"Do I detect a *but* in there somewhere?"

Lovie closed the cash register drawer. "I haven't been able to put my finger on it yet, but something about the girl troubles me. Not necessarily in a bad way. I feel like I've known her for a long time, yet we only just met. The way she looks at me with those dark eyes is unsettling somehow. Makes the little hairs on my neck stand up straight, if you know what I mean."

"Speak of the devil," Sam said when she noticed Annie

and Mack crossing the street together, struggling under the weight of a large Igloo cooler.

Sam held the door open for them. "If you have shrimp in there, I'll have to turn you away. Thanks to Cooper and Sean, I have enough to last the summer."

"Lord no!" Mack said. "Been a long time since I cast a shrimp net."

They dropped the cooler on the floor and Annie lifted the lid. "Check this out, Miss Sam. Captain Mack took me out to the Gulf Stream today. We found a piece of carpet floating in the ocean, and guess what?"

"Under the carpet, you found a school of fish," Sam said, peering down at the filets of mahimahi.

"How'd you know?" Annie asked, letting go of the lid.

"I've been fishing a time or two myself," Sam said. "My father was a boat captain like Mack. In fact, they were best friends."

"Oh, really? I didn't know that."

Mack removed his cap from his head and wiped the sweat from his brow with the back of his arm. "We had a good day, but I'm awfully tired. We reeled 'em in for more than three hours. Could've kept going if we'd had another set of hands."

The twins emerged from the kitchen. "You should've taken us with you," Cooper said.

"Yeah! Why don't you ever take *us* fishing?" His voice carried a joking tone, but Sam could tell from his tight smile that Sean's feelings were hurt.

"I never knew you wanted to go," Mack said.

"To the Gulf Stream fishing?" Sean stared at Mack, incredulous. "Are you kidding me?"

Mack squeezed Sean's shoulder. "Be at the dock at six tomorrow morning."

"Yes!" Sean pumped the air with his fist.

Mack snickered. "But you're in charge of bringing the sandwiches."

Cooper turned to Annie. "We've been worried about you. You should've told somebody where you were," he said, like a father to his teenage daughter who'd missed her curfew.

Annie stiffened. "I didn't realize I had to check in with anybody."

"That's why my mom gave you a cell phone," Sean said.

Annie patted her pockets in search of her phone. "I must have left it at the cottage. I've never owned a cell phone before." She flashed a smile that reached her eyes. "I'm sorry if you guys are mad at me."

"Nobody's mad. We were just worried." Sean elbowed his brother. "Come on. Help me with this cooler."

The two boys hefted the cooler and hauled it to the back.

Mack leaned against the wall. "Boy, am I beat." He folded his arms across his ample gut and bowed his head.

Sam and Lovie conducted a final check of the showroom, before turning out the lights. Sam was eager to go home and shower the smell of seafood from her body before meeting her new sponsor at seven for an AA meeting. She shooed everyone out of the back, locking the door behind them. She was backing out of the parking space when Eli's cruiser turned into the lot.

"Eli!" Jamie opened the door and hopped out of the Jeep.

From the car window, Sam watched her son and her ex greet one another in a man hug. They talked for several minutes in what appeared to be a serious conversation. Jamie's shoulders slumped and his expression grew stony, clearly disappointed in whatever news Eli was sharing. When Eli play-fully cuffed him on the ear, Jamie responded with a resigned shrug before returning to the Jeep.

"Eli wants to talk to you," Jamie said, slamming the door.

Sam checked the time on the clock on the dash. "I have a meeting in an hour. I need to shower first."

"Your meeting can wait. You need to hear what Eli has to say."

Sam got out of the car and approached Eli with caution. She hadn't talked to him since the night they'd broken up. She decided it best to remain concerned but friendly. "You gave us all quite a scare the other day."

"Did I, Sam?" Eli's soulful gray eyes met hers, daring her to look away. "Did I really scare you?"

"Of course," Sam said, raking her fingers through her hair. "You've become quite the celebrity. America's hero of the week."

"It's an off week for news," he sighed. "So I scared you, just not enough to want me back?" When he smiled, his dim-ple appeared on his cheek to the right of his lips, making Sam's knees go weak.

That damn dimple.

Willing herself to be strong, Sam held her back ramrod straight and her head high. "If you came here looking for a reconciliation, I'm sorry. I can't offer you one."

"Can we at least talk about it? Maybe go somewhere for coffee."

She shook her head. "I have a meeting at seven with my new sponsor."

A surprised look crossed his face. "You have a new sponsor?"

"Considering the circumstances, I don't think it's a good idea if you continue to be my sponsor. I'm moving on with my life, Eli. I suggest you do the same."

He swallowed, his Adam's apple bulging in his throat. "Won't you please give us a chance?"

"I'm sorry, but I can't." She inhaled a deep breath, the salty air steadying her nerves. "If anything, this whole hostage crisis has made me realize how toxic our relationship is for me. The danger your job presents and the stress of worrying every day whether you'll make it home safely from work at night is more than I can handle."

"Come on, Sam. We're talking about Prospect here. The hostage situation is the biggest crisis we're likely to see this century."

She cast a nervous glance at the Jeep. She needed to get to her meeting. "Look, I see no sense in rehashing everything we talked about the other night. It's not going to change anything. We both need to move on. Find someone younger, Eli. Start a family. You'll love being a parent."

"I don't want anyone younger. I want you." He took hold of her arm. "You and Jamie are my family."

She tugged her arm free. "Jamie said you had something to tell me."

Rubbing the back of his neck, Eli sighed. "I'm considering a job offer. In New York."

Sam's jaw dropped. New York was so far away. "When do you have to let them know?"

"They've given me the weekend to decide."

The sudden thirst for alcohol overcame her. Staying sober was proving to be a bigger challenge than she'd imagined without Eli's support. When they were together during the evening cocktail hours, they did other things, like take long walks on the beach or go to one of the barrier islands in his boat. All she'd wanted to do in the five days since they'd broken up was lock herself in her bedroom with a bottle of booze.

"That's very considerate of them to give you three whole days."

Eli winced at the anger in her voice.

"I assume they've offered you a promotion," she said, more a question than a statement.

"I'd call it a lateral move, but I will be assigned to a special unit that works with the homeless, many of them kids."

Sam smiled. Eli was getting his dream job.

"Speaking of runaways, is Annie around?" Eli asked. "I was hoping to have a word with her."

"You just missed her. Do you really think she's a runaway?"

"She's something. I haven't figured out what yet, but I aim to find out."

Sixteen

FAITH

"FAITH, CAN YOU come help me for a minute," Mike called from the front door Thursday night when he arrived home from work. "I brought some of my things over from the other house I need to bring them in."

She slid her casserole in the oven, removed her apron, and went outside to help her husband, stopping dead in her tracks when she saw the shiny Buick SUV in the driveway. "Whose car is that?"

With a mischievous grin, he dangled the car keys in front of her face. "Yours."

She stared at the car, then back at him. "What do you mean, mine?"

"I mean, I bought you a new car. Technically it's used, but it has less than ten thousand miles on it." He placed the key in the palm of her hand and wrapped her fingers around it. "Your bucket of rust is headed for the truck graveyard."

Faith chewed on her bottom lip. "I can't believe you did this for me."

"I've been thinking about this for weeks. It's a husband's responsibility to make sure his wife drives a safe car, especially when his daughter is riding with her."

Not my last husband, Faith thought.

Mike chucked her chin. "Red would not have been my first choice, but I got a good deal on it."

"I think the red is kinda sporty." She ran her hand across the hood of the car. "You are too good to me."

"I like making you happy." He handed her the key and opened the driver's door. "I'll get Bitsy, and we'll go for a spin."

"No, please, don't!" She stepped in front of him blocking his path. "I just got her to sleep."

He glanced at his watch. "But it's only six thirty."

"She, *we*, had a difficult day." Mike's eyebrows shot up in question, and Faith added, "I'll tell you about it later. I want to check out my new ride first." She climbed onto the driver's seat and sniffed. "It smells like leather."

He went around to the passenger side and slid in beside her. With country music playing from the Bose speakers, Faith and Mike spent the next thirty minutes exploring the car's many features. They punched buttons and turned knobs, consulting the manual whenever they couldn't figure out how to work something.

"Thank you Dr. Neilson." She leaned over the center console to kiss him. "You just made your bride a very happy woman."

He kissed her back with more passion. Pulling away from her, he eyed the backseat. "Shall we check it out?" he asked, his voice husky with desire.

She traced his lips with her finger. "We're married now, babe. We have a bed for this kind of thing."

He laughed. "Where's the fun in that?"

Starting at his collarbone, she nibbled a trail of kisses on his neck all the way up to his ear. "There's lots of fun in that," she whispered. "We just haven't had much chance to explore it yet." Faith turned off the ignition and opened her door. "As much as I hate to leave my new car, I need to check on the crab casserole in the oven. Are you hungry?"

"Not right now. I ate a late lunch." Off in the distance, a streak of lightning lit up the darkening sky. "Why don't we have a glass of wine and watch the storm roll in from the porch?"

Leaving the french doors ajar so they could hear Bitsy if she needed them, Faith and Mike settled in the rockers on the screened porch with a bottle of Pinot Noir and a plate of cheese on the table between them.

"So tell me, what happened that made your day so difficult?" he asked.

For the past three days, Mike's twelve-hour shifts at the hospital hadn't allowed time enough for her to tell him about the week's events. While they sipped wine and ate slices of cheese, she told him about Bitsy's growing obsession with Annie Dawn. She also explained how Annie had disobeyed her, not once but twice, by going into Jackie's house when she'd specifically asked her not to, and by entering their bedroom even though Faith had closed the door and declared the room off limits.

"Are you sure you didn't lose your necklace at work?"

"I'm not a hundred percent sure. I've looked everywhere at the market, but it may have accidentally gotten thrown away in the trash."

Mike carved off a chunk of cheese and popped it into his mouth. "Have you told Jackie any of this?"

Faith nodded. "She came by yesterday on her way home from Charleston. She didn't say it outright, but I got the impression she thinks I'm overreacting—although she suggested I have Eli run a background check on Annie. I talked to him earlier today, but I haven't heard back from him."

"I don't like the sound of any of this. And you still haven't told me what happened today."

"Bitsy whined and pouted and complained all day. She demanded, kicking and screaming, that I call Annie. When I tried to explain that we needed to respect Annie's privacy on her day off, she had a full-on nuclear meltdown. She wouldn't take a nap, or eat anything. I was lucky to get her in the bed when I did."

"That doesn't sound like Bitsy at all."

"I know," Faith said, shaking her head. "She hasn't been herself since Annie showed up."

Mike sat back in the rocker, sipping his wine. "She's made a new friend, and she wants to spend time with her. I get that."

As she stared out over the inlet at the approaching storm, Faith contemplated whether her daughter's recent behavior changes could be so easily justified. Bitsy was only seven years old after all. "I'd like to think that's all it is, but she said some things today that really worry me."

"Such as?"

"She asked me if I thought she was a bad girl. When I questioned her about it, she clammed up. But later on, I heard her punishing Dolly for being a naughty girl, right before she stuffed her in a drawer and slammed the drawer shut."

Mike let out a soft whistle. "You don't think that has anything to do with Annie, do you?"

"I have my concerns about the girl, but she doesn't seem

the type who would abuse a child." Faith took a sip of wine. "Until Saturday night, Bitsy hadn't spoken to anyone about anything in nearly a year. She might simply be expressing some pent-up emotions over the way Curtis treated her."

Mike rubbed his chin. "Sounds like post-traumatic stress disorder to me. Did you tell Moses about any of this?"

"I left a message for him today, but he hasn't called me back yet." Faith let her head fall back against the chair. "I don't know how many more days like today I can take. I feel like a monster has suddenly possessed my daughter. She was never a bad little girl. What if she's scarred for life from what Curtis did to her?"

Mike reached for Faith's hand and squeezed it. "Bitsy is going to be fine. I promise you that. She just needs more time. I'm sure Moses will tell you that when you speak to him. It's a process. One step at a time."

"I hate to say it, but I almost wish the silent Bitsy would return."

"No you don't." Mike brought Faith's hand to his lips. "The silent Bitsy might have been easier to control, but think of all the hurt and anger she was keeping inside, eating away at her soul. At least she's expressing herself. Maybe not with the emotions you want to see, but it is a step in the direction toward healing."

Faith tilted her head to the side as she thought about it. "That actually makes a lot of sense."

Mike massaged her knee, his hand creeping up her thigh. "Someone needs to take care of Bitsy's mama." A naughty boy grin appeared on his lips. "And I think that someone should be me."

She walked her fingers up his arm. "What did you have in mind?"

Mike poured them both a little more wine. "I say we take our wine to the bedroom. We have the whole night ahead of us. If what you say is true, our daughter is likely to sleep uninterrupted until morning."

Seventeen

JACKIE

THE THREAT OF bad weather put a damper on Jackie's plans for dinner. The twins wanted to grill steaks, despite the lightning crackling in the sky around them, but Jackie insisted it was too dangerous.

"Come on, Mom. It's fine," Sean argued. "We can move the grill into the garage."

A bolt of lightning flashed, followed by a loud clap of thunder. "Nobody is cooking outside." Jackie stepped back from the window in the dining room. "In the garage or otherwise. We can order a pizza."

"Or I can make shrimp salad," Annie offered.

They all groaned. "No more shrimp. Please!" Cooper said.

Sean refused to give up. "When will Dad be home? He'll let us cook on the grill."

"Not anytime soon. He was still in surgery when I called a few minutes ago." Jackie's phone vibrated on the kitchen counter and her mother's face flashed on the screen. She snatched up the phone.

"Do you know where Sam is?" Lovie asked, sounding short of breath. "I've been trying to call her. She's not answering her phone."

Why does our mother always call Sam first?

"I have no idea, Mom. Is something wrong?"

"It's Mack! He's gasping for air and clawing at his chest."

The blood drained from Jackie's face. "You need to call an ambulance, Mom." She felt three pairs of teenage eyes staring at her. "I'll meet you at the hospital. Bill is still there. I'll let him know we're coming."

"I don't understand. Why is Bill at the hospital? What can he do to help us?"

Jackie's concern mounted at the panic and confusion in her mother's voice. "He's a cardiologist, a heart doctor, remember?"

"Oh, yes, of course."

"Listen carefully, Mom," Jackie said in a calm but firm voice. "I need for you to hang up the phone and dial 911. Tell them your friend is having a heart attack and you need an ambulance right away. I want you to ride with Mack to the hospital, and I'll see you there. Do you understand?"

Lovie muttered her understanding and hung up.

"What's wrong, Mom? Is it Mack?" Cooper asked.

"Yes. Sounds like he might be having a heart attack. I need to get to the hospital." Jackie retrieved her purse from the chair by the back stairs where she left it when she returned from the store earlier.

"I'll go with you, Miss Jackie," Annie said.

More often than not, Jackie was unable to interpret the looks her twins exchanged with one another. But this one she understood. They didn't want to go unless she made them.

They'd gotten their fill of hospitals last year when Cooper spent a week in ICU after fracturing his skull in a hiking accident.

"You boys stay here. I'm putting you in charge of dinner." Jackie removed two twenties from her wallet and placed them on the kitchen counter. "This should be enough for two large pizzas." Starting down the stairs, she called over her shoulder, "But be sure to save some for the rest of us."

The first drops of rain fell as Jackie and Annie were climbing into the SUV. Jackie punched Bill's number into her cell phone as she maneuvered the big vehicle down the narrow, curvy driveway. He answered on the third ring. "I'm so glad I caught you," she said, and explained the situation to him. "Mom seemed confused when I spoke to her."

"A crisis like this can cause an older person to become discombobulated. Why don't you call her back to make certain the ambulance is on the way?"

Lovie answered on the first ring. "The rescue people are here. They're putting him on a stretcher now. I'm scared, honey. What if something happens to Mack?"

"He's in good hands, Mom. I promise we'll get him the best possible care."

Jackie ended the call and focused her attention on the road. Torrents of rain decreased visibility, making it necessary for Jackie to drive the five miles to the hospital at a snail's pace. Annie and Jackie settled into the only two available seats in the crowded ER waiting room. She called Sam first, and then Faith who sounded groggy as though Jackie woke her up.

"Poor, Mack. I have to say I'm not surprised though. He hasn't looked well lately." Faith sighed. "I can send Mike if you need him, but I think it's best if I stay here with Bitsy. She's been going through a rough patch lately."

"I see no sense in either one of you coming out in this weather. I'll keep you posted."

Jackie and Annie waited for what seemed like an eternity. As the storm grew worse, more people entered the emergency room. A woman with a bloody towel wrapped around her right hand. A man with a three-inch gash above his left eye. With no empty chairs, they stood against the wall or sat on the floor. Annie gave her seat to a little boy who was gripping his arm in pain, his right wrist bent at an unnatural angle.

Sam and Jamie arrived just as Bill, dressed in scrubs with his stethoscope draped around his neck, emerged from the examining rooms with Lovie in tow. Her eyes were red-rimmed from crying and her hair stood on end as though she'd been raking her fingers through it.

Bill left Lovie in Sam's care and pulled his wife to a corner of the room.

"How bad is it?" Jackie said, reading her husband's grave expression.

"Bad." Bill massaged the back of his neck. "Preliminary tests show that Mack has suffered a major heart attack. To make matters worse, he has atrial fibrillation. God only knows how long he's been living with that, the crusty old fart. Do you have any idea when he last had a checkup? I asked your mom, but she didn't know."

Jackie shook her head. "I have no idea."

"He's stable for the moment, but he's going to need surgery. And soon."

"How soon?"

"Tonight soon. Tomorrow morning at the latest." He leaned in closer and lowered his voice. "Listen, Jack. I don't feel comfortable performing this surgery. Mack is like an uncle to me. His A-fib makes a critical situation life threatening. I don't trust anyone in my practice with his case. I'm sending him to MUSC. An air ambulance is already on the way and a colleague is standing by in Charleston."

Jackie clutched her purse. "Is he going to die?"

Bill looked at her square in the eye. "I honestly don't know."

Inhaling a deep breath, Jackie straightened. "Okay, then. I guess I'm taking my mother to Charleston. Can you look after the kids?"

"I can do that. I'll head home as soon as I get Mack off."

Jackie returned to her family who were huddled together near the exit door. "Bill is sending Mack to Charleston in an air ambulance for surgery."

Lovie's hand flew to her throat. "In a helicopter. In this weather?"

Jamie pulled the radar up on his phone. "The storm is almost over, Gran," he said, showing her the screen. "Why isn't Uncle Bill performing the surgery? He's the best."

"Some doctors aren't comfortable operating on their own family. And he thinks of Mack like an uncle." Jackie smiled at Jamie. "But thanks for your vote of confidence." She turned to Lovie. "I guess that means you and I are going to Charleston."

"I'd like to go with you, Miss Jackie, if that's okay." Annie lowered her head, staring at her feet. "I don't know him all that well yet, but I'd like to be there for him."

Jackie gave Annie's arm a quick squeeze. "Of course you can go with us. Anybody else?" She looked at Sam and Jamie.

"You go ahead, Mom. Faith and I can manage the market tomorrow," Jamie said to Sam and she nodded.

Jackie looked to the sky when she heard the thumping beat of a helicopter's rotating blades overhead, the sound of impending doom. "Okay, then. I guess we better get going."

Eighteen

SAM

"ANNIE SEEMS TO have a calming effect on Mom," Sam said when she saw her mother and Annie talking softly to one another in the backseat, their heads held close together. "I'm glad we brought her along."

Jackie glanced in the rearview mirror. "That girl can talk to anybody about anything at anytime." She cleared the last light on the outskirts of town and increased her speed. "So. Now that we have forty-five minutes ahead of us, tell me, what's going on between you and Eli?"

Sam ignored her sister, staring instead at the headlights of oncoming cars. Since her encounter with Eli in the Sweeney's parking lot earlier, she'd tried not to think about him, about his job offer and the idea of him moving all the way to New York. She'd been fighting the urge for a drink all night. The crisis with Mack had set her nerves on end and made the craving that much stronger. She was relieved to be surrounded by her family, to be heading to MUSC where they would hold vigil in a hospital waiting room instead of at home where the temptation for alcohol might prove too great.

Sam thought about calling Megan. She'd hit it off with her new AA sponsor, but she didn't want to scare her away by dropping a load of baggage on her too soon, only hours after their first meeting. Making friends with other women had never come easy for Sam. She'd always had a hard time finding things in common with them. She liked being outdoors, engaging in recreational activities like hunting and fishing. Most women she knew preferred shopping and playing tennis, pastimes more suited to Jackie, things Sam knew little about.

Sam brought her phone to life and texted Moses: "*En route to MUSC with Mom. Mack had a heart attack. I'll call you when I know more.*"

He texted back right away: "*Please do. I will say a prayer for him. How are you holding up?*"

Sam returned her phone to her lap, leaving his question unanswered.

"You're avoiding my question, Sam. What is going on with you and Eli?" Jackie asked, keeping her eyes glued to the road. "It hurt my feelings to hear about your breakup from Annie. After everything you and I went through last summer, I thought we'd grown closer."

"What's left to say if Annie already told you about us? Eli and I broke up. Our relationship is over."

"I hope this isn't your old fear of marriage coming back to haunt you."

Sam's face tightened. "My fears never went anywhere. The situation is complicated. And I'm sick and tired of talking about it."

"When you find someone who is so obviously perfect

for you, like Eli is for you, making the commitment is the easy part."

"He may be perfect for me," Sam said. "But I'm clearly not perfect for him."

"Says who, you? You don't get to make those decisions, Sam. If you're not careful, you will end up alone."

"Can we please forget about Eli for now and focus on Mack?"

For the rest of the drive to Charleston, Jackie and Sam spoke in hushed tones, so Lovie couldn't overhear them discuss the complications of Mack's condition and the chances of his survival. Being married to a cardiologist had its benefits. Sam marveled at how much her sister knew about the risks associated with open-heart surgery and the recovery times for someone Mack's age.

Slippery roads doubled the time it normally took them to drive to Charleston. Bill had texted Jackie detailed directions on where to go once they arrived at the Heart and Vascular Center. They turned the SUV over to the valet parking attendant and entered the building. A security guard pointed them to the nearly empty surgery waiting room where they checked in with the receptionist before making themselves comfortable in a group of oversized chairs clustered around a square coffee table.

"Should I go find us some coffee?" Annie offered. "I think we're in for a long night."

"That'd be great, Annie." Jackie removed several bills from her wallet. "Get some sandwiches and snacks too, if you can carry it all."

While Annie was gone in search of the cafeteria, a nurse—her hair pulled into a severe bun with the facial expression to match it—came to the waiting room to brief them. According to the nurse, the surgery team had whisked Mack into the operating room as soon as they got him prepped.

"He's been in the OR for about thirty minutes now. You can expect the operation to take up to six hours." After promising to update them periodically, the nurse disappeared once again behind the closed double doors.

Lovie got up and began pacing the floor, her shoulders slumped, her hands twisting in knots. "I don't understand why I can't see him."

"He's in surgery, Mom, in the operating room," Jackie said. "The doctors and nurses are taking good care of him. Mack is a fighter. He will make it through this just fine."

Sam took Lovie by the arm and led her back to her chair. "Annie will be back in a minute with sandwiches. I bet you're starving. You didn't eat any dinner tonight, did you?"

"How can I possibly think about eating, knowing what they are doing to Mack in there?" Lovie pointed at the double doors.

"It's important that you keep up your strength," Jackie said. "Mack is going to need your help when he gets out of the hospital. Who will take care of him if you get sick?"

Annie returned with a turkey sandwich, chips, and coffee for each of them. Scooting her chair closer to Lovie, she helped her old friend unwrap the plastic from her sandwich and pour cream into her coffee.

Sam shot her sister a look. *Is this kid for real?*

Sam and Jackie did their best to direct the conversation away from Mack's surgery while they ate. But Lovie was too distraught, dazed, and confused to talk lucidly about anything. Finally, frustrated, Jackie removed a pill bottle from her bag, broke a white tablet in half, and insisted their mother take it. "Xanax," she mouthed to Sam.

Sam raised an eyebrow. "Do you always carry around a supply of narcotics?" she whispered.

"I have anxiety, Sam. After what I've been through the past year with my husband, that shouldn't surprise you." She dropped the pill bottle back in her bag. "Besides, Xanax is not a narcotic. It's a carefully controlled substance."

"Which is all the more reason we shouldn't be giving it to our mother without her doctor's approval."

The nurse returned around midnight, reporting that everything was going smoothly in the operating room. The others nodded off sometime later. But Sam, no matter what she tried, couldn't get comfortable enough to fall asleep. She was dozing when she heard Annie stir sometime around four. Through a cracked eyelid, Sam watched the girl leave the waiting room.

Curious, and a tad suspicious, Sam got up and followed her. Her unease mounted as Annie bypassed the ladies' room and exited the front of the building. Careful to keep her distance, she walked as quietly as she could manage in her rubber-soled Sperrys. She trailed Annie down Doughty Street and around the curve onto Jonathan Lucas. Her concern escalated into full-fledged alarm when Annie entered the Hollings Cancer Center. When Annie got on the elevator, Sam waited on the ground floor, watching until the signal light indicated the elevator had stopped on the third floor. To save time, she opted to take the stairs. Bolting up three flights, she arrived on the third floor in time to catch a glimpse of Annie's green work shirt as she was disappearing through double doors marked ICU. Sam punched in the button on the wall that released the lock and opened the doors. She spotted Annie down the hall, speaking to a petite brunette at the nurses' station. Sam hid behind a tall metal cart, her back pressed against the wall, watching and waiting until Annie crossed the hall and entered one of the patient's rooms. She allowed five excruciatingly slow minutes to pass before she followed her.

In all the twenty years since she'd last seen him, Sam had not forgotten the face of the man she'd once planned to marry, the man who'd broken her heart. She would have recognized Allen anywhere despite his bald head, sunken cheeks, and skin the color of an overripe banana. Once so handsome and alive, the man lying in the bed in front of her reminded Sam of a baby bird.

What the hell is Annie doing visiting Jamie's father?

Of course. The eyes. Sam had never noticed it before, but she'd sensed it many times. And it wasn't just Sam. Her whole family had commented on that odd feeling of familiarity, like they'd known Annie all her life when they'd only just met her. The shape of the eyes was the same—wide set and upturned—but Annie's were more the color of dark chocolate whereas Jamie's were as black as soot. Like his father's. Like their father's.

Sam stared first at Allen, then at Annie. "Which one of you wants to explain what's going on here?"

Allen's lips spread into a smile, revealing teeth stained and rotting from chewing tobacco. "It's good to see you, Sam. You're looking well."

"Unfortunately, I can't say the same about you." Sam smacked herself in the forehead. "God! How could I have been so stupid?" She glared at Annie. "You've been lying to us all this time, living in my sister's guest house, babysitting for my niece, working in my place of business. It wasn't a coincidence that you"—she pointed at Annie—"showed up out of the blue on our doorstep. Because you"—she jabbed a finger in Allen's direction—"sent her there to find us. You need something don't you, a kidney or bone marrow?"

The guilty look on Allen's and Annie's faces told Sam everything she needed to know.

"Well, you won't get it. At least not from my son. You're not getting one drop of Jamie's blood. You gave up all rights to his body parts when you abandoned us twenty years ago."

Fury raged through her body, threatening to blow her mind to pieces. Her chest tightened and her throat constricted. She needed air and fast. She dashed out of the room, shot past the nurses' station, and flew down the hall, then the stairs, and out of the building. Gripping her purse to her chest, blinded by tears, she ran as fast as she could down the deserted dark sidewalks. She ran until her lungs ached and legs finally gave out. She slowed to a walk, gasping for air. First Eli and their breakup followed by the hostage situation. Then Mack. Now Allen. Four major crises in less than a week. Too much for an alcoholic to face without comfort from a bottle.

She looked around, surprised to find herself surrounded by the stately buildings of the College of Charleston. There did not appear to be a bar or restaurant nearby, at least not that she could see. Everything was closed at that hour, anyway. And it was still dark outside. She roamed the downtown streets of Charleston, block after block with no set direction in mind. When she passed a bum on one of the street corners, she considered asking him for a sip, but that seemed desperate, even despite her unbearable craving.

Where was Annie's mother in all this? The woman who'd

beaten Sam out of the job as Allen's wife. Sam thought back to the night of Faith's wedding. "I'm from Florida," Annie had said. "My mom is a maid at a seaside motel and my father works in construction, but he's been out of a job for going on three years." All lies. Except the one about Allen being currently out of work. That much was obvious.

All these years she'd wondered what had happened to him, where he lived, whether he still worked as a fisherman. He'd never tried to contact her, and she had no idea how to get in touch with him. Not that she'd ever wanted to. He'd made his feelings for her clear when he left her at the altar to raise their child on her own. There'd been times when she'd worried about how she'd track Allen down if Jamie became ill and needed stem cells or an organ donation. How ironic. No way in hell would she let her son donate any of his precious body parts to a man who had never so much as sent him a birthday card.

What was so special about Annie's mother that Allen would choose to marry her? How was it fair that Annie had been raised by her father when Jamie had spent every day of his life wishing he knew his? The old hurt, the sense of loss that had consumed her for years after Allen left, came rushing back. She couldn't bear the pain, not after breaking up with Eli and the threat of losing Mack.

When the sky grew pink over the houses and buildings of downtown Charleston, she entered the first establishment she could find that served breakfast and booze. She slid onto a stool at the empty bar and ordered a coffee and a double shot of whiskey. She drank the shot in one gulp and ordered another. Her cell phone vibrated in her pocket with an incoming text, and she realized she had seven missed calls from Jackie.

Sam read the text from her sister: "*Where are you? Great news! Mack made it through surgery. The doctor says he's going to be fine. He's still in recovery. Mom has gone back to be with him now. I assume you've gone out for breakfast. Please bring us some.*"

Sam didn't have the strength to explain the situation to Jackie. She kicked back the second shot and ordered a third. Another text came in from her sister fifteen minutes later: "*You're scaring me, Sam. Did something happen? Please let me know you're okay.*"

As much as Sam wanted to keep Allen's condition a secret from Jamie, she knew Annie wouldn't let that happen. She'd recognized the determined set of the girl's jaw—the same stubborn willpower she'd seen on her own son's face many times. Annie aimed to get whatever her father needed to keep him alive.

She texted back: "*Ask Annie.*" And then powered off her phone.

Nineteen
JACKIE

JACKIE SLID HER phone back in her oversized black bag and turned to face Annie who was sitting next to her. "What's going on with Sam? She said you would know."

The color drained from Annie's face. "So she told you."

"She didn't give me any details. She just said to ask you."

"I haven't been completely truthful with you about who I am." Annie slumped back against her chair. "My last name isn't Dawn. It's Bethune. Allen is my father. And he's here." Annie aimed her thumb over her shoulder. "A block over at the cancer center. Sam followed me there earlier when I went to see him."

"Allen Bethune… You mean Jamie's father?"

Biting her lip, Annie nodded and looked away.

Jackie's mind raced as she considered Annie's revelation. "Which makes Jamie your half brother. Which makes everything you told us about hitching a ride with the family with the cute baby a lie. You came to Prospect with a specific agenda in mind."

"I came to Prospect to meet Jamie."

Jackie sprang to her feet and began pacing back and forth. For the past hour, a steady flow of people had filed into the waiting room to await the outcome of their loved one's surgery. The room was already full, but people continued to arrive. Jackie sat back down, lowering her voice. "You tricked us. You led us to believe that you are destitute, that you live in Florida with your family, when all this time you've been on a mission. What exactly is it that you need?"

"Part of Jamie's liver," Annie said without hesitation.

"Whoa," Jackie said, exhaling loudly. "I can only imagine how Sam responded to that."

"She seemed pretty upset. I didn't mean to hurt her, Miss Jackie. You've gotta believe me. Sam has been nothing but kind to me. This isn't about her. This is about me trying to save my father's life. Unfortunately, I don't think she sees it that way."

"She's very protective of her son. But I'm sure you already figured that out for yourself."

"Yes, ma'am. This hasn't been easy for me, you know. Especially once I started to get to know your family. I'm sorry for taking advantage of you. You're all so nice. You're lucky to have each other. My daddy is the only family I have."

Jackie's head jerked up. "Where's your mother? I take it she's not working as a maid in a motel in Florida"

"No, ma'am. My mama took off when I was a baby. I haven't seen her since." Annie looked Jackie straight in the eye. "Go ahead and say it. My father deserved it after what he did to Sam."

"You know about what happened? About what Allen did to Sam?"

"I only found out about it recently. I love my father, Miss Jackie. I don't want him to die. He's all I have."

Jackie and Annie were too deeply wrapped up in their conversation to notice Lovie approaching until she was standing right in front of them. "They're moving Mack up to the ICU on the fourth floor."

Jackie moved her bag out of the chair she'd been saving next to her. Gripping the arms of the chair, Lovie lowered herself to the seat. She seemed to have aged ten years in the past twelve hours.

"How is Mack, Mom?"

"He's going to be just fine. I was relieved to hear him ask the doctor how long before he could go fishing again."

Jackie laughed and Annie covered her mouth to hide her smile. She turned toward her mother. "We need to figure out our plans. I assume you want to stay here with him."

"I don't think Mack should be alone," Lovie said.

"I agree." Jackie squeezed her mother's arm. "We need to prepare for an extended stay, five or six days according to Bill. I suggest we go home, pack our things, and come straight back. It won't take us more than a few hours. We won't need to stay in a hotel. My carriage house is only a couple of blocks over from here. We can take turns sitting with Mack."

"You would do that for me?" Lovie asked with a sigh of relief.

"I've already cleared it with Bill and the boys. They will have it no other way."

Lovie clutched her bag. "Let's go, then. Where's Sam?"

"She—" Annie began, but Jackie shut her up with a warning glare.

"Sam had some business she needed to take care of," Jackie said. "She may or may not be riding home with us."

Too preoccupied to question this explanation, Lovie nodded. "I need to go to the restroom before we leave."

Jackie stood and helped her to her feet. "We'll wait right here for you."

Once Lovie had exited the waiting room, Annie said, "We're not just going to leave Sam here, are we? She needs to talk to Jamie. He's gotta get tested, to see if he's a match for a liver transplant. I haven't seen my dad in a week. He's gotten so much worse. We need to do something soon."

Jackie removed her phone from her bag and clicked on Sam's number. Her call went straight to voice mail. "You don't know Sam like I know Sam. She's gone into hiding. She'll come out eventually, but only when she's ready.

"How's she gonna get home?" Annie asked, her lip trembling.

"Don't worry," Jackie brushed a stray strand of hair off the girl's cheek. "Sam is resourceful. She'll come home when she's ready."

As much as she hated the idea of leaving her sister alone and vulnerable in Charleston, Jackie knew she must put their mother's needs first. "We can always send one of the boys back to pick her up if necessary."

That seemed to appease Annie, but Jackie knew the rest of her family wouldn't be so easy to convince.

Twenty

FAITH

FAITH FELT ANOTHER whopper migraine coming on. As the company's accountant, her primary duties included balancing the books and paying the bills. Sam made juggling the rest of the operations look easy. But Faith had quickly become overwhelmed with the burden of it all. The credit card machine wasn't working properly. One of the refrigerator units was making a strange noise. And it was nearing one o'clock but the wine distributor who arrived like clockwork every Friday morning had yet to show up.

Mike had dropped Bitsy off an hour ago on his way to work. They'd spent the morning together at the hardware store buying supplies for their weekend project—a backyard playhouse for Bitsy. They'd eaten an early lunch at the Sonic Drive-In and gone to Sandy's for an ice cream cone afterward. Mike reported that Bitsy had been in a great mood all morning, but her spirits plummeted once she arrived at Sweeney's and discovered Annie was not there. Faith had put her daughter to work refilling the bins on the vegetable carts, but every five minutes or so, Bitsy tugged on the hem of Faith's shorts and whined about wanting to see Annie. As much as she wanted to be the calming influence her daughter needed, her patience was quickly growing thin.

Faith finished up with a customer and nudged Jamie who was working the fish counter, standing by patiently while a lady decided between grouper and salmon. "Keep an eye on Bitsy for me," Faith whispered. "I need to get some Advil out of the back."

While searching the desk for the office supply of Advil, she stumbled upon Sam's black-leather card file that housed all the contact information for their business associates. She swallowed three Advil with the cold coffee from the mug on her desk and took the card file back to the front.

She waited for Jamie to finish ringing up his fish lady. "Does your mom usually call in an order to the wine supplier, or does he come automatically? We're running low on several varieties. We'll be out completely by the end of the weekend if he doesn't restock today."

Jamie thought about it for a minute. "I'm not sure. He's usually here by now. Why don't you call her?"

"I've been trying all morning. She hasn't returned any of my calls or texts."

"Let me try." Jamie pulled out his phone and held it to his ear. "That's weird. The call went straight to voice mail. Mom never turns off her phone."

"I'm beginning to get worried. We haven't heard anything from anyone in Charleston about Mack." Faith removed her phone from her apron. "I'll call Jackie."

Faith could barely hear her sister when she answered. "Why are you whispering?" she asked.

"Because Mom and Annie are asleep in the backseat," Jackie said.

"Why haven't you called us? How's Mack?" Faith retreated to the corner of the showroom, away from a cluster of noisy customers.

Jackie gave her a brief update on Mack's condition. "We're on our way home to get some clothes. Mom and I are going back to Charleston for a few days so we can help Mack through the worst."

"I have a couple of fires here that I need to put out. Sam's not answering her phone. Can I speak to her?"

Jackie groaned. "Brace yourself, Faith. I have some unpleasant news."

Faith listened, a finger stuffed in one ear and the phone pressed close to the other, as her sister recounted the latest development in the mysterious phenomenon named Annie Dawn.

"That actually explains a lot about Annie," she said, more to herself than her sister. Faith's skepticism of Annie began to make sense. Her comment to Bitsy about them becoming cousins. Her knowledge of fishing she'd obviously learned from Allen. Her resourcefulness—all the things she innately knew how to do were talents she'd developed over a lifetime of taking care of herself.

"Including but not limited to her untimely appearance in Prospect," Jackie said.

"I knew there was something off about that girl." Faith cast a nervous glance across the showroom at her daughter. How would Bitsy react when she found out that her teenage idol was a liar who had manipulated everyone in the family to get close to Jamie, her stepbrother whose liver she needed to save their father's life? The same father who had abandoned

Jamie before he was even born. Faith rubbed her throbbing temples. "And you have no idea where Sam is?"

"None. She's been missing since around five this morning."

"So you just left her in Charleston? I'm sure that went over well with Mom."

"She's too preoccupied with Mack's situation to care. I'm sorry, but I didn't know what else to do, Faith."

"You did the right thing." Staring at the floor, Faith paced in small circles. "Poor Sam. She's toughed it out as a single parent all these years only to find out that Allen has been this perfect father for his other child."

"I've heard Annie's side of the story, Faith, and I would hardly call her life perfect. Her mother abandoned her when she was a baby."

"What goes around comes around, I guess." Another throng of customers entered the market. "Listen, I need to get back to work. We're swamped. We could use Annie's help, but I'm not sure she should be around Jamie. I'd hate for her to say anything about their father to upset him until we find Sam."

"I don't think you need to worry," Jackie said. "I talked to Annie. She understands the seriousness of the situation, and she knows Sam should be the one to tell Jamie about Allen."

"What am I supposed to tell Jamie about his mother's whereabouts?"

Jackie sighed. "Honestly, I don't know. We need to let the situation unfold on its own. My main priority right now is getting Mom back to Charleston."

Faith watched her nephew working through the line of customers at the checkout. She loved Jamie like her own son. She sensed big trouble on the horizon. Sam and Jamie would need help, more than she or Jackie could provide.

"And my priority is to call Moses, first chance I get."

When Jackie dropped her off at the market twenty minutes later, Annie went immediately to work restocking the display cases. Thrilled to have her playmate back, Bitsy jumped in to help. She handed plastic containers of seafood salad and cold soups from the rolling cart to Annie, who then stacked them neatly on the shelves.

Faith kept one eye and ear on Annie while she waited on customers, and saw Jamie corner her the first chance he got. "Where's my mom? Why isn't she with you?"

"She stayed in Charleston." Avoiding his gaze, Annie removed a notepad from her pocket and began jotting down a list of items that needed replenishing.

"What about Gran and Aunt Jackie? Did they come back with you?"

"Yes, but only to get some clothes. They're going right back to Charleston." Annie tucked the notepad under her arm and began pushing the cart toward the back. Jamie stepped in front of her.

"Wait a minute, Annie. I'm worried about my mom. When is she coming home, and why isn't she answering her phone?"

Annie looked past Jamie to Faith, who shook her head no, warning the girl not to say too much. "Something happened that upset her, and she took off. We haven't seen her since this morning. That's all I can say." Annie wheeled the cart around him.

Jamie crossed the showroom to Faith. "I don't understand any of this. You talked to Aunt Jackie. Did she mention anything about my mom?"

"We didn't have much time to talk," Faith said, willing herself to sound calm.

"It probably has something to do with Eli." Phone in hand, Jamie stepped outside the market.

"I don't like lying to my nephew," Faith said the moment Annie returned to the showroom. When the girl avoided her gaze, Faith grabbed her by the arm. "You dropped this bomb on my family. Now you need to help us sort it out. I'm concerned about my sister."

Bitsy tugged at Faith's apron. "Why are you being mean to Annie, Mama?"

Faith released Annie's arm and stroked her daughter's hair. "We're having a little adult talk, honey. Nothing for you to worry about."

"I didn't plan for any of this to happen, Miss Faith," Annie said, tears puddling in her doe-brown eyes. "My dad is getting worse by the day. I'm sorry Sam is so upset, but if she doesn't show up soon, I'm gonna tell Jamie."

Jamie came back inside, bringing with him a surge of hot air. "Tell me what?"

"Tell you that Annie's coming to my house tonight for pizza," Bitsy said, pulling on his arm. "And you're invited too."

Faith and Annie exchanged a look of relief.

Jamie scooped Bitsy up. "Hey squirt, I think you'd better ask your mama before you go inviting everyone over for dinner."

Bitsy's tiny fingers brushed a lock of hair off Jamie's forehead. "I thought since Aunt Jackie and Aunt Sam are gone, we could all eat supper together. Besides, you haven't been to my new house yet."

"You have a point there, kiddo." Jamie blew a raspberry on Bitsy's neck before putting her back down.

Faith winked at Jamie. "Let's get through the day before we worry about supper." She gave her daughter a nudge toward the kitchen. "Bitsy honey, why don't you and Annie finish the restocking before we get busy again?"

Annie wheeled the cart off with Bitsy skipping alongside her.

"Eli hasn't heard from Mom," Jamie said as soon as they were gone. "I'm worried, Aunt Faith. Should we call Moses?"

"I've already left messages on his cell and with his receptionist."

"So you're worried too?"

"A little. It's not like your mom to disappear without checking in. Especially since you and I are the only ones manning the shop today. But we have to remember that your mom is a very strong, capable woman who can take care of herself. I'm sure she just needed a little time to herself. She has a lot on her mind with her breakup with Eli."

"A lot on her mind? You saw her the other night. She was wrecked. If this breakup is really what she wants, she wouldn't be drinking herself blind. Did you hear he might be moving to New York?"

"Eli?" Her eyebrows shot up. "No!"

"Yep. He's been offered a job with the police force up there. He has until Monday to decide if he wants the job or not. You know we'll never see him again if he moves. We can't let that happen! I know deep down my mom wants to be with Eli."

"I can try to talk some sense into her, but she rarely listens to me."

Jamie leaned across the counter toward her. "I've never told anyone this, but I know I can trust you. I've always had this weird empty feeling inside of me, like I'm missing one of my vital organs or something. Uncle Bill was always good about including me in father/son kind of stuff, but it was hard watching Cooper and Sean go home with him afterward when I had to go home alone. Eli and I are more like friends than father and son, but I still love him like a dad. And I think he loves me like a son. And our relationship makes sense because he doesn't have kids and I don't have a father. If he moves to New York, I would have to deal with that empty feeling all over again. I don't want to lose him, Aunt Faith."

Faith saw the gleam of tears and rubbed his arm. "I understand, honey. Everyone knows that Sam and Eli belong together. Everyone except your mama. Her head is harder than most, but maybe, if we work real hard, we can come up with a way to prove it to her."

Sniffling, Jamie pulled away and swiped at his eyes. "But first we need to find her."

"She'll show up eventually. She loves us too much, and she loves this business. You know Sam. She's a hands-on kind of gal. She won't be able to stay away but for so long."

"What if something happened to her, if someone tried to hurt her or something?"

Faith pointed her finger at him. "Don't even go there, Jamie." She squeezed his shoulder. "You need to keep the faith."

Another wave of customers entered the showroom, and the rest of the afternoon passed in a flurry of activity. Faith was grateful for the distraction, but, judging from Jamie's pinched expression and the faraway look in his eyes, he was having a hard time thinking about anything but his mom.

When Eli and Moses came through the front door together a few minutes before six, Faith figured they'd been out in the parking lot contemplating how best to help the dysfunctional Sweeney sisters out of their latest crisis.

Jamie rushed to their side. "Have you heard anything from Mom?"

Moses shook his head. "She's not answering my calls. We were hoping she'd gotten in touch with one of you."

Faith joined them. "Jackie texted a little while ago when she got back to Charleston, but there was no sign of Sam at the hospital. I'm worried. We need to do something."

Eli rested his hand on the revolver at his waist. "Technically, we can't file a report until a person has been missing for twenty-four hours. But I have a couple of buddies on the force in Charleston. I spoke to them earlier. They are on the lookout."

Annie and Bitsy came out from the back office where they'd been playing Old Maid for the past hour. "Can we go home now, Mama? I'm tired of being here."

"Sure, honey." Faith picked up her daughter, and Bitsy hid her face in her neck.

"I can't sit around here doing nothing." Jamie removed the Jeep keys from his pocket. "I'm going to Charleston to look for her."

"Wait, Jamie, don't go." Annie placed a hand on his arm. "There's something I need to tell you first."

Moses's phone vibrated in his hand. "Hold that thought, Annie. I got a text from Sam." Everyone stared at Big Mo as he silently read the text. He looked up from the phone. "She's in trouble."

Twenty-One

SAM

SAM SAT BOLT upright in bed. Where the hell was she? Was she in someone's house? The homey decor—four poster bed, lace curtains, and ornamental rugs—didn't look like any hotel she'd ever stayed in. Last thing she remembered... Ugh. What was the last thing she remembered? She fell back against the mountain of pillows. Peeking under the covers, she was relieved to find she was still wearing her bra and panties. The door to the adjoining bathroom was open. As best she could tell she was alone. Not that she was in the habit of picking up strange men. But she hadn't felt like herself lately. Nothing surprised her about her own behavior anymore. She seriously needed to get a grip.

The last thing she clearly remembered, she was drinking shots of whiskey at Halo. But that was early this morning, at breakfast. If the clock beside the bed was right, it was almost time for dinner. Which left a lot of unaccounted for hours in between. She covered her face with a pillow, the dense down muffling her anguished shriek. "Aargh!" *So this is what rock bottom feels like.* She pulled the pillow away from her face and hurled it across the room, knocking a lamp off the chest of drawers. "Fuck you, Rock Bottom," she yelled. "And fuck you, Allen."

She sat up slowly, waiting for the dizziness to pass before trying to stand up. She found a terry cloth robe on the back of the bathroom door and went outside to the balcony adjacent her room. Down below, people meandered on the sidewalks on the other side of the iron fence that surrounded the property. From her second-floor piazza, Sam spotted a street sign—the corner of Ashley Avenue and Bee Street. She felt some comfort in knowing she was still in Charleston.

Bile rose from her stomach. She had no recollection of coming here. Sam had never blacked out before. Sure, she'd had instances where she'd lost bits and pieces of memory after drinking too much, but never hours erased from her mind. It terrified her to think of what could've happened to her. Alone and drunk in a town she barely knew.

She went back inside and searched the drawers for a pack of matches, stationery, anything that would give her the name of the inn. She located her purse beside her discarded pile of clothes on the bathroom floor. Stuffed inside one of the interior pockets, she found a receipt from The Ashley Inn Bed and Breakfast for $181.69. It was time stamped 12:09 p.m. She powered on her phone and, ignoring the texts and voice messages that came flooding in, googled the address of the inn.

She texted Moses: "*I'm in trouble. 201 Ashley Avenue. Charleston. Please come alone.*"

He responded: "*Be there in 45 minutes. Don't move.*"

She texted Jamie: "*I'm sorry for worrying you. I'll be home tonight. I'll explain everything then.*"

She didn't wait for his response, couldn't bear the thought of him being angry with her. Or disappointed. She stripped naked and stepped in the shower, letting the steaming hot water wash away the day's drunkfest.

I've got to get ahold of myself. Forget about Eli and Allen. Focus on Jamie. What kind of example am I setting for him?

She dressed in the same clothes, sans underwear, which she balled up and stuffed in the wastebasket. She dried her hair and put on a little mascara, eyeliner, and lip gloss.

When Moses texted that he was in the lobby, Sam hurried downstairs to meet him.

The girl behind the check-in desk greeted her with a snide, "Are you leaving so soon?"

Sam slapped her room key on the counter. "I just needed a little nap. Thanks."

Moses offered his arm and Sam accepted it, grateful for his *steadying force* to guide her down the front steps."

"How much do you know?" she asked Moses, once they were tucked inside his compact car.

"Only that you disappeared for most of the day without a word to your family. They are worried sick about you, in case you're wondering. Judging from the smell of alcohol on your breath, you spent part of that time in a bar somewhere." He started the car. "Are you hungry? When's the last time you ate?"

"I ate dinner. Last night."

"Then I'm taking you to my new favorite restaurant." He sped off down Ashley Avenue.

"Who called you?"

"Faith and Jamie both called me," Moses said, taking a left

onto Calhoun Street. "I was at Sweeney's when I got the text from you."

"I figured as much. That's why I told you to come alone."

She stared out the car window at the people strolling down the sidewalk, out walking their dogs on a pleasant summer's evening. Why couldn't her life be so uncomplicated? Maybe she needed to get a dog.

"Was Annie at the market?" she asked, and braced herself for the answer.

"Yes, why?"

"Because she knows."

Moses took a right onto E Bay Street, drove a few blocks, and then whipped his car into a parking space in front of 167 Raw. "What does Annie know, Sam? I can't help you until I know the whole story."

"Do you ever think about coincidences, how ironic they can be sometimes? It turns out that Annie isn't a stranger after all. She and Jamie share something in common. They have the same father."

"What?" Moses placed a finger to his ear. "Did I just hear you say Jamie and Annie are half brother and sister?"

"Yep. Small world, ain't it?"

Moses placed his big hand over his face, rubbing his cheeks and chin. "Wow. That actually explains a lot about a lot of things."

"I can't believe we're eating at a raw bar," Sam said, opening the passenger door. "Oysters on the half shell aren't exactly my idea of hangover food."

They entered the restaurant, and Moses asked for a private table in the corner. The hostess greeted him with a smile of recognition, as though he'd been there many times before.

Once they were seated, Sam said, "I like the vibe of the place."

Perusing the menu, Moses said, "If you're looking for something that will stick to your ribs, the lobster roll is the best I've eaten. Po' Boy is not a bad choice either. And, they have great craft beer on tap." He winked at her.

Her face took on a green tint. "The thought makes me want to vomit."

Moses set his menu down and reached for Sam's hand. "Why didn't you call Megan?"

"Because, Mo, I only just met the woman yesterday. I didn't want to scare her off with all my problems."

"She's a veteran sponsor. That's why I picked her for you. That's what the whole sponsorship program is about. You know this."

Sam hung her head. "I made a lot of bad decisions today. I was already feeling vulnerable after breaking up with Eli. Then Eli was held hostage with a bomb handcuffed to his arm. Then Mack had his heart attack, and I was terrified we would lose him. When I saw Allen lying in that hospital bed, with Annie at his side, I just lost it."

"Wait a minute. Allen is sick?"

"Yes, he has some sort of cancer. Probably liver, judging from his sallow-looking skin."

The waiter—a young man about twenty with muscular tatted-up arms—arrived to take their order. Moses ordered a dozen crab claws with iced tea and Sam opted for the lobster roll and a diet coke.

After the waiter left, Sam filled Moses in on what little she knew about Annie and Allen.

"Knowing how you feel about Jamie's father, I can only

imagine how hard this is for you," Moses said, when she'd finished talking.

"I thought I'd put this business with Allen behind me a long time ago. But all the pain and loneliness came rushing back to me today. With something new mixed in—jealousy."

"And that's totally understandable. When Allen abandoned you, he stripped you of your self-esteem. You've never been able to devote yourself to anyone else, because you don't see yourself as worthy. And now you feel jealous not only that Allen picked someone else to marry but that he's parenting someone other than Jamie."

The tension drained from Sam's shoulders and she slumped back in her seat. "No wonder I pay you the big bucks. You've just solved all my problems."

"That's where you're wrong." Mo wagged a beefy finger at her. "I've identified your problems. Now you and I need to work together to come up with a solution on how to work through them."

"I was afraid of that. What did you have in mind, Dr. Ingram?"

Lacing his fingers together, he placed them on the table and settled back in his chair. "You can start by going to see Allen."

"What?" Sam's forehead shot up to her hairline. "Are you crazy? No way."

"I'm not crazy at all. I'm dead serious. And you need to do it tonight."

Twenty-Two

SAM

"**R**EMIND ME AGAIN why we're doing this?" Sam asked on the way to the Hollings Cancer Center an hour later.

"Because, Sam, you've made some assumptions about your relationship with Allen that may or may not be true. Those assumptions have controlled your emotions all these years."

"Are you saying the truth will set me free?"

"In the end, yes. How long it takes to travel the road to freedom depends on Allen's reason for leaving you. Maybe he joined the Marines for a tour of duty in the Gulf, planning to one day come back and claim you as his bride. Which, to me, would be admirable and easier to forgive than if he got cold feet because he didn't like the way you styled your hair."

Sam rolled her eyes. "Both seem highly unlikely to me."

"Of course I'm exaggerating, but you get my drift. Either way, you and I will face the reality together, and you will begin the process of healing."

"Did I ever tell you how much your logical approach to

everything irritates me?" Sam propped her head against the window. "I wish I could go home and crawl into my bed."

"You tried that already today, and it didn't work out so well for you."

Moses pulled up in front of the cancer center. "I'll let you out here, then go park the car."

"You promise you're coming in?"

Moses placed his hand over his heart. "I'll be waiting for you in the lobby with my cell phone in hand. If you get in trouble, all you have to do is text me." When she reached for the door handle, he grabbed her arm. "One more thing before you go. You need to know the details about Allen's disease before you talk to Jamie. You can't ask Jamie to donate an organ when you don't even know which organ he needs to give."

She swallowed hard. "I understand."

Sam made her way to the third floor of the cancer ward for the second time that day. She'd been too preoccupied earlier to notice that Allen had a roommate, an older man who was currently puking his guts up into a bedpan.

Sam wanted to help him, but she didn't know how. "Can I call the nurse for you?"

Wiping his mouth with the sleeve of his robe, he shook his head. "Nothing she can do. But thanks."

Sam pulled the drape tight to allow the man his privacy.

Allen gestured toward the chair beside the bed. "I'm surprised to see you again so soon."

"My shrink insisted I come," Sam said, her tone more hostile than she'd intended.

"Ouch."

Sam softened. "I'm sorry. I didn't mean that the way it sounded. It's been a long day."

"For the record, this organ donor business was not my idea. Once Annie gets something into that stubborn head of hers, it's hard to shut her down."

"What kind of cancer is it?"

"Liver. Even if Jamie turns out to be a match, my guess is, it's too late for a transplant. The doctor won't admit it, but I can hear it in his voice. I'm dying, Sam."

The sudden lump in her throat surprised Sam. She'd spent the last twenty years wishing ill will on Allen. Shouldn't she be happy to find out he was going to die? "Does Annie know?"

"I've tried to break it to her as gently as possible. Deep down inside, I think she understands what's happening. She's just too darn bullheaded to accept it." Allen traced the pattern on the quilt covering his legs. "She made this for me. Lord knows where she learned how to sew. Probably from watching some program on TV. " He pulled the quilt close to him. "The truth is, I didn't discourage her from going to Prospect. I wanted her to meet Jamie. No matter how you feel about me, my daughter has a right to know her half brother. After I'm gone, she'll be all alone."

"Where's Annie's mother?"

"Long gone. She took off when Annie was a baby." He looked pointedly at Sam. "I know what you're thinking. I deserve every bad thing that happened to me because of the way I treated you."

"I won't argue with that. So you married her."

He nodded. "But I didn't love her. Not like I loved you. I didn't mean to hurt you, Sam."

"Then why did you? I thought we made a good team. We were ready to set the world on fire."

A smile parted his lips. "*You* were ready to set the world on fire. *I* never had that kind of drive and determination. You are the best person I've ever known in my whole life, Sam."

"I don't under—"

He held up his hand. "I wasn't good enough to be your husband. Or your child's father. I had in mind to make my mark on the world, and then come back for you. But it didn't work out that way. I realized pretty darn quick that I would never be anything but a poor, dumb fisherman."

How was it possible for twenty years of hurt and anger to dissipate in a matter of minutes? If only he'd talked about his feelings instead of walking out on her. If only he'd reached out to her, contacted her, she could have helped him.

Is this what it feels like to be set free?

Sam smiled. "I come from a long line of fishermen, remember?"

"Yeah, but Oscar Sweeney had something I never had. Smarts." His face grimaced with pain when he repositioned himself against the pillows. "Annie is smart like that. She takes after her mother."

"I have to admit, I'm curious about Annie's mother. Tell me about her."

"There's not much to tell. I met Sandra a few years after I left Prospect. I married her when she got knocked up with Annie. I'd already run out on one innocent child. I couldn't bring myself to abandon another. I'm not surprised Sandy took off like she did. She always had her heart set on making it big in Hollywood."

"Did she? Make it big, I mean."

"I honestly don't know. We haven't heard from her since she left."

"I know what that feels like."

"I deserved that." An awkward silence filled the room and they heard the man in the bed next to Allen retching. "As you might imagine, I've spent my life jumping from one fishing boat to the next. I managed to keep Annie in school, but she hasn't had an easy life. Most of the time we barely scraped by."

The misgivings Sam had initially felt toward Annie subsided. "She's a good kid, Allen. You did right by her. She's a hard worker and easy to get along with. She's not like most teenagers I know."

He shrugged. "I'm a lousy provider, but it turns out I'm not such a bad father." He hesitated, as though trying to decide whether to continue. "I know I don't have any right to ask, and I understand if you say no, but I'd really like it if you'll allow me to meet Jamie."

When Sam entered the lobby, Moses rose from his chair and she walked straight into his arms, his powerful muscles giving her the strength she needed to hold herself together.

"How'd it go?" he asked, his chin atop her head.

"As you predicted. I'll fill you in on the way home." She took a step back from the giant. "But I want to check in on Mack before I leave, if that's okay with you. I need to see him now."

"Of course."

As they exited the Hollings Cancer Center and walked a block to the parking deck, Sam told Moses she planned to come back to MUSC on Sunday and bring Jamie to see his father depending on how her son received the news.

"I'll get the car," Moses said, "and wait for you in front of the Heart building. Give Mack my best."

As Sam retraced her steps from early that morning, she thought about how much had happened during the last sixteen hours. With all the issues she needed to work through, she would undoubtedly need Moses to help her in the days and weeks ahead. Part of her felt ready to flap her wings and fly. Allen had left her all those years ago—not because of his feelings for her but because of his own feelings of inadequacy. The other part of her felt tethered to the earth, burdened by the blow she would soon deliver to her son. She had no idea how to tell Jamie that his father suddenly wanted to see him after all this time, that his father was also Annie's father, and that his father would die if Jamie didn't undergo an organ transplant to save his life.

The attendant at the information desk in the lobby gave Sam the room number and pointed her to the elevators leading to the fourth floor. She was relieved to find Mack alone. She wasn't in the mood to explain her day's whereabouts to her mother and sister.

"You gave us quite a scare, you know," she said, approaching Mack's bed. His appearance shocked Sam. In addition to the tubes and wires covering his face, arms and chest, his eyes, now cloudy, were sunken and his skin translucent. Sam thought her old friend looked as though he was on death's doorstep, like he'd aged ten years in the last twenty-four hours.

"I even scared myself this time. All those damned cigars finally caught up with me." He reached for her hand. "I have to admit, the idea of fishing the great big ocean in heaven with Oscar Sweeney sounds appealing."

"Stop being morbid, Mack. It's not your time."

"I wouldn't be too sure about that." He brought her hand to his cheek, his prickly gray whiskers rough against her skin. "You just missed your mom and Jackie. I sent them down to the cafeteria for dinner. Lovie, bless her heart, has been fussing over me all afternoon. I couldn't take it anymore."

"Let her fuss. She's grateful you're alive. We all are." Sam lowered herself to the edge of the bed. "How do you feel?"

"Like a cargo ship crossed my chest." He peeled his hospital gown back and showed her the angry incision marching down his chest.

"Ouch, you poor man." She patted his arm. "I'm not going to stay long. You need your rest."

"Don't go just yet." He gripped her hand tighter. "I've been lying here for most of the afternoon, thinking about how blessed I've been to share my life with the Sweeney family. You and your sisters are like daughters to me—the children May and I were never able to have. Your father was the best friend a man could ever ask for. And Lovie ... well, I always had a bit of a crush on her, even when we were married to other people. The past year has been one of my happiest." He was quiet for a minute, the sound of his shallow breathing mixed with the beeping of the monitors. "I wish I'd gotten the nerve sooner to tell your mother how I feel about her. But I kept those feelings to myself for fear of betraying Oscar."

It scared Sam to hear Mack speak with such melancholy. "Dad would never have wanted Mom to be alone. Who else to take his place but his best friend?"

"I realize that now. Now that it's too late." He looked

159

away, staring out the window for a long minute before returning his attention to her. "Don't let that happen to you, Sam."

"Let *what* happen, Uncle Mack?"

"Don't let your stubborn notions get in the way of your happiness. I know you, girl. You're as bullheaded as your father. And not unlike me. You can talk yourself into believing the ocean is red when you know damn well it's blue. You and Eli belong together. Don't let your misguided conscience convince you otherwise."

"How did you know we were having problems? Did Eli tell you?"

"He didn't have to. When you get to be my age, Sam, you see things most people don't see. I've been catching fish nearly all of my life. Eli has cast his line. And while my gut tells me he's prepared to wait awhile for you to take the bait, I'm not sure that's a risk you should take." Mack stared over at the monitor, beating a perfect rhythm of his heart as the blood pumped through his newly bypassed arteries. "I've just had a hell of a reminder of how precious our time is on earth."

Twenty-Three
FAITH

AFTER MOSES'S ABRUPT departure for Charleston, Eli and Jamie had taken off together, and left Annie and Faith to close up the market.

"Hop in, Annie. I'll give you a ride home." Aiming her key at the car, Faith clicked the doors unlocked.

Annie hesitated. "Thanks, but I think I'll walk."

"And *I* think that's a really bad idea. There is a lot of traffic on the road this time of day." Faith opened the front door for her.

"Come on, Annie," Bitsy said, taking her by the hand. "Don't you want to ride in my new car?"

Once they were all buckled in, Annie said, "This is nice," running her hand across the wood-paneled dashboard. "What did you do with your truck?"

"Mike took it to the truck graveyard." Faith started the engine. "That old truck has seen me through a lot, good and bad. I was sad to see it go, but it'd become pretty unreliable."

"Can Annie come over for a sleepover?" Bitsy asked, kicking her feet against the back of Faith's seat.

Faith was too exhausted to entertain company, but she couldn't bring herself to tell the girls no. "Sure, if she wants to."

"I'm not sure that's such a good idea." Annie looked down at her khaki shorts and work shirt. "I've been wearing these clothes for two days. I feel pretty grimy."

"Why don't I run you out to the farm to get your things? Then you can have a long hot shower in our guest room."

"Or a bubble bath," Bitsy threw in.

Faith winked at Annie. "She loves the new spa tub. I promise I won't let her get in with you."

"I'm not much on taking baths," she said over her shoulder to Bitsy. "But a long hot shower sounds perfect."

Faith waited for traffic to clear before turning right onto Creekside Drive. "Bill is taking the boys to Charleston to see Mack anyway. I don't think you should be alone. Not tonight."

"Yay!" Bitsy clapped her hands. "Can we get pizza takeout?"

"Of course," Faith said in the rearview mirror. "We'll pick it up from Angelo's on the way back from the farm. Mike has to work late at the hospital. How about we have ourselves a girls' night in?"

Bitsy clapped her hands again. "What kind of pizza do you like, Annie? Pepperoni is my favorite."

Annie turned her head so she could see her little friend in the backseat. "I like anything on my pizza, Bits. Pepperoni, sausage, mushrooms, anchovies."

Bitsy crinkled her nose. "Ooh, gross. What's an anchovy, Mama?"

For the rest of the drive, they discussed the various options for toppings and grew hungry for pizza in the process. By the time they arrived home with two large steaming pizza boxes on the backseat beside Bitsy, they were starving. But an hour later, Annie's two slices remained untouched on her plate on the table beside her. Her left hand resting on her iPhone in her lap, she rocked slowly back and forth on the porch, staring out across the water at the disappearing sun. Bitsy gobbled down the last bite of her crust and crawled onto Annie's lap with her coloring book and Dolly. Opening the book, Annie absent-mindedly thumbed through the pages until Bitsy picked out the one she wanted to color.

Faith and Annie sat together in comfortable silence while Bitsy scribbled away with her crayons. Several boats passed by, out for an evening cruise, the passengers waving up to them. When Bitsy grew tired of coloring, she put her book down and reached for Dolly. She curled up in Annie's arms, stuck her thumb in her mouth, and was asleep within a matter of minutes.

Faith knew what it was like to watch one's father dying from cancer; and despite her grievances toward the girl, she was worried about her. Usually talkative, Annie had hardly completed a sentence since they'd gotten home. Taking a sip of Chardonnay, Faith said, "I was a little hard on you at the market earlier. I'm worried about Jamie. And I'm worried about you too. I'm truly sorry about your father, Annie. If there is anything you want to talk about, I'm a pretty good listener."

After several long minutes of awkward silence, Annie said, "I know all of you hate my dad after what he did to Sam. But he's not the same man anymore. Believe me, his life would have been a lot easier if he'd just dropped me off in some foster home. But he didn't do that. He made sacrifices for me, and I'm grateful to him for that."

"I gather your mother's not involved in your life?"

Annie shook her head. "She took off when I was a baby. I'm better off without her."

Faith thought back to the night of her wedding reception at Jackie's, and wondered how much of what Annie had said was true.

"Did you ever live in Florida?"

"I was born in Fort Lauderdale, and that's where we lived until I was about eight, when my dad lost his job. After that, we went to the Keys, moved around a lot down there, living in motels mostly. I went to nine different schools in five years."

"I imagine that can be tough on a kid," Faith said.

Annie shrugged. "I got used to it. My dad is not a drunk, Miss Faith, and he doesn't steal. He just has really rotten luck. Every time he found a fishing job he liked, the owner would sell the boat or move it to the Bahamas."

"Did your father ever work construction?" Annie rolled her head to the side, facing Faith. "He did, actually. When I was fourteen, we moved back to Lauderdale, and Dad got a job building houses. He really liked it, too. That was the most normal year we had. But then he got sick and had to quit. I got a job waitressing after school to support us while he had chemo. He made it through one round, and we thought he was going to beat the cancer, but then he got sick again. This time it's really bad. The doctors say he needs a transplant. I got tested. When we found out I wasn't a match... that's when Daddy told me he had another kid."

Faith nearly choked on her wine. "You mean Allen never mentioned Sam or Jamie before then?"

"Nope. He didn't even know if his kid was a boy or a girl."

Settling back in her chair, Faith watched a man and his

young son putt-putting down the creek in their boat, two fishing rods hanging over the back. She would never understand what made some parents treat their children so poorly—beating them or becoming alcoholics or leaving home to chase their own selfish dreams. Women were often just as guilty as men. Annie's mother was a perfect example.

"I wonder why he never bothered to find out."

Annie shrugged. "I guess he was ashamed of the way he'd treated them. Now that I know the truth, I think maybe the reason he has taken such good care of me is to make up for what he did to them."

Faith considered Annie's assessment before answering, "That's one way of looking at it."

"I had to beg my dad to come here. He refuses to ask Jamie for his help. But I think he wants to meet him. You know, in case he dies." Annie's voice cracked.

"I'm so sorry, Annie." Faith stroked the girl's arm. "I can't imagine how hard this has all been on you. You're so young to have been through so much."

"We spent every last penny we had on our bus tickets to Charleston. Daddy got sick during the trip. An ambulance met us at the bus station and took him straight to the hospital. He's been there ever since."

Annie checked her phone, and let out a sigh when there were no messages. "I wish someone would call from Charleston and let us know everything's okay."

"Don't worry. Moses will call when he has something to report."

"What if something happened to Sam?"

"No news is good news. Moses knows this family well.

He'll know how to handle the situation and how to break the news to Jamie."

Annie relaxed. "I hope you're right."

Bitsy woke up when Faith tried to move her to her bed. She insisted Annie read her a bedtime story. Faith peeked in on them a half hour later when Mike came home and found them both sound asleep in Bitsy's bed.

"Let's not disturb them." Faith turned out the overhead light and closed the door halfway. "I have some pizza in the warming drawer. Are you hungry?"

"Starving." He followed her to the kitchen. "Sounds to me like you've changed your mind about Annie." He removed a Coast craft beer from the refrigerator for himself and refilled Faith's empty glass with Chardonnay.

"I think that's fair to say." Faith transferred some Greek salad from the Angelo's plastic container to a plate and added two slices of warmed pepperoni pizza. "Annie opened up to me about her past tonight. Which has helped me to understand her better." She handed Mike his plate. "Let's go out on the porch and I'll tell you about it."

Once they'd settled into the rocking chairs, Faith said, "All this time I thought Bitsy was the one who needed Annie, but after what she told me tonight, I think it may be the other way around. The two of them are kindred souls."

While Mike ate his dinner, she told him all about Sam's discovery and subsequent disappearance, and then her talk with Annie that evening.

"Whoa." Mike wiped his mouth with his napkin and set his empty plate on the table in front of them. "I'd say the Sweeney sisters have had a rough day. Poor Sam. And poor Annie."

"And poor Jamie," Faith added.

Mike nodded. "What's he like, Jamie's father?"

Faith had to think about Allen for a minute. She didn't remember that much about him, it'd been so long ago. "He seemed like a nice enough guy at the time. We were all surprised when he ditched Sam the way he did. I think her breakup with Eli stems from all the pain Allen caused her back then."

"Maybe Moses can talk some sense into her."

"I certainly hope so." Faith sat back in her chair and pulled one leg underneath the other. "What's up with you? How was your day?"

"Well..." Mike took a long swig of his beer. "I've been dealing with my own share of craziness today. I'm hesitant to tell you about it with all you already have on your plate, but I think you need to know."

"Are you kidding me? I'm constantly burdening you with my family's drama. I want you to talk to me about your problems."

He drew in a deep breath. "Well, there's this nurse at work. She kind of has a thing for me."

Faith's stomach lurched. She'd been married less than a week and already there was another woman. "Should I be worried?"

Mike reached for Faith's hand. "No! It's nothing like that. Several years ago, she made it known that she had a crush on me. I asked her out once, but I felt absolutely no chemistry toward her. She took a job in Columbia shortly after that. She moved back to Prospect about a month ago, apparently to take care of a sick parent. At least that's what she told everyone."

"What does she look like?" Faith asked.

"She's pretty, if you like female wrestlers."

Faith popped Mike's arm with the back of her hand. "Seriously?"

"She's alright-looking, I guess, if you can get past the hook nose. She has blonde hair and blue eyes, but she recently dyed her hair dark brown and started wearing green-tinted contact lenses."

"That's strange. I thought all women wanted to be blonde."

He tugged on Faith's ponytail. "I prefer brunettes, myself."

"They call my color mousy brown, but I'm glad you like it," Faith said, running her hand across the top of her head. "Do I need to take up weight lifting to defend my territory?"

He chuckled. "You have nothing to worry about."

Faith raised an eyebrow. "But she's been hitting on you at work?"

His chubby cheeks flushed red. "It was innocent enough at first. She'd bring me coffee or a soft drink from the cafeteria. Then, she began leaving heart-shaped chocolates on my desk and texting me with sexual innuendos. When I blocked her number from my cell phone, she started writing me notes. Finally, today, I confronted her. I told her I have a new bride, whom I love very much, and that her advances are making me uncomfortable. She apologized, said she only meant to be friendly."

"This is kind of creepy, Mike."

"I know. I'm sorry." He squeezed her hand. "We haven't exactly had the easiest first week of marriage with Annie, Sam, Mack, and now Chloe."

"Chloe? I knew a girl name Chloe in high school."

"Did she have thunder thighs and huge biceps?" Mike teased.

Faith giggled. "She had bad BO and bucked teeth. That's all I remember."

"I suggest we go on our honeymoon sooner rather than later," Mike said, cupping his hand behind her head. As he was drawing her in for a kiss, Faith caught a flash of movement in the living room behind them.

She jerked away. "Did you lock the front door?"

He followed her gaze. "I'm sure I did. Why?"

She pointed to the french door, which they'd left cracked. "I thought I saw someone in the living room."

He jumped to his feet. "I'll go check."

Too freaked out to stay on the darkened porch alone, Faith went inside and closed the door behind her. She was placing Mike's plate in the dishwasher when he returned several minutes later, carrying a glass of milk.

"Everything is locked up tight, and the guest room door is closed. You probably saw Annie when she moved to her room. I found this"—he held up the glass of milk—"on Bitsy's bedside table. Annie must have gotten it for her. I'm surprised she hasn't learned yet how much your daughter despises milk. Bitsy told me the first time I took her to lunch."

Faith broke out in a cold sweat. "Annie knows all right. I heard her mention it the other day."

Twenty-Four

JACKIE

JACKIE WAITED FOR Bill and the boys out in front of the Heart and Vascular Center. "What took you so long?" she asked when they finally arrived a few minutes after eight.

"Cooper and Sean were starving. I had to stop and get them something to eat," Bill said.

Jackie smiled. "Imagine that."

"You know how much we hate hospitals, Mom," Sean said, an irritating whine in his voice. "I don't understand why we couldn't wait for Uncle Mack to come home before we visited him."

Jackie placed a hand on her son's back. "Some things just shouldn't be put off."

Cooper shot his father a look of alarm. "I thought you said Mack was going to be fine."

"I said he made it through the surgery." Placing his hand at the small of Cooper's back, Bill guided him toward the entrance to the building. "He's a long way from being fine. I'm sure he will appreciate seeing the two of you."

On the way to the fourth floor, the boys gave a spirited recounting about the day's escapades on the water. They'd gotten stuck on a sandbar at low tide. While waiting for the tide to come in, they dug up three buckets of clams. And then, on the way home, they ran out of gas and had to flag down help from another boat.

"It was so embarrassing." Sean hung his head. "We've never run out of gas before. Some of our friends came by while we were getting towed in." He looked up at his father. "Something must be wrong with the gas gauge."

Lovie was pacing back and forth in the ICU family waiting room when they arrived. "Thank goodness you're here," she said to Bill, wringing her hands. "I'm worried about Mack. He's talking out of his head. I can't understand a word he's saying."

"Calm down now, Lovie," Bill said, taking her by the shoulders. "There are any number of things that can cause confusion after a major surgery. His oxygen levels could be low, or his electrolytes might be out of whack. Has his doctor been in to see him tonight?"

Lovie shook her head emphatically. "I told the nurse to call him, but I don't think she did."

"I'll go check on him. I don't have privileges at this hospital, but I can at least take a look at his chart." Bill motioned for the twins to follow him and they disappeared behind the double doors leading to the intensive care unit.

Jackie walked her mother to the closest vacant seat. "I know you're worried, Mom. But you need to try and calm down." She dropped to the love seat, pulling her mother with her. "You need to stay strong for Mack." She wrapped her arm around Lovie, drawing her near. "We can't have you getting sick on us, now can we?"

Shaking her head, Lovie collapsed against Jackie. They sat in silence, watching a ceiling-mounted TV across the room as the Atlanta Braves' pitcher struck out the Yankees. Fifteen minutes passed before the twins reappeared and plopped down in the chairs opposite them.

Lovie sat up straight. "Where's your father?"

"He's back there with Mack," Sean said, aiming a thumb at the ICU.

"Something bad happened." Cooper raked his fingers through his orange mop of hair. "We were talking to Mack, or trying to anyway—he didn't seem to know who we were or what was going on—when all these alarms and buzzers started going off."

Nodding his head vigorously, Sean added, "A whole basketball team of nurses came rushing into the room at once. It freaked me out."

"Dad kicked us out of the room," Cooper said. "He seemed worried."

Jackie cut her eyes at her mother, signaling the boys to be careful not to upset their grandmother, but it was too late.

"Oh dear." Lovie's hand flew to her mouth. "That doesn't sound good."

"Okay, let's try not to panic," Jackie said, rubbing circles on her mother's back. "Bill will be out in a minute to tell us what's going on." She gestured at the TV. "Why don't you boys go watch the ball game while we wait?"

Cooper and Sean lumbered across the room and made themselves comfortable on the sofa in front of the TV.

Jackie's attempts to placate Lovie met with little success. Her patience was wearing thin when Bill returned twenty minutes later.

"Dad?" Cooper leapt to his feet. "Is everything okay?"

Bill motioned him to sit back down. "Don't get up, son. The doctor is in with Mack now. He promised to give us an update as soon as he knows something."

Lovie stared Bill down. "What do you know that you're not telling me?"

"I know nothing, Lovie. I promise," Bill said. "There is no point in speculating about anything until we know something for sure."

"Is he conscious?" Lovie asked.

"Not at the moment, no," Bill said with a grave expression.

"I need to be with him." She slowly rose to her feet.

"You can't go back there, Lovie. I'm sorry. They won't let you in his room."

"I can't just sit here and twiddle my thumbs. I'm going to the chapel down the hall," she said as she pushed past him.

Bill waited until his mother-in-law was gone before he sat down by Jackie. "Be honest with me, Bill. I need to prepare myself so I can be strong for Mom."

Bill sighed. "It doesn't look good, honey. It appears as though he's suffered a stroke." When tears filled Jackie's eyes, Bill handed her his linen handkerchief.

"I've known Mack all my life. I can't imagine what it will be like without him." She blew her nose into Bill's handkerchief. "And poor Mom. He has kept her grounded this past year. They are practically living together, you know. I'm not sure she can handle it if he dies."

Bill patted her thigh. "Let's not get ahead of ourselves, Jack. Mack is a tough old salt. Don't give up on him yet."

She smiled, thinking about how Mack had seen her family

through so many good and bad times in her life. "He is a tough old salt, isn't he?"

"Have you heard anything about Sam since we talked?"

"Not a word." She settled in closer to her husband, comforted by his presence. "Do you ever wish you worked for a big teaching hospital like this one?"

He rested his arm on the back of the sofa behind her. "MUSC didn't offer me the job when I interviewed here, remember?"

"That was years ago." Jackie tilted her head back to look at him. "Your reputation is solid now. I'm sure they'd love to have you."

"Where would I live? Unless you're willing to share your carriage house with me?" He kissed the top of her head. "Our little love nest tucked away at the back of Clara's property."

"Now who's getting ahead of himself?"

"Admit it." He nuzzled her ear. "You're giving in to my charms."

"You underestimate my willpower," she said, laughing and pushing his face away from hers. "I'm serious, though. After living on three acres in a five–thousand-square-foot house, we wouldn't survive a day together in the carriage house. If we bought Clara's house, now that's a different story."

"Actually, I've been giving it some thought since we talked about it the other day. I'm not ready for retirement, but working at MUSC might provide the midlife challenge I need." He propped his elbow on the arm of the chair, sinking his chin into his palm in thinking mode. "What would we do with the farm?"

"Keep it as our weekend retreat, of course," she said, half joking. "Aside from the problems in our marriage, I've been happier this year than I've been in a long time. I really like working in Charleston during the week and coming home on the weekends."

"It's certainly worth considering. A big change like this might be just what we need to survive our empty nest," he said, his expression suddenly glum.

Jackie glanced over at the twins, who were engrossed in the baseball game, their long legs stretched out with their feet propped up on the coffee table in front of them. "You're going to miss them, aren't you?"

He looked at the boys with longing. "Very much. Aren't you?"

"Of course," she replied, thinking about how Bill had always been more hands-on with their sons than she had. "But I'm excited about this next stage in life as well. I'm banking on them going to Georgia. I'm ready for football games and parents' weekends."

"Who says they're going to choose your alma mater over mine?"

"Last time I heard, it snows a lot in Boston. I can barely get them to put on a coat during the winter as it is."

He laughed. "You're probably right."

She dropped her smile. "Football weekends and spending the workweek in Charleston—none of that will be possible if Mack dies. I can't expect my sisters to bear the responsibility of taking care of Mom alone."

"We aren't talking about a cross-country move, Jack. Your sisters work with your mother. They can look out for her during the week, and we can pick up the slack on the weekends." He crossed his arms and settled them atop his spare tire. "I'm not ready to start applying for jobs, but it's definitely something to think about. We're entering a new phase in life. We'll once again be husband and wife, not mom and dad." His lips curled into a mischievous grin. "Does this mean we can have sex soon?"

"Typical man." She play-slapped him on the chest. "All you ever think about is sex."

Twenty-Five

SAM

O N THE DRIVE home from Charleston, Moses helped Sam get prepared for breaking the news to Jamie. But seeing Eli's police cruiser parked on the curb in front of her house threatened what little composure she had left.

"What's he doing here?" she asked, as Moses whipped his sports car into the driveway behind Sam's Jeep.

"I assume he's here to offer Jamie moral support." Moses killed the engine and turned to Sam. "You need to stay focused on the job at hand. And remember, you haven't done anything wrong aside from reacting poorly to some disturbing news."

Jamie and Eli were camped out in the sitting room, watching the Atlanta Braves on TV, the coffee table at their feet littered with foil wrappers from DoubleDees BBQ.

Eli tipped his head in greeting. "We've been worried about you."

"I know, and I'm sorry for that," she said.

When Jamie got up from the sofa, she relished the warmth of his hug for longer than usual.

Sam and Moses took seats—she, next to Jamie on the sofa, and Moses, opposite them in a club chair. She leaned forward and took a deep breath to compose herself.

"I found out something today that upset me quite a bit. I'm ashamed to say, I let my emotions get the best of me. Moses came to my rescue, as always, and I'm on the road to straightening out my issues."

"What happened that made you so upset?" Jamie asked.

When Sam looked at Eli and said, "Do you mind giving us a few minutes alone?" Jamie shot him a look that dared him to leave.

"No, stay. I want you here, regardless of what my mom wants."

Eli waited for Sam to nod her approval before settling back in his seat.

She took another deep breath to steady her nerves. "I saw your father today, Jamie. He's at MUSC in Charleston in the Hollings Cancer Center."

Jamie's body went stiff, and an awkward silence fell over the room. After several long minutes, Eli dared to ask, "What kind of cancer does he have?"

"Liver."

"Well, that sucks for him," Jamie said. "But as far as I'm concerned, that has nothing to do with us."

"There's more." Sam combed her fingers through her hair. "I learned today that Annie is Allen's daughter."

Jamie's head shot up. "You mean our Annie, as in Annie Dawn?"

"Yes, except her name isn't Annie Dawn. It's Annie Bethune." When her son's brows knitted in confusion, Sam added, "I know. It's difficult to wrap your mind around it."

Jamie's eyes bounced all over the room, hitting on all of them but focusing on no one. "Are you suggesting that Annie is my stepsister?"

"She's more than your stepsister, sweetheart. She's your half sister. Your blood."

Jamie's face darkened as he considered the implications. "Then it's not a coincidence that Annie showed up at Aunt Faith's wedding. She wants something from us?"

Sam reached for her son's hand. "Your father needs a liver transplant. Annie is not a match, but there's a good chance you might be."

Jamie stared down at their hands, clasped together. "So what you're saying is this man—we'll refer to him as my 'sperm donor' since I can't bring myself to call him my father—has shown up after twenty years of radio silence asking for one of my vital organs. I might think it was funny if it wasn't so damned pathetic." He looked up at Sam. "That's some fucked-up shit. No wonder you hit the bottle when you found out about all this."

"Watch it, Jamie," Eli warned. "You're way out of line. I know you're upset, but your mom didn't do this to you. She's your biggest fan."

Moses leaned forward. "Eli is right, Jamie. Your mom has had a difficult day trying to cope with all this. You owe her some respect."

Jamie hung his head.

"There are two separate issues on the table here, Jamie." Moses placed his hands on the wooden coffee table in front of him. "The first is the matter of your liver, whether or not you'd be willing to donate part of it if it turns out you're a match."

"But I—"

Moses cut him off with a firm shake of his head. "You can't make that decision until you've had some time to research the risks involved with surgery, and until you've had a chance to talk about it with each of the three of us individually. On the one hand, we want you to do what's right for you, Jamie; after all, this is your body. On the other hand, your feelings for your father aside, we are talking about saving another human life. A decision made for the wrong reasons could come back to haunt you five or ten years down the road."

"How much time does Allen have? Does anyone know?" Eli asked.

"Not much," Sam answered. "He's a very sick man. Jamie might be the only one who can save his life."

"That's ironic," Jamie said, "because I appear to be the only one who thinks his life isn't worth saving."

"I don't see any harm in getting tested," Eli said. "If you're not a match, it becomes a nonissue."

"Good point," Moses said. "The second issue that needs to be decided is whether or not you want to meet your father."

A flash of anger raced across Jamie's face. "No thanks. I have no interest in hearing his sorry excuses about why he missed the last nineteen years of my life. Unless he's going to tell me that he joined the Marines, that he's been off fighting the Taliban in Afghanistan. And we already know that's not true. He's been too busy parenting his daughter. His other child. The one he chose to acknowledge. Sorry, Moses, but no. I have zero interest in meeting him."

Sam stroked her son's arm. "I know how much it hurts, honey. I feel the same way about Allen marrying someone else and not me. About him choosing another family over us. I think talking to him will help you understand why he made the choices he did."

Jamie shot to his feet. "All the alcohol you've been drinking has made you soft, Mom. I can't believe this guy shows up out of the blue, with some sob story about having cancer, and just like that"— he snapped his fingers—"you forgive him for knocking you up and walking out on you."

Sam stood to face him. "I haven't forgiven him for anything, Jamie. You and I toughed it out through some difficult times because of *his* choices, the decisions *he* made for *us*. But I've been carrying around a lot of misconceptions, unfortunately ones that I passed on to you, which turned out not to be true. Talking to Allen answered a lot of questions for me. He didn't leave me because of anything *I* did. He didn't love me any less than I thought he did. He let his own pride get in the way of doing the right thing. And that had nothing to do with me. Or you."

Jamie stared her down. "Nothing you can say or do will change my mind, Mom. I have no interest in meeting the sperm donor anymore than I have in giving him part of my liver."

"If you won't talk to him, will you at least talk to Annie?" When Sam reached toward him to stroke his cheek, he brushed her hand away.

"Why would I do that? I don't even like that girl."

"That's not true and you know it," Sam said. "We all like Annie. We may have had our suspicions about her in the beginning, but she has proven to be reliable and hardworking. None of this is her fault."

Moses stood and stretched. "I could use a cup of tea. Jamie, will you help me find a mug?"

Hearing the stern tone in his voice, Jamie trailed after Moses.

Sam left the room and went outside to the front porch. She hoped Eli wouldn't follow her, but when he did, she was glad for his presence. She moved over to make room for him on the swing. "I'm exhausted. Can we please not talk?"

"Of course. Just know that I'm here for you if you need me." Their companionship was easy, like it'd always been, neither feeling the need to fill the silence with unnecessary chatter. The sound of a neighbor's dog interrupted the quiet night, the bark becoming more urgent with each passing moment. Eli and Sam smiled at one another. They knew that bark well. They'd taken care of Belle several times while her owners were out of town. She was a sweet dog, but impatient and demanding.

"With his busy schedule, Moses won't always be around for you. Do you have someone you can call when you need to talk?"

"Moses found a new sponsor for me. Her name is Megan Flanders. I've only met her once, before my meeting last night. That was right before Mack had his heart attack. I didn't feel like I knew her well enough to call her today. My bad, I guess."

"Megan is a friend of mine. She's the kind of person you can call anytime, night or day. She's been through hell herself. Get her to tell you her story sometime."

"Thank you for being here for Jamie tonight. He really counts on you, you know. Just because you and I are no longer together doesn't mean your relationship with him has to end."

"I love Jamie like a son. I'm going to miss him when I move to New York."

Sam stiffened. "If you're trying to make me feel guilty, it's not going to work." She hopped off the swing. "You should probably leave now." Turning her back on his baffled expression, she went inside and closed the door.

Why do I always have to be such a bitch? She leaned back against the door, her heart pounding in her chest.

She went to her room, waiting until she heard Moses's car back out of the driveway before venturing to the kitchen for her own cup of Sleepytime tea. Mug in hand on her way back down the hall, she heard Jamie murmuring into the phone in his room. She pressed her ear against his door. She could only catch every third word, but his voice sounded serious. At first, she thought he might be talking to Sophia until she heard him say her name. Annie.

Twenty-Six

SAM

IN THE PREMARKET hours at Sweeney's on Saturday morning, Sam noticed Jamie and Annie huddled together on several different occasions. Mostly, serious expressions on their young faces accompanied their whispers, but once or twice, she caught a flash of a smile and a playful gesture toward one another.

While Sam was relieved to see her son accepting his new reality, she also felt a twinge of jealousy toward the girl. She'd never had to share Jamie's affections with anyone before. With the exception of Sophia—but Sam had never seen them together and didn't know how Jamie treated his new girlfriend—and with the exception of Eli, which wasn't the same because her son's relationship with him was all about guy stuff like baseball and fishing. Of course Sam enjoyed those activities as well, but Jamie didn't look at Eli the way he was looking at Annie. With that special tenderness in his dark eyes that he once reserved only for Sam.

As was typical of a Saturday, they were slammed with

business from the moment they opened the door at ten. After the first wave of customers left, they had to scramble to restock.

"Thank goodness Mike took the day off today," Faith said in passing. "Last thing we need is Bitsy underfoot."

"Having your daughter here is never a problem for me. You know that. But it's nice for you when you don't have to worry about her while you work." Sam squirted a green cleaner on the counter and wiped it down with a clean cloth. "Have you heard anything from Charleston? I'm a little worried. Neither Mom nor Jackie is answering my texts."

"Not since yesterday evening," Faith said. "I assume no news is good news."

Sam hoped that was the case, but when Bill entered the showroom an hour later, she knew something was terribly wrong. She could count on one hand the number of times her brother-in-law had visited Sweeney's in his lifetime. He stood off to the side, waiting for the customers to clear out before he approached the counter.

"Jackie wanted me to tell you the bad news in person." He coughed to clear his throat. "Mack died early this morning."

"No!" Faith cried. "How can that be?"

Sam bit back a sob. "I don't understand. He was doing so well," she said, even though she knew Mack was less than well when she'd visited him the previous evening.

"He suffered a massive stroke around nine o'clock last night and never regained consciousness." He looked first at Sam, then at Faith. "I'm so sorry. I know how much Mack meant to both of you."

Sam noticed a car pulling up alongside the curb out front.

"Considering the circumstances, I guess we should close the shop."

"I can't tell you how to run your business," Bill said. "But your mother is hoping you will stay open. In fact, Jackie has taken her home to shower and change. Lovie insists on coming to work this afternoon. She says that once word gets out about Mack, his friends will gravitate here to pay their respects."

Sam thought that was the most ridiculous thing she'd ever heard, but it turned out to be true. Lovie arrived within the hour, and for the rest of the day, a continuous stream of patrons came to Sweeney's—the usual Saturday traffic of vacationers headed to the beach mixed with locals stopping by to pay their respects to Captain Mack Bowman's adopted family. Mack's closest friend, Noah, arrived shortly after Lovie and stayed until well past closing. Sam fought off exhaustion, using her mother as a role model of strength. Lovie accepted condolences with a gracious smile, never shedding a tear or exhibiting a sign of weakness. Sam could see Jamie was suffering, but she never got a break from waiting on customers to reach out to him.

Even after six o'clock, when they closed the market to the paying clientele, the townsfolk continued to come. Jackie, Bill, and the twins arrived, followed by Mike, Bitsy, Eli, and Moses. Mack's fishing buddies showed up reeking of their day's work. And the marina employees ventured across the street in waves. Faith opened bottles of wine while Sam passed the trays of hors d'oeuvres that Jamie helped Annie prepare—mostly tuna and shrimp salad served on Bremner Wafers.

"How're you holding up?" Jackie engulfed Sam in a hug, a rare show of affection from her older sister. "It's been a difficult thirty-six hours for you. Have you had a chance to talk to Jamie about Allen yet?"

"I told him last night as soon as I got home. He didn't take it well at first, but he seems to be adjusting. He and Annie have been awfully secretive today. I'm glad they're bonding. I just don't want him to confuse the two issues—the excitement over finding out he has a half sister and the discovery that the father he's never met has cancer and needs part of his liver to survive."

"Poor Jamie. That's an awful lot to process at once."

"It is, especially when you add Mack's death to the mix. The old man was like a grandfather to Jamie. To all the Sweeney cousins." Sam gestured at the twins.

"I still can't believe he's gone."

"Neither can I," Sam said. "Mom seems to be processing Mack's death, but I don't think she should be alone tonight. I would offer to have her stay with me, but I need to spend some time alone with Jamie."

"I'm one step ahead of you. I asked her to stay with us indefinitely. Her townhouse is going to feel empty without Mack. He was such a positive influence on her. He kept her grounded. I don't know how we would have made it through this past year without him."

"I think she'll be fine as long as we keep her busy. We don't want what happened before to happen again—when the market was under renovation and she went a little cuckoo with too much time on her hands."

Twenty-Seven

FAITH

IT WAS NEARING eight o'clock when Mack's attorney showed up at their impromptu visitation. Craig Smalls pulled Faith and Sam over to the corner away from the crowd.

"I realize this isn't the most opportune time for this discussion. But considering that funeral arrangements will need to be made, and since you all are the closest thing Mack has to a family, I wanted to apprise you of the terms of his will."

"I don't understand," Sam said. "Why us? Why not our mother?"

"Because Mack named the two of you the executors of his estate. Mack lived well below his means." Smalls paused, choosing his words carefully. "He wasn't a wealthy man by any stretch of the imagination, but he inherited a sizable sum from his parents. He hasn't spent a dime of it with the exception of the money he used to buy the property where he keeps his houseboat. Which, alone, is worth several hundred thousands of dollars."

"Wait, what?" Sam shook her head as if to clear it. "I never knew Mack had money."

"He never wanted anyone to know. Because he was an only child, with no children of his own, this is the end of the road for the Bowman family."

"What will happen to the money?" Faith asked.

He looked at Faith. "Your mother will inherit half of it, and the rest will be divided between your sisters and you."

Sam and Faith stared at each other in disbelief.

"We can talk about the logistics next week after the funeral. The important thing now is to make the arrangements. Mack has left very clear instructions that he wants his body cremated and his ashes spread on the water. He left it to Lovie to pick the right spot."

"Some of the folks here tonight suggested to Mom that we have a brief service followed by a fish fry out at Mack's place," Sam said.

Smalls smiled. "I think Mack would like that." He handed business cards to Sam and Faith. "Have the bills sent to me. I'll make sure they get paid." He surveyed the room as the crowd gathered. "Mack was quite a guy. Prospect will not be the same without him." He looked back at Faith and Sam. "I'll be in touch soon, and I'm truly sorry for your loss."

Once Smalls had gone, Bitsy skipped across the showroom to Faith. "Who was that man, Mama?"

"Oh, he was just a friend of Mack's." Faith stroked her daughter's matted hair. "Did you and Mike work on your playhouse today?"

"Uh-huh," she said, bobbing her head up and down. "We dug a big hole in the ground, and Mike's friend filled it with cement."

"Wow!" Sam said. "That sounds like some playhouse."

"Bitsy came up with the floor plan all on her own," Mike said, joining them. He removed a crumpled piece of paper from his pocket and showed it to Faith and Sam. Using crayons, Bitsy had colored an elementary house in yellow with two windows, a door, and window boxes with pink flowers.

"I can't believe you poured a concrete floor," Faith said.

Mike shrugged. "One of my patients owns a concrete company."

Staring up at her mother, her hazel eyes wide, Bitsy asked, "Why did Mack have to go to heaven, Mama?"

Faith lifted the little girl into her arms. "God called Mack to heaven to help him do angel work for him."

"What kind of angel work?"

Faith touched her daughter's nose. "Important stuff like guarding over you."

"You mean, so Daddy can't get me anymore?"

The color drained from Faith's face. "Yes, that's exactly what I mean."

"You have lots of people watching over you." Mike tickled Bitsy's belly button with his finger. "In heaven and down here on earth, like me."

Bitsy giggled and squirmed but quickly grew serious again. "Jamie and Annie aren't being very nice." Her lip stuck out in a pout, she pointed at her cousins across the showroom. "They're over there in the corner telling secrets."

Faith exchanged a knowing look with her sister.

Sam said, "Your cousins love you, Bits Babe. They would never hurt your feelings intentionally."

"Sometimes your cousins need to talk about big kid stuff, just like I talk to your aunts about grown-up things. It's the kind of stuff that isn't appropriate for little ears like yours," Faith said, nibbling on Bitsy's earlobe. She spotted Jamie and Annie making their way through the crowd. "Here they come now, to check on you."

"Aww, Bits, what's the matter?" Jamie tugged on his young cousin's sandal. "I know you're sad about Mack. We all are." He turned to Sam. "I know this isn't exactly the best time to bring this up, but Annie and I were wondering if you would go with us to Charleston tomorrow to see her dad."

Faith watched her sister closely. If this request came as a surprise, Sam didn't show it.

"I don't think we'll have Mack's funeral until Monday, so I don't see why not," Sam said.

Annie rested her head on Jamie's shoulder. "He's agreed to get tested to see if he's a match."

"Get tested for what?" Bitsy asked.

Faith and Mike exchanged looks, and he gave a slight shrug of his shoulders.

"Jamie is going to get tested to see if his blood matches Annie's," Faith answered. "Turns out they might be brother and sister."

"Which makes Annie your sort-of cousin." Mike gave her little pink sneaker a tug. "Isn't that cool?"

Bitsy's face scrunched up in confusion. She opened her mouth and inserted her thumb, burying her face in her mother's chest.

"I'm proud of you," Sam said, squeezing her son's shoulder. "One step at a time."

"Can Annie stay at our house tonight?" Jamie asked. "We want to leave early for Charleston in the morning. Besides, we have a lot to talk about. I can run her out to the farm now to get her stuff."

A flash of disappointment crossed Sam's face, but she quickly recovered. "I guess that will be fine. But come straight back. I'll be ready to go home as soon as our guests leave." Sam cleared her throat, nodding her head at Bitsy.

Taking the hint, Jamie asked, "Do you want to ride with us, Bits?"

Biting down on her lip, she nodded. Jamie turned his back to her and she grabbed hold of his shoulders, jumping on for a piggyback ride.

"Looks like Annie is here to stay," Mike said, once the kids were gone.

"Yep." Sam sighed. "And somehow I need to get used to the idea that my son has a half sister."

Faith pulled her sister in for a half hug. "I know, honey. This can't be easy for you."

"I was hoping for some time alone with Jamie tonight," Sam said. "I'll have to settle for a cup of green tea and a long soak in the tub since wine is out of the question."

Faith motioned toward Eli, who was engrossed in conversation with Lovie across the room. "I don't understand why you have to settle for anything when you can have that hunky man, who obviously adores you, holding you in his arms tonight."

Mike chuckled. "I don't want to overstep my boundaries as brother-in-law here, but I have to say, I agree with my wife. Eli is one of the good guys. I'd hate to see you let him go."

Twenty-Eight

JACKIE

WHEN JACKIE HEARD someone stir during the night, she assumed it was her mother and got up to check on her. She found Lovie sitting at the breakfast room table staring out the window into the dark night.

"Are you having trouble sleeping? Let me make you some tea," Jackie said, popping a Pure Camomile K-cup into her Keurig. When the machine finished brewing, she added a drop of milk and a pinch of sugar the way her mother liked it.

"Thank you, honey," Lovie said when Jackie slid the mug in front of her. They sat in silence for a minute while she sipped her tea. "You don't need to fuss over me. I know you girls are waiting for me to collapse, but that's not going to happen as long as I keep busy."

"We've all suffered a great loss, Mom, and we should grieve together. Expressing our sorrow over losing someone we love is not a weakness. It is part of the process of healing." Jackie reached for her mother's wrinkled hand. She rubbed Lovie's knuckles, gnarled from years of hard work. "Pampering *you* makes *us* feel better. You've done so much for us over the years. Let us do this one thing for you in return."

Lovie tugged her hand free of Jackie's. "I know how this will go. Tonight you're offering me a cup of tea. Next week you'll be moving me to a retirement home."

"Please don't bring that up again, Mom. I learned my lesson last summer. If you move anywhere, it will be into my guest cottage. And only on your own terms."

Lovie appeared hopeful, as though she liked the idea, then her face fell. "I couldn't possibly do that. What would I do with all my things?"

"Put them in storage. Or leave them in your townhouse. You wouldn't have to make a permanent move. Just until you felt better." Jackie got up and poured herself a glass of milk. "For the record," she said when she returned to the table, "I thought I was doing the right thing by taking you to visit the Hermitage. You were so confused back then. A different person than you are now."

"I know what you're thinking." Lovie set her mug down. "You're thinking I've been better off this past year because I've had Mack in my life."

Jackie wagged her finger at her mother. "Don't go putting words in my mouth, Mom. It's true. I think you've been in a much better frame of mind since you started seeing Mack. But that's because you were happy. And not so lonely. Contrary to what you believe, none of us is *waiting* for you to go off the deep end now that he is gone. But there is nothing wrong with us fussing over you. You don't always have to be the strong one. You can lean on your family for a change. We're here for you."

"I already miss him so much. I feel this ache deep down

inside, and I know it'll only get worse. I'm afraid to face my life without him. The only thing I know to do is stay busy so I don't have to think about it."

"Until it's four o'clock in the morning and you can't sleep."

Lovie smiled a sad smile. "When I can't sleep at home, I refuse to lie in bed tossing and turning. I get up and make good use of my time. Do you have any silver that needs polishing?"

Jackie laughed. "Even if I did, I wouldn't ask you to polish it."

"I used to bake brownies for Mack during the night when I couldn't sleep." Lovie smiled at the memory. "He would eat them for breakfast with a big glass of milk. His presence is in every corner of my home."

"All the more reason for you to move into my guest house. If only for awhile."

Lovie sniffled. "Isn't Annie living in your guest house?"

"Not indefinitely." When Jackie had volunteered the guest house to Annie, she'd been thinking in terms of weeks, not months. Now, knowing that Annie's father might die and that Jamie was her only other family shed a new light on the situation. While Jackie had grown fond of the girl, appreciated her resourcefulness and companionship, she wasn't ready to foster a teenage girl on a permanent basis. Especially now that she was so close to empty nesting. She had plans—for her husband to apply for a position at MUSC and to renovate Clara Graves's house. Not that she wanted to see Clara go. She would miss the charming lady. But she knew the upkeep on such a large house was taking its toll on Clara's old bones, and she feared she might have another fall.

Jackie patted her mother's arm. "We don't have to make a decision about this now. Just think about it. It would be nice for the twins to have their grandmother around, especially during the school year while I'm in Charleston."

"In other words, you're looking for someone to do the cooking and cleaning for your family while you're off gallivanting around in Charleston. You need someone to take Faith's place as their stand-in mother."

Jackie pushed back from the table. "The twins are almost seventeen years old. They hardly know when I'm in the same room with them. They need someone to buy groceries and make dinner for them every now and then. And to hand out twenty-dollar bills, which is their father's responsibility. I'll remind you that Faith lived here for free while she got back on her feet after her breakup with Curtis. She helped me out, and I helped her out in return. It was a win-win situation for both of us. I was trying to do something nice for you, Mom, by offering you a place to live while you mourn your loss."

Lovie stared up at Jackie, her face set in stone. "And I'm trying to tell *you* that I don't need your help."

I'm a fifty-one-year-old woman, not a disobedient child caught with her hand in the cookie jar five minutes before dinner. Why is it my mother can zap my self-confidence with one cock of her penciled-on eyebrow?

"Fine, then." Jackie rose. "Enjoy your tea. I'll see you in the morning."

Jackie bypassed the master bedroom and went straight to Bill's study down the hall where he'd been sleeping on his pull-out sofa bed for the past nine months. Without knocking, she opened the door and nudged him to move over on the lumpy mattress. She crawled under his thin blanket and spooned him from behind. She kissed his bare shoulder, and then his neck and ear.

He woke slowly at first, but then came to life when he realized what was happening. He rolled over, facing her. "Does this mean..."

She wrapped her arms around him, pressing her body close. "I think you've suffered enough."

"No, baby." His voice was husky in her ear. "I haven't suffered nearly enough."

Twenty-Nine
SAM

NO ONE SPOKE a word on the ride home from Charleston on Sunday afternoon. Jamie slept in the backseat while Annie stared out the passenger window, wiping at her eyes and sniffling. Sam was afraid to ask, and neither of them seemed willing to volunteer a report of their visit with Allen. Judging from their despondent demeanors, she guessed that things had not gone well.

She had refused the opportunity to see Allen, having already heard everything she needed to hear from him. She stayed in the waiting room while Jamie and Annie went back to ICU. Jamie wasn't gone long, and didn't have much to say when he returned. They went down to the lab together for the preliminary tests that would determine if Jamie was donor material. After a simple blood test, Sam wasn't surprised when the oncologist intern, an arrogant kid not much older than Jamie, declared him a potential match.

"We'll need to conduct several other tests to be certain," the boy doctor said.

Sam jotted her number down on a piece of paper and handed it to the intern. "I'll need to speak to the doctor before we make our decision."

The intern consulted his chart. "With all due respect, ma'am, your son is nineteen. He can make the decision on his own."

Hands on hip, Sam stared the boy down. "I don't care how old he is. No one is carving off a slice of my son's liver without my blessing."

"Yes, ma'am." The intern attached the slip of paper to his file. "I'll have the doctor call you as soon as possible."

Annie spent more than an hour alone with her father, finally emerging from his room with swollen, red-rimmed eyes.

"Annie, honey." Sam wrapped her arm around her. "There are organizations that can provide housing if you want to stay in Charleston to be near your dad. I can help you find the right people to talk to."

"Daddy doesn't want me here." Annie sniffled. "He says I shouldn't be wasting my time sitting by his bed watching him die." She cried on Sam's shoulder. "He's not going to die, is he, Sam?"

"The doctors are doing everything they can for him." Although she intended her words to offer comfort, she suspected there was not much more the doctors could do.

Annie stirred as they drove down Jackie's winding tree-lined driveway. "I'm doing the right thing, aren't I, Miss Sam? By coming back here instead of staying with my dad at the hospital."

Sam offered Annie's arm a soft squeeze. "Yes, honey. Let the doctors and nurses take care of your father. You're only a phone call away. They know how to contact both of us in an emergency."

Sam's heart went out to the girl. Her future looked bleak. Allen's recovery could take weeks, months even, above and beyond the operation. That is, *if* he was well enough to have the transplant and strong enough to survive the surgery. Annie didn't earn enough money through babysitting for Bitsy and working part-time at the market to support them. And who knew how long it would be before Allen could return to work? Sam couldn't imagine Allen and Annie living in Jackie's guest cottage. After all the years she'd spent getting over him, Sam didn't want to be in such close proximity to her ex, whether he was a dying man or not.

Annie drew in a deep breath and sat ramrod straight in her seat when Sam pulled up at Jackie's. "Okay, then. Thank you for driving me to Charleston."

"You're welcome, sweetheart. I know it's hard to do, but try not to worry. You're not alone in this. We are all here for you."

Sam and Jamie were almost home when, instead of turning left onto Main Street, she made a quick right into the marina parking lot. She switched off the engine and turned to Jamie who was still riding in the backseat. "What say we get some ice cream?"

When Jamie was little, an ice cream cone from Sandy's was the answer to all his problems.

He rubbed his eyes with his balled fists. "Two scoops of salted caramel won't fix this, Mom, but I'll take you up on the offer. I'm starving."

Sugar cones in hand, mother and son strolled down to the dock, surprised to find it nearly deserted on a Sunday afternoon. They walked to the slip where Mack kept his forty-five-foot Bertram and sat down on his fiberglass dock box.

"What's going to happen to his boat?" Jamie asked.

"We'll sell it, I assume." Sam felt it premature to tell Jamie about the terms of Mack's will.

"As much as I hate to admit it, you were right, Mom."

"What was I right about?" She tried to appear nonchalant, but her stomach was in knots with worry over what had transpired between her son and his father.

"About Allen. I'm glad I got the opportunity to meet him. Because now I won't spend the next twenty years wondering what he was like. Just so you know, I'm not buying his lame excuses about needing to prove himself to the world before claiming you as his wife. What kind of man does that? There's no rocket science here. The idea of having a wife and kid freaked him out and he took off."

Sam licked her salted caramel. "If that's true, why did he marry Annie's mother when she got pregnant?"

"That's like comparing a shiny red apple to a rotten banana. Allen knew he could count on you to raise me right. Based on what Annie told me about her mother, if Allen hadn't stuck around to support kid number two, she would've ended up in a foster home. Not that the support he offered her was worth a damn."

Sam stopped licking. "I disagree. I think Allen has done a nice job with Annie. She's hardworking and resourceful and pleasant tempered."

"Those are qualities she's gained from having to cope with all the hardship he placed on her. She's barely had a roof over her head or enough food on the table for most of her life."

"But Annie loves him, and we have to respect her feelings."

"I'm aware. She's ready to take a scalpel to my gut to save his life." They sat in silence for a few minutes, eating their ice cream and watching the pelicans dive for fish. "I googled the procedure. The liver immediately begins to rejuvenate itself, which is cool, but the surgery requires a sizable incision in my stomach. Not a good thing for my six-pack abs." He ran his free hand across his belly.

"I googled it too. You would likely lose your gall bladder. I don't think that's a big deal, but it is on my list of questions for the doctor. And you'd have to stay in the hospital for up to a week. Which, to me, is a huge indicator as to the seriousness of the surgery."

"After what Allen did to us, I don't feel like I owe the guy a thing. But I would do it for Annie, if there was any chance it might save his life. If the odds aren't in his favor, I don't want to go through major surgery for nothing."

"Of course not. You have your baseball scholarship to think about, among other things. It won't be long before you start training again. You just got back on your feet. I'd hate to put your poor body through unnecessary trauma. Have you talked to Sophia about any of this?"

"A little. She doesn't really understand, though. Sophia is an only child like me, but she has both her parents, who are happily married. She says she would do anything to save her father's life."

"You would too, Jamie, if the circumstances were different."

Jamie tossed the last of his cone in the water and a flock of seagulls immediately attacked it. "He's going to die anyway. He told me so himself. He said days, Mom, not weeks or months. Annie will have no money or family to support her except a half brother she's known for five minutes."

"I'm surprised he was so up front with you about dying," Sam said, wiping her mouth with a napkin.

"He doesn't want my liver. According to him, the transplant wouldn't do any good anyway. He doesn't want Annie to know, though, because he doesn't want her to lose hope."

"He basically told me the same thing." Standing, Sam placed a hand on her son's shoulder. "This situation will play itself out, Jamie. We just need to give it some time."

Thirty

SAM

FAITH AND MIKE invited the extended Sweeney family and a few of Mack's closest friends to their house for a
cookout. Faith texted the group: "*Leave the tears at home. Mike
and I want this to be a happy occasion to celebrate Mack's life and
our love for him.*"

Sam and Jamie had just arrived when Bill offered Eli a
toast. "Congratulations on your new job, Lieutenant. You
deserve it not only for what you've done for this family but
for what you've done for the town of Prospect. We will miss
you." Bill held up his tumbler of scotch, and the small crowd
cheered, "Here, here."

Not one for making speeches, Eli offered his appreciation
to Bill and clinked his nonalcoholic beer with those around
him. As soon as he could free himself from the well-wishers,
he made his way over to Sam and Jamie. Avoiding eye contact
with her, Eli said to Jamie, "I'm sorry, buddy. I was hoping to
have the chance to tell you myself."

Jamie stared at the ground, kicking pebbles with his flip-flop clad feet. "I can't believe you're moving to New York."

"Actually, I'm not. I received an offer late yesterday afternoon. I've been offered a job, which includes a promotion, from the police department in Columbia. You and I are going to be neighbors."

Jamie's head jerked up. "Really?"

Eli beamed. "Yep. Really."

Jamie engulfed him in a big hug. "That's awesome, Eli."

Eli pushed back and held him at arm's length. "You mean a lot to me, Jamie. Even though things didn't work out between your mom and me, I hope you and I can still be a part of each other's lives. That is, if you'll have me?"

Jamie hugged him again. "Of course I'll have you." He slapped Eli on the back. "I'm going to get a beer... uh...I mean a soda."

Sam and Eli smiled at his retreating back. So far Jamie had managed to keep his partying in check. He had chosen not to join a fraternity; and when he wasn't in class or playing baseball or hanging out with Sophia, he spent what little free time he had in the library. Sam knew all too well that certain factors of alcoholism were genetic. But she also knew that not all children of alcoholic parents became alcoholics. As far as she knew, Allen had never had a drinking problem, but she made a mental note to ask the doctor. Especially considering liver was his brand of cancer.

"How long before you leave?" Sam asked.

"I start my job two weeks from tomorrow." Eli smiled at her, a smile that portrayed all the love he felt for her. "If you'll excuse me, I need to check in with Annie. I haven't spoken to her in a day or so."

Sam turned away from the group so no one would see her tears. She wandered down to the dock, sat down on the end, and hung her legs over the side.

Jackie joined her a few minutes later. "Are you sure this is what you want, Sam? To send Eli away to Columbia?"

"I'm not sending Eli anywhere. He made that decision on his own."

Jackie held up three fingers. "Three words will stop him from going. I don't think I need to tell you what those three words are."

Sam leaned back against the piling. "I'm not sure about anything anymore after everything that's happened this week. With Eli being held hostage, Allen showing up with cancer, and Mack suddenly dying." She ticked the points off on her fingers. "All these things have reminded me how fragile life is. For the past twenty years, I've lived with the assumption that the man I loved left me because I wasn't good enough for him. Even though I now know that's not true, I'm having a hard time accepting it. I've dedicated my life to my child and my business, believing that I didn't deserve happiness with a man. And then Eli came along. And he was perfect for me. He *is* perfect for me. I can look you straight in the face and admit that I love him like mad. I know he's my one big chance to be happy. Yet I'm paralyzed to do anything about it."

"The stakes now are not the same as they were with Allen, Sam. Regardless of his reasons for leaving, Allen not only broke your heart—he broke your spirit. He left you to raise your child on your own. Every hardship you experienced— every long night you suffered when your baby had a fever or an earache, every school and sporting event you attended as a single parent, every holiday you and Jamie celebrated without a husband and father—they were all reminders of that heart-ache. It's different with Eli. You don't stand as much to lose. If the two of you got back together, what's the worst thing that could happen?"

Sam picked at the pressure-treated wood of the dock. "He could have an affair."

"Look at me." Jackie aimed her thumb at her chest. "Although I don't recommend it, I'm living proof that your relationship will survive if that happens. What else?"

"He could get killed in a shootout. Or a bank robbery."

"The most certain thing about life is death, Sam. Look at Mom. Dad was her life partner, her one great love, yet she allowed herself to be vulnerable again. Ask her. I bet she'll tell you that every minute she spent with Mack this past year was worth the pain she's feeling now."

Sam grabbed at the opportunity for a change of subject. "Speaking of Mom. She appears to be holding up okay."

"On the surface. She's a boiling pot of emotional stew deep down inside."

Sam's head jerked up. "Uh-oh. What happened?"

"We had words last night. Why does she always take it out on me?"

"Because she is counting on you to be strong for her. She sees herself in you, and she knows she can trust you with her feelings, that you won't back down, that you will match her strength."

"Sounds like you've given this some thought," Jackie said.

Sam raised her shoulders. "She used to count on me like that. Until I cracked. Until I started running straight to the bottle every time my burden became too heavy to bear." Sam tucked a leg up underneath her. "Mom's always been that way with you. Because you're the oldest."

Jackie pointed at the group of men gathered around the grill at the side of the house. "Go. Talk to Eli. Tell him how you feel. He won't move, if you ask him not to. He doesn't want to leave Prospect. It's written all over his face. This is his home. Here, with you."

"I will. When I'm ready."

"Fine. But I'm warning you, don't wait too long, Sam. Nothing lasts forever."

Thirty-One

FAITH

FAITH HAD NEVER hosted a party before. Not for family or friends or for any of her daughter's six birthdays. She set out big displays of food—corn on the cob, deviled eggs, and bowls of potato and mixed green salads—on a folding banquet table covered with a red gingham cloth. When the hamburgers and hot dogs were ready, friends and family loaded their plates with food and found a place to eat, either in one of the beach chairs Mike had arranged on the deck or on one of the blankets Faith had spread on the grass. While they ate, they made toasts to Mack and told stories of his escapades from his fifty-plus years spent on the water. His generosity toward those in need, his remarkable kindness to the townsfolk, and his genuine camaraderie with his friends were all duly noted.

As the sun began to set, the crowd grew lazy from bellies full of beer and burgers. Moses and Bill left immediately following dinner to attend to patients in need. Mack's closest friend, Noah, had brought his eight-year-old granddaughter along. Bitsy and Mary Beth chased fireflies and played tag around the group of teenagers hanging out at the water's edge.

"It's hard to believe he's gone," Sam said to Faith, who was sitting next to her in an Adirondack chair. "I can't remember a family gathering that didn't include Mack."

"It's eerie. I can almost feel him here with us." Faith inhaled a gulp of salty air. "He's as much a part of the inlet as the marsh grass."

"I know what you mean. I'm gonna miss watching him lumber across the street every afternoon with his catch of the day."

Faith gestured at their mother, who was speaking with a group of Mack's friends over near the grill. "Mom seems okay for now. She's stuck in the moment of Mack's passing, surrounded by family and friends. I'm worried about how she will be tomorrow, after the service, when she's forced to face life without Mack."

"At least she knows what to expect, having been through it before with Dad."

Bitsy appeared before them, ice cream sandwich in hand. "Mama, I'm sad," she said, crawling into Faith's lap. "Mary Beth had to go home."

"It's getting late, honey. Time for little girls to go to bed." Faith helped Bitsy tear the wrapper off the ice cream sandwich. "Maybe you can play with her another time."

Bitsy bit down on her sandwich. "Maybe I'll get to see her tomorrow."

"I bet you will. The two of you can run around together after the service."

Sam nudged Faith. "Do you know who that woman is talking to Eli?"

Faith stiffened at the sight of a stranger standing by the cooler of beer. She was laughing at something Eli said as though it was the funniest thing she'd ever heard. Eli had a lot of admirable qualities, but Faith didn't think humor was necessarily one of them. Something about the woman seemed vaguely familiar. She wasn't necessarily pretty but attractive in a muscular, masculine way. "I feel like I know her, but I can't put my finger on it. I wonder who she is?"

"That's Chloe," Bitsy said, licking the chocolate wafer off her tiny fingers. "She works at the hospital with Mike. She came to our house once, when Annie was babysitting for me."

Tidbits of her conversation with Mike from Friday night came back to her, making the little hairs on her arm stand to attention.

She's pretty, if you like female wrestlers.

I knew a girl name Chloe in high school.

Did she have thunder thighs and huge biceps?

This is kind of creepy, Mike.

"What'd she come to our house for?" Holding in her breath, Faith tried to keep a straight face so as not to show her daughter her fear.

Bitsy used the hem of her dress to wipe the ice cream off her mouth. "She came to pick up something for Mike."

Faith and Sam exchanged a concerned look over Bitsy's head. "Hop up, honey," Faith said, patting Bitsy's bottom. She eased herself up from the low-slung chair. "You sit here with Aunt Sam while I go welcome our new guest."

As she marched across the yard, Faith surveyed the crowd for Mike but didn't see him anywhere. He couldn't have gone far. He'd been handing out ice cream sandwiches on the porch a few minutes earlier.

"I'm Faith Neilson," she said, extending her hand to Chloe. "Are you a friend of Mack's?"

211

Chloe looked confused at first. "You mean of Mike's?"

"No, I'm mean of Mack's. Mack Bowman. He is a close family friend who passed away yesterday morning. We are having a private gathering in his honor."

Chloe held her shoulders back and thrust her large perky breasts out. "Mike invited me to come," she said, but the way her eyes darted around told Faith the woman was lying.

"That's funny. He didn't mention it to me." Faith eyed the gold cross at Chloe's neck. "That's pretty. I used to have one exactly like it."

Eli took a step away from Chloe and moved closer to Faith. "Is there some sort of problem here?"

"Actually, yes. I have reason to believe this woman is stalking my husband." Faith caught sight of Mike rounding the corner from the front of the house and waved him over.

"What're you doing here?" he asked when he saw Chloe.

"You invited me, silly. Don't you remember?" Taking a step closer to Mike, Chloe pressed her body against his in a way that made Faith want to smack her.

"I did no such thing, and you know it." He pried her fingers off his arm. "This is a private party, Chloe. I thought I made myself clear the other day. There has never been anything between us, nor will there ever be. I am a happily married man." He wrapped his arm around Faith and pulled her close. "Eli, if you would be so kind as to show Chloe to her car."

Eli removed his badge from his back pocket and flashed it in her face. "I'm Officer Eli Marshall with the Prospect Police Department. If you'd be so kind as to come with me." He took her by the arm and forcibly led her away.

Mike's shoulders slumped and he shook his head. "I don't

know what to say, honey. I'm so sorry. I have no idea how she found out about the party."

Suddenly chilled, Faith wrapped her arms around herself. "Because she's stalking you, Mike. She was in our house."

"Wait. What?"

"I told you about it. The other day when Annie was babysitting for Bitsy—about our photograph being turned face-down on the chest, that it looked like someone had been lying in our bed." Faith pointed at Chloe, who was getting into a silver sedan at the end of the driveway. "It was that woman. She stole my necklace. Didn't you see it? She was wearing it around her neck."

Mike's face darkened. "This is serious. We need to get confirmation before we start hurling accusations. I'll wait for Eli to come back, if you'll grab Annie and Bitsy. We'll all meet inside in a minute."

Faith left her husband and strode back to where Bitsy and Sam were still sitting, deep in conversation. She pulled her daughter to her feet. "Time for you to get ready for bed. Why don't you run ask Annie if she'll read you a bedtime story? I'll be in in a minute to tuck you in."

"What's going on?" Sam asked, once Bitsy had skipped off.

Faith leaned in close to her sister's ear. "Mike is being stalked by a crazy woman. She just showed up here out of the blue. I have reason to believe she stole my gold cross necklace, the one you and Jamie gave me for Christmas."

"I'm so sorry, Faith. 'And just when you thought it was safe to go back in the water.'"

Sensing the sudden negative vibe, the guests made moves to

213

leave. Friends and family swarmed Faith, offering their appreciation for a memorable evening and the opportunity to celebrate Mack's life.

"You seemed flustered, honey. Is something wrong?" Lovie asked.

"I'm just tired. And we have a big day ahead of us." Faith could tell by her curious expression that her older sister suspected something amiss. As she gave her mother a hug, she mouthed to Jackie, "I'll call you later."

By the time Faith and Sam got inside, Annie had helped Bitsy change into her pajamas and was reading her a bedtime story. Mike and Eli were at the dining room table studying the video surveillance tapes from last Tuesday on Mike's laptop computer.

Faith and Sam peered over their shoulders, watching the screen as a shadowy figure made her way down the hall to the master bedroom.

"We didn't install cameras in our bedroom," Mike explained to Eli. He fast-forwarded through the tape until they saw the woman emerge from the bedroom, a shiny object dangling from her left hand. Faith's gold cross.

Faith jabbed her finger at the computer. "Pull up the footage from Friday night." Mike looked up from the computer, confused, and she added, "Remember, the night we were out on the porch and I thought I saw someone in here? When you found the glass of milk beside Bitsy's bed, and commented that Annie should know by now that she doesn't like milk."

"Right. I forgot all about that." Mike's fingers flew across the keyboard. "Here."

Snippets of surveillance video appeared on the screen, flashing images of Chloe entering the front door, pouring a glass of milk in the kitchen, watching Faith and Mike through the french doors, then going into Bitsy's room.

"That woman was in my daughter's room, standing beside her bed while she slept!" Faith said. "I want to know how the hell she got in this house."

"I hate to question the obvious, but were the doors locked?" Eli asked.

"We always keep the doors locked," Mike said. "But I checked them all anyway after I discovered the milk."

Eli rubbed the stubble on his chin. "Which means this woman has somehow gotten a key to your house."

"I always keep my keys in the top right drawer of my desk at work," Mike said. "Maybe she had a copy made."

Eli's cell phone rang and he took the call into the kitchen. He returned less than a minute later. "That was dispatch. Chloe's preliminary background check is clean, but I plan to do a lot more digging tomorrow."

Annie appeared at Faith's side. "What's wrong, Miss Faith?" she asked, her face ashen. "Did something happen with my dad?"

"Oh no, sweetie. It's nothing like that." Faith took a seat at the table and pulled Annie down to the chair beside her. "Bitsy mentioned that a woman who works with Mike stopped by the house the other day when you were babysitting. We were wondering what you could tell us about her."

Annie took a minute to collect herself. "Well, Bitsy and I were playing Connect Four in the fort we built under here." She tapped the table with her finger. "When the doorbell rang, I went to answer it. I could see through the peephole that it was a woman wearing a nurses' uniform. I asked her through the closed door what she wanted, and she said that she worked with Mike at the hospital and he'd sent her to pick up a patient's file that he left at home. When I told her I wasn't supposed to let anyone in, she said if I opened the door a crack she would show me her credentials. I hope I haven't done anything wrong." Annie appeared stricken. "Her badge looked legit, and her uniform had little dogs with smiley faces on them. She seemed nice."

Faith patted Annie's hand. "Of course not. You had no way of knowing. What happened then?"

"The woman said she'd only be a minute. She seemed to know where to go, like she'd been here before. I went back to Bitsy in the fort. I'm not sure how long she was here. She said she'd let herself out." Annie turned to Mike. "She wasn't here for a file, was she?"

Mike shook his head. "Patient files belong to the hospital. It's against regulations to remove them from the property."

"Have you ever seen this woman before or since that day?" Eli asked.

Annie stared up at the ceiling for a moment before answering. "No. I think I'd remember her eyes."

Eli smiled the gentle smile that instilled trust in everyone he met. "I know what you mean. They're really fake looking, aren't they? The color of a tree frog."

Annie covered her mouth to hide her smile.

Eli slid a business card across the table to Annie. "If you ever see her again, I want you to call or text me right away. Do you understand?"

"Yes, sir." Annie stuffed the card in her pocket.

Eli rose to leave. "I'm on duty tomorrow afternoon, but I will stop by Mack's memorial service when I get a chance. I should know more then. In the meantime, you need to get your locks changed. As soon as possible."

Thirty-Two
JACKIE

JACKIE WRESTLED WITH her conflicted emotions as she sat at her dressing table, performing her bedtime beauty routine and carrying on a conversation with Bill. On the one hand, she felt hopeful that by working hard all her dreams would come true. On the other hand, she felt confused and uncertain about which path to take.

"Do you think I'm doing the wrong thing by expanding my business so quickly?" she asked Bill who was lying in bed behind her with the latest Michael Connelly novel open on his chest.

"Not at all." Bill peered at her over the top of his reading glasses. "You're in a prime position to expand. Why wouldn't you take advantage of the opportunity while you have it?"

"I don't know. Something my mother said last night," Jackie said, running her brush through her hair. "When I offered for her to live in the guest cottage while she grieved, she accused me of trying to find someone to take Faith's place as a stand-in mother for the boys. She said I was neglecting my

family while I gallivanted around in Charleston. She insinu-
ated that I was behaving inappropriately. I've worked hard this
past year. I'm proud of what I've accomplished."

"You have every right to be. And, for the record, I'm
proud of you too."

She smiled at him through the mirror. "Thank you. I'm
glad someone appreciates my efforts." Jackie set the hairbrush
down and opened her jar of night cream, dabbing a dollop
on her face. "Because Mom made it sound like I had taken
advantage of Faith. The arrangement was mutually agreeable.
At least I thought it was. Did you ever hear Faith complain?"

"On the contrary. She told me more than once how
much she appreciated the opportunity to live here for free.
After what they went through with Curtis, Faith and Bitsy
needed the peace of mind that being around family provides."
Bill closed his book and placed it on the nightstand. "Look,
honey, your mom has suffered a major loss. She's not thinking
straight. Try not to let her get to you."

"Normally I don't. I just can't shake this feeling that my
priorities are not in the right order." She screwed the lid back
on the face cream and turned around to face her husband.
"I overheard the boys talking to Noah about college tonight.
Cooper told him he was thinking about going to Tulane, and
Sean said he was applying to SMU. I always assumed they
would stay together, close to home. Then it dawned on me.
I've never even asked my own sons where they want to go to
school. What kind of mother is too self-absorbed to talk to her
children about college?"

"The kind of mother who is not afraid to have a life of her
own. Come here," he said, lifting the covers back on her side
of the bed.

She slipped off her robe and crawled in beside him.

"Don't be so hard on yourself, Jack. Ignoring your ambition is part of the reason we got into trouble. Staying true to yourself is vital for your mental well-being." He tapped her head. "Don't worry about the boys. They have always been independent and resourceful."

"Exactly. They have each other for support. They have rarely needed either one of us. Which is one of the things that worries me about them going to two different schools. They won't have each other. New Orleans and Houston aren't exactly neighboring cities." Jackie sighed. What's wrong with me? Most women dread facing an empty nest. Yet here I am making plans to expand my design firm and renovate the house of my dreams on the Battery."

Bill chucked her chin. "It works both ways, you know. Whether they go to school in South Carolina or in California, whether they end up working on Wall Street or on an ice-fishing boat in Alaska—the boys are starting new lives of their own. You and I will be out of their sight and out of their minds the minute we drop them off at whatever college they choose." Bill set his glasses down and turned on his side to face her. "We need to look at our empty nest as a good thing. The past eighteen months have not been easy for us, sweetheart. But we have fought our way back together. We're in love all over again, and I, for one, am damn excited about entering this next stage in our lives."

"Me too." She kissed the tips of her fingers and pressed them to his lips. "But Cooper and Sean aren't gone yet. Maybe I should plan to spend more time with them instead of less during their last year of high school."

"That's easy enough to do, if that's what you decide you

want. Let Lexie and Cecilia handle the day-to-day operations in Charleston. You can make all the major decisions from here. You can use my study, turn it into your home office."

"I can't believe it." Jackie brought her hand to her mouth in mock horror. "You're offering to relinquish control of your sacred man cave to me?"

He kissed her lips. "If it makes you happy, my love."

When he tried to kiss her again, she pushed him away. "You know, that's actually not a bad idea," she said. "I could postpone my expansion for a year, which would give me time to decide whether I want office space or a physical storefront. If I restricted my travel to Charleston to day trips, we could turn the bedroom I've been using at the carriage house into another office." Jackie plumped up the bed pillows and settled back against them. "Which brings up the matter of Annie."

"What about Annie?"

"At the time, I thought I was offering her the use of the guest cottage for a few weeks. Definitely no longer than the summer. Since it turns out she's Allen's daughter and Jamie's half sister, and since he's probably gonna die and leave her without any other family, we can't just turn her out into the cold."

He furrowed his brows. "Are you suggesting we adopt her?"

"Adopt? No. But perhaps we can foster her. Or in my case, I'd like to mentor her. We have a chance to make a difference in a child's life, someone who really needs some positive parental guidance. She's tough on the outside, but vulnerable deep down inside."

He lay back against the pillows. "You're making my head spin, Jack. The kid is only sixteen. She has two more years of high school, maybe three depending on how far behind she is in her classes. A minute ago you were struggling to postpone expanding your business in order to spend more time with the boys, and now you're talking about fostering a child for three years. And where does your mother fit in? Didn't you say you offered the guest cottage to her?"

"Living in the guest cottage isn't appropriate for a teenage girl. She could have boys over and throw wild parties right under our noses."

"I hate to tell you, but living in the guest room down the hall from Cooper and Sean isn't exactly appropriate either, considering their feelings for her." Bill rolled onto his back and stared up at the ceiling. "If something happens to Allen—although he may very well end up making a full recovery—but if he dies, I'm inclined to let someone else throw their hat in the race to be that girl's parents."

Thirty-Three

SAM

SAM HADN'T BEEN out to Mack's property since Thanksgiving. They'd closed the market at two o'clock and then stopped at Sam's house for a quick change of clothes before heading to Mack's memorial service. Lovie was riding shotgun next to Sam, while Jamie and Annie spoke in hushed tones in the backseat. As they approached the property, Sam was surprised to see that Mack had cleared most of the land close to the water leaving several of his prized live oaks and not much else. The openness provided a breathtaking view of the creek that Sam had previously found uninspiring.

"Was Mack planning to build out here?" Sam asked.

"Not that I know of," Lovie said, gazing out the window. "Maybe he planned to surprise me. It is certainly a lovely spot to build a home."

Sam maneuvered her Jeep into the coned-off parking area and pulled into the first available spot. They gathered their belongings and got out of the car.

"Do I look all right?" Lovie asked. "Now that I'm here,

I'm not sure wearing white was such a good idea. I dressed for Mack today. He hated for me to wear black. He said women should always wear bright colors, that it made us look vibrant and youthful."

Sam suspected her mother had owned that particular white cotton dress since the eighties, perhaps even longer, but she was certain the hot-pink straw hat was a gift from Mack this past Easter. "You look nice, Mom. Mack would be proud that you wore his hat."

They walked toward the water, marveling at the setup in front of them. Pine farm tables with matching benches displayed vases of daisies in various shapes and sizes. Rows of white wooden chairs were positioned along the water's edge in front of a podium from which the minister would conduct the service. Several bartenders wearing skinny black ties and crisp white shirts with the sleeves rolled up waited to take orders from the attendees.

Jackie emerged from the crowd that had already begun to gather. "What do you think?"

"I think someone has outdone themselves in planning this service," Sam said. "And my guess is, that someone was you."

"Noah asked me to help," Jackie admitted. "Mack's friends had good intentions with their grandiose plans, but they got in over their heads when they tried to execute them."

"He would have loved the communal seating," Sam said.

"Although I'm not sure how he would've felt about having bartenders," Lovie said. "You know Mack. He was all about fending for himself. He hated for anyone to fuss over him."

"In this particular case, Mother, the bartenders are needed to accommodate the crowd," Jackie said in a clipped tone that drew Sam's attention.

"I think everything is perfect." Sam gave Jackie's arm a gentle squeeze of encouragement. "Remember we're supposed to send the bills to Mack's attorney. I have his address."

Jackie held out a Bible, its leather worn and edges frayed from years of use. "I found this on Mack's nightstand on the boat."

Sam took the Bible from Jackie, running her hand over the cover. "I haven't seen him carry this in years."

"Back when Dad was alive, Mack took this Bible wherever he went," Jackie said with a smile. "I've chosen several of the most dog-eared passages for his friends to read. I hope that's okay."

Lovie bowed her head. "I can't believe he's gone," she said, biting on her fist to stifle a sob.

"I know, Mom." Sam draped her arm around Lovie's shoulders and pressed a tissue in her hand. She heard the minister testing the microphone. "Looks like they are getting ready to start the service. Why don't we go find a seat?"

"We've reserved the front row for family." Jackie pointed to the cluster of chairs in the shade of the oak tree where Faith, Bitsy, and the boys were already seated.

The service included the usual litany of prayers, passages, and hymns. Noah offered the eulogy, evoking fits of laughter from the congregation with antics of the time he spent with Mack, both on the water and off. The minister dipped his hand in the urn the crematorium had provided, and then held his palm open, allowing the breeze to blow Mack's ashes across the water. A flutist ended the service with "America the Beautiful." Although not a military man, Mack was known for his patriotism. Short but moving, the service was just the way Mack would have wanted it.

Afterward, parched from the heat, the crowd migrated to the bar for refreshments.

Sam pulled Jackie to the side. "It was a lovely service."

Jackie dismissed the compliment with a wave. "These old men mostly knew what they wanted." Something caught Jackie's attention at the makeshift kitchen where the caterers had set up commercial fryers and prepped tables. "I need to get the fish frying." She snickered. "Funny, that's usually your job." She pointed at a table two rows over that boasted an elegant arrangement of pink roses. "I've reserved that table for our family. Noah sent those flowers to Lovie. He says they're from Mack."

Sam helped her mother get settled at the table while Faith went for drinks. "You haven't seen Mike, have you?" Faith said when she returned, juggling several glasses of lemonade. "He was supposed to have been here an hour ago."

"I don't see Bill anywhere either," Sam noticed.

"Bill has an excuse," Faith said in a snarky tone. "He was called into surgery."

Sam arched an eyebrow. "Trouble in paradise already?"

"With everything that's going on with this Chloe woman, what else am I supposed to think? He's not answering his phone."

Sam reached for her sister's hand. "Faith, honey, I know you're worried, but you're letting your imagination get the best of you. Did you sleep at all last night?"

Faith shook her head. "Not much."

"Mike has never let you down. He'll be here. He probably just got tied up with a patient." Sam noticed the caterers putting out the first trays of fried flounder. "Why don't we go fix ourselves a plate?"

The Sweeney cousins, plus Annie and Mary Beth, ate at one end of the table while the adults occupied the other. The kids inhaled their food, and then excused themselves in search of dessert.

Bitsy appeared at Faith's side with her new freckle-faced friend in tow. "Mama, can Mary Beth and I go play on the swing with the big kids." Bitsy pointed at the live oak where Annie, the twins, and Jamie were hanging out, eating slices of cake.

Faith patted Mary Beth's yellow head. "As long as Annie promises to keep an eye on the two of you. I want her to wave at me, so I know she's watching you."

The girls ran off, Bitsy's flowery sundress flapping behind her, with Dolly under her arm, yellow ribbons in her hair, and pink sneakers on her feet. "Bitsy looks adorable," Sam said. "She seems so happy."

Faith placed a hand over her chest. "It does my heart good to see her make new friends after all she's been through."

They continued to watch the girls as they approached the big kids. When Bitsy tugged on Annie's arm, she bent down to listen to her. Annie shot Faith a thumbs-up. *Yes.* She would keep an eye out for her daughter.

Faith and Sam returned their attention to the table. During the next half hour, the remaining members of the Sweeney family somehow managed to sneak bites of food despite the continuous flow of Mack's friends stopping by the table to offer condolences.

Sam's cell phone rang and she suspected from the area code that it was the call from Allen's doctor she'd been waiting for. She left the table and walked out on the dock for privacy. Dr. Garcia knew the complexities of the relationships involved in his patient's case, and answered all of Sam's questions regarding the liver transplant procedure from the donor perspective.

"Am I correct in assuming that you are in a position to offer Annie support? Because, I'll be frank with you, Ms. Sweeney—her father's health is declining. Rapidly. At this point, I can't recommend a transplant. He simply isn't strong enough. That may change. Miracles happen all the time with my cancer patients. But, I'm afraid to say, it seems highly unlikely in this case."

"What am I supposed to tell Annie?" Sam asked, pacing back and forth on the dock. "She is pressuring Jamie to go ahead with the transplant. I don't want her to lose hope."

"Frankly, I'm not sure what's worse—losing hope or being in denial. For me, as her father's doctor, and for you, as her friend, we owe it to Annie to prepare her for the worst."

Thirty-Four
FAITH

FAITH KEPT ONE eye on her sister, who was pacing the dock with her cell phone glued to her ear, and one on Bitsy and Mary Beth, who were taking turns on the rope swing Mack had hung from a low branch on the tree nearest the water. Annie and the three boys stood with a group of local teenagers on the other side of the tree. Faith was relieved to see Annie cast an occasional glance Bitsy's way to check on her.

Faith didn't know whether to be furious or frightened with Mike over his absence. She felt certain he had a logical explanation. As a busy emergency room doctor, showing up late for family events was typical, but he'd always texted her in the past whenever he was running behind. Her gnawing doubt reminded her that she'd only known him a year. Based on her mama's standards, twelve months was not enough time to learn enough about someone to marry them. She dismissed the negative thoughts with a vigorous shake of her head. Mike was not complicated. He was kind, caring, and compassionate. She'd learned her lesson with Curtis. Surely her Rotten Bastard

Radar would have alerted her to impending disaster if Mike posed a threat to her well-being.

Faith spotted Eli at the edge of the crowd and waved him over. In his uniform, the handsome policeman turned more than a few heads as he made his way to their table. Most knew him by name and returned his friendly smile.

When Faith stood to greet him, Eli took her by the arm and led her away from the table, out of her mother's earshot. He scanned the gathering. "Where's Mike?"

Faith sighed. "I wish I knew. He was supposed to meet me here two hours ago. He's not answering any of my calls or texts."

"Don't worry, Faith. I'm sure Mike has a legitimate reason for missing the service."

"I hope you're right. I'd hate to consider the alternative with this stalker on the loose. Speaking of Chloe, do you have any news?"

"I do. But I'm afraid you're not going to like it. I was hoping to brief you and Mike at the same time." Eli paused to wave to a friend across the party. "I heard back from my contact at the Charlotte-Mecklenburg PD who did some digging for me. It turns out our friend, Chloe Morrison, was recently released from a psychiatric hospital there. According to my source, Ms. Morrison is bipolar. Six months ago, one of Chloe's coworkers at Piedmont Hospital where she worked accused her of stalking him. Instead of bringing charges against her, the doctor convinced Chloe to seek psychiatric help."

"And let me guess. The hospital refused to give her back her job when she got out."

"Bingo." Eli pointed at her, his fingers in the shape of a gun.

"Which is why she moved back to Prospect. She told Mike she came home to take care of an aging parent."

"That's simply not true. Both of Chloe's parents were killed in a suspicious house fire thirty years ago. Chloe was only fifteen years old at the time."

Faith snapped her fingers. "That's it! I knew I was forgetting something important about her. Chloe was a year older than me, but we went to the same high school. The story was all over the newspapers. The police thought she had something to do with setting the fire."

"Initially, they did. But the police eventually cleared her. She moved to Atlanta after that, went to live with a spinster aunt."

"Sounds to me like Chloe's been unstable for a long time. And now she's set her sights on my husband." She stared him down. "What is it about me, Eli? Why am I the magnet for crazies?"

Eli smiled. "This time, Faith, it's not on you. Your husband is the target."

Faith noticed Sam ambling across the lawn with her head bowed as though deep in thought. "Who were you talking to? Was that Mike?" Faith asked her sister when she joined them. The sound of desperation in her voice brought back memories—a different summer, a different stalker.

"Why would Mike be calling me?" Sam asked, poking at her chest.

Faith's shoulders slumped. "I guess he wouldn't. I'm sorry for jumping down your throat. I'm just on edge."

"That was Allen's doctor," Sam said. "He refuses to do the transplant. He said we need to prepare Annie for the worst."

"Poor kid. That's too bad," Eli said. "Where is Annie anyway?"

"Over there with Bitsy and the boys." Their eyes followed Faith's finger to the oak tree. They watched, laughing, as Bitsy leapt on top of Jamie, tackling him to the ground. "Jamie is a good sport to put up with her nonsense."

"Are you kidding me? He loves the attention." Sam stood on her tiptoes to see over the crowd. "I think I just saw Mike's truck pull up."

Sure enough, several seconds later, Mike came marching toward them, his shoulders hunched, his face set in a deep scowl. He put his arms around Faith and hugged her tight. "I'm so sorry I missed the service. You have no idea what I've been through today."

Faith rubbed the tense muscles in her husband's back. "I'm afraid to ask. I'm sure it has something to do with Chloe."

"The crazy bitch won't leave me alone." He rubbed his balding head. "Just as I was leaving to come here, the chief of staff called me into his office. The doctor on call in the ER last night reported a significant number of pain medicines missing. Chloe claims she saw me take them."

Faith's mouth dropped open. "I don't understand. First of all, you were at home last night. And secondly, why would she do that to you, if she's supposedly in love with you?"

"Because she's psychotic," Eli answered. "I was just filling Faith in on what I found out from Charlotte." Eli gave Mike the details of the report he'd received from his contact at CMPD.

Mike drew Faith closer to him. "We need to press charges." He kissed the top of her head. "I can't let anything happen to you or Bitsy."

Once again all eyes traveled to the tree by the water where the younger generation was gathered. Cooper and Sean were captivated by something Annie was saying to them. Mary Beth was propped up against the trunk of the tree sucking on a blade of grass, and Jamie was standing nearby talking to Noah. Bitsy was nowhere in sight.

Faith's stomach lurched. "Where is she?" She conducted a quick survey of the grounds. "I don't see Bitsy anywhere!"

All four of them took off running across the property. Sam got there first. "Where's Bitsy?" she asked Jamie.

His head jerked up in surprise. "What'd you mean?" He glanced at the tree, then back at his mother. "She was literally just here." He pointed to a spot near them on the ground where the grass was flattened. The concern growing in his voice, he said, "We were sitting together right there a minute ago. She was telling me about her playhouse."

Faith saw them then—Bitsy's little pink sneakers lying abandoned beneath the swing. She covered the ground to the tree in three long strides. Grabbing hold of Mary Beth's arm, she yanked the little girl to her feet. "Where's Bitsy? Where'd she go?"

"Easy now, Faith," Noah said, prying her hand off his granddaughter's arm. "She's just a child." He lifted a now-crying Mary Beth into his arms. "Do you know where Bitsy went, honey?"

Nodding, the little girl planted her face in her grandpa's chest.

"You need to tell us, Mary Beth," Eli said, his voice kind but stern. "This is very important."

Hiding her face in the crook of her arm, Mary Beth pointed her tiny finger at the split-rail fence separating Mack's lot from the property next door. "She walked over there, to the fence with that lady."

Faith forced herself to sound calm despite the panic gripping her chest. "What lady, Mary Beth?"

"The one who offered her a Snickers bar. Bitsy said her name was Chloe."

His hand pressed to the headset in his ear, Eli raced to the edge of the property, jumped over the fence, and disappeared through the row of magnolia trees on the other side. He returned seconds later, shaking his head. "I just missed them. There's still dust in the air from the dirt driveway." A crowd had begun to gather around them and he raised his hands to get everyone's attention. "Listen up. We don't have much time. I've already initiated an Amber Alert. I know the make and model of the car this woman drives. I'm going after her. Reinforcements should be here any minute. They will want to search the property and talk to each of you."

Eli took off again, this time with Sam on his heels.

Faith picked up her daughter's pink sneakers and clutched them against her chest, her anxiety increasing as she remembered the parent safety class she had when Bitsy was in preschool. *Never let your guard down. It only takes a few seconds for an abductor to snatch a child.*

Thirty-Five

JACKIE

THE SUDDEN COMMOTION startled Jackie. People were leaving their tables and running down toward the water. She assumed someone must have fallen off the dock, a child perhaps, until she heard mention of kidnapping and abduction. Who would take a child from a funeral reception? Must be some mistake.

Sitting next to her, Lovie said, "Wonder what on earth is going on?"

Out of the corner of her eye, Jackie saw Eli and Sam hop in his police cruiser and speed away. Alarm mounting, she helped her mother to her feet. "I'm not sure, but we'd better go find out."

Unable to see over the heads of those gathered, Jackie tapped the person on the shoulder in front of her. "What's going on?"

A look of recognition crossed the woman's face, although Jackie couldn't place her. "You don't know?" the lady said, her hand gripping the fabric of her blouse.

"Obviously not," Lovie said.

"It's your granddaughter. Someone has taken Bitsy." The woman stepped aside so they could pass.

"Oh dear lord. Who would want to take that precious child away from her mother?" Lovie leaned against Jackie for support as they elbowed their way to the front of the crowd.

Jackie knew there were a lot of pedophiles who would take a child away from his or her mother. But in Bitsy's case, based on the phone conversation she'd had with Faith earlier in the day, Jackie suspected the woman currently stalking Mike was somehow involved.

They found Faith a blubbering mess, holding tight to her daughter's pink tennis shoes. Desperate to console her inconsolable daughter, Lovie tried to wrench her arm free from Jackie's grip, but Jackie held tight. Faith had enough to contend with without having to comfort their mother. "Stay here, Mom. Let Mike take care of Faith."

An army of police officers arrived on the scene. They surrounded Faith, asking her more questions than she could possibly answer at once.

Jackie searched the crowd for her boys, anxious to put her eyes on them and make certain they were safe. She spotted them at the same time Cooper saw her. He grabbed his brother and they rushed over.

"It's all our fault, Mom," Cooper said near tears. "We were supposed to be watching her."

"She was with us one minute, then gone the next." Sean's face was full of anguish. "That woman is not going to kill her, is she, Mom?"

Lovie groaned in agony. The blood drained from her face, and her eyes rolled back in her head. When she collapsed and fell limp against Jackie, a collective gasp came from those standing close by.

The twins sprang into action. Cooper wrapped his arms around his grandmother from behind while Sean lifted her feet. They found a shady spot in the grass to lay her down. She was already coming to by the time Mike rushed to her aid. He checked her pupils and her pulse. "She just fainted. She's going to be fine." He stood and dragged Jackie off to the side. "It's awfully hot out here, and with the emotional distress… You should probably take her home."

"She's not going to leave Faith. You should know that by now." Jackie wiped the sweat from her brow with the back of her hand. "But I agree it's hot as blazes out here. I'll get Mom in the car and turn on the air conditioner."

"Why don't you take her to our house? We are headed there now. The police are going to search the area again and talk to all the attendees individually. But they are sending us home with several officers in case Chloe tries to contact us or decides to bring Bitsy back."

Jackie pressed her sticky cheek against Mike's. "We're here for you. Whatever you need, we are at your disposal. This woman fancies herself in love with you. She's not going to hurt Bitsy. She's just trying to get your attention."

"Well, she sure as hell got it." Mike squeezed Jackie's arm. "I need to get back to Faith. I'll see you at the house."

The twins helped their grandmother to the car while Jackie spoke to one of the police officers, explaining her connection to the missing child and giving them her number in case they needed to get in touch with her. They rode in silence to Faith's house—the boys in the back with gloom etched in their faces and Lovie in the passenger seat, wringing her hands and fidgeting with her hat.

"Just take the hat off, Mom," Jackie said when she'd finally had enough. Not only was pink her least favorite color and a poor choice for a funeral, it reminded Jackie of a happy little girl with hot-pink sneakers on her small feet, a child who was only just beginning to recover from the trauma inflicted by her cruel father.

Unpleasant thoughts began to invade Jackie's mind— images of Bitsy's hands and feet tied, her mouth gagged, a crazy woman refusing to give her food and water. Jackie had meant what she'd said to Mike. She didn't think this Chloe person would sexually molest her niece or harm her in any way; she wanted to impress Mike. She was delusional, that much was certain. She probably had some grandiose notion that Mike would leave his wife and the two of them would run off together to Tahiti, taking Bitsy with them.

Forcing the unwelcome visions from her mind, Jackie punched in her husband's cell number, but the call went straight to voice mail. He was still in surgery. She snuck a peek at the twins in the rearview mirror. Cooper's face was hidden behind his large hands, and tears streamed down Sean's cheeks. She choked back a sob at the sight of her boys in pain. She needed to stay strong for her family. All of them. She thought about Sam and her recent habit of reaching for the bottle at the first sign of trouble. She said a silent prayer, asking God to give Sam strength.

It dawned on her then what had been nagging at her ever since the talk she'd had with her mother two nights ago. When their father died six years ago, even before that, really, everyone in the family had counted on Sam to be the tough one. The middle sister was the keystone of the family, their rock. Aside from her downward spiral into alcohol after all that had happened with Curtis the previous summer, Sam had recovered, with Eli's help, and had resumed her place as the family rock—even when staring at Curtis's evil face for three days during the trial in November. She had held herself together throughout the months that followed until this past week. When she broke up with the man of her dreams. When that man was held hostage during a bank robbery. When Mack died, and her son's father, after a nineteen-year absence, showed up on his deathbed with his teenage daughter in tow, a poor girl with no family of her own, destined to become an orphan. When her sister's husband was being stalked and her niece was kidnapped. No person, strong or weak, should have to cope with all of that.

And what had Jackie done? She'd run off to Charleston to satisfy her own selfish needs. Her mother was right. She was neglecting her family. All of them. Not just the two loves of her life in the backseat. Whether they showed it or not, they needed her now, and they'd need her in the months and years to come. Just as her mother would need her as she grieved for Mack. Just as Annie, Jamie, and Sam would need her as they coped with the Allen situation. Just as Faith would need her as she waited the return of her daughter. Jackie's family had allowed her a year to sort through her midlife crisis, and now she would show her appreciation by granting them the same support and understanding they'd given her.

She turned into Faith's driveway and drove up to the house. After putting the engine in park, she turned around to face her family. "Chin up, everybody! Faith and Mike are counting on us to remain positive. We will do whatever it takes to bring our Bitsy home."

Thirty-Six

SAM

"**Y**OU REALLY SHOULDN'T be in the patrol car with me, Sam" Eli said as they raced toward the main road. "Promise me, if we get into a situation you'll stay in the car."

"Cross my heart," Sam said, drawing an *X* on her chest with her finger. "I can't just sit around and twiddle my thumbs while some insane woman leaves town with my niece. Tell me again the make and model of the car."

Eli came to a rolling stop before peeling out onto Creek-side Drive toward town. "We're looking for a silver late-model Hyundai Elantra."

"That pretty much describes fifty percent of the cars in Prospect."

"Unfortunately." He removed a notepad from his shirt pocket and read, "South Carolina plates 3-4-9, R-S-B." He set the notepad on the console between them.

When Eli said, "Roger that," Sam understood he was talking to dispatch. "We'll check it out. I'll call for backup if needed."

"What're we checking out?" Sam asked.

"Chloe's house. Her address is 1502 Old Beach Highway."

Lights flashing and siren blasting, Eli sped down Creekside through the Main Street intersection and out past Moss Creek Farm. Sam kept her eyes peeled for Chloe's car as best she could considering the speed at which Eli was driving. Three miles outside of town, he turned off the siren. "Best not to alert Chloe to our presence, although I seriously doubt she's here."

They arrived at a nondescript brick rancher set back from the main highway with few trees to shield it from passersby. "This place is too exposed to hide from the police," Sam said.

Eli turned into the driveway and pulled up to the enclosed detached garage. "Stay here. I'll be right back."

He peeked in the garage window first, and then shook his head, letting Sam know Chloe's car was not in the garage. Shifting in her seat, Sam watched him make his way around the house, turning doorknobs and peeking in windows.

"She's not here," he said when he climbed back into the car. He reported his findings to dispatch, ending, "Roger that."

"Let's head back toward town. We can stop by Jackie's on the way."

There were many places to hide in the vast acreage at Moss Creek Farm, and while neither Sam nor Eli had much hope in finding signs of Bitsy or Chloe, they searched the property from top to bottom anyway. Process of elimination.

Sam's initial panic had worn off and real fear was setting in. When she choked back tears, Eli said, "You've had a tough week," pulling her in for a half hug as they were getting back in the car. "You need to lean on someone. Whether we're together or not, I'm here for you. I understand how hard it is to resist the temptation to drink in times of crises. Don't give in to it. Reach out to someone instead, anyone who can help. If not me, then your sponsor or Moses."

"Thanks, Eli. I appreciate it," Sam said, sniffling. "You've had a difficult week too, considering the hostage situation and all. And I know how much my family means to you, especially the younger generation. Why is it that you seem better equipped to handle difficult situations than me?"

He chuckled. "Trust me, I'm not better equipped. I've just been at it a hell of a lot longer than you." He smiled down at her. "Believe it or not, thinking I had a bomb handcuffed to my wrist wasn't the worst part of my week. Nor was Mack's death, and I really loved that old salt. The worst part of my week was when you jabbed a knife through my heart."

This time she didn't try to hide the tears. "In all the craziness that's happened this week, I've done a lot of soul searching and come to some important conclusions. I miss having you in my life, Eli. This isn't the time or place, but once Bitsy is home safe and sound, I'd like it if you and I could talk. About us."

He opened the car door for her. "In that case, the sooner we find Bitsy the better."

For the next hour, they drove around town searching in alleys and parking lots and side streets. Eli stayed in constant communication with police headquarters, and so far none of the other officers had spotted the silver Hyundai, its owner, or the missing little girl wearing the flowery sundress.

"This crazy bitch appears to have disappeared off the face of the planet and taken my niece with her."

Eli turned off Creekside and pulled in beside the other police cruisers parked in Faith's driveway. "Brace yourself, Sam. This is going to be rough. Hiding our fears from Faith and Mike will not be easy. But we need to try."

The police had turned Faith's house into Command Central. Several uniformed officers huddled with Faith and Mike in the living room discussing their options. In the kitchen, Lovie had donned an apron and was making pitchers of fresh lemonade and perking pots of coffee. With heads bowed and shoulders slumped under the weight of the world, the four teenagers sat around the breakfast room table with Jackie, her attempts to console them falling on deaf ears.

Sam sat down in the empty chair beside her sister. "Okay, kids, listen up. We're not accomplishing anything by moping around."

Jamie looked at his mother as if she'd lost her mind. "What else are we supposed to do?"

"Paper the town with missing person's flyers," Sam said.

Jamie sat up in his chair. "That's actually a good idea," he said, and the others nodded their agreement.

"Does anyone have a recent photograph of Bitsy?" Sam asked.

Four iPhones appeared at once. The teenagers compared photographs until they decided on one Annie had taken earlier in the day. A sweet image of Bitsy with a great big toothy grin. "We need a laptop," Cooper said, looking around the room. "I'll see if we can borrow Mike's."

Cooper got up and returned a minute later with Mike's laptop. "He has Photoshop, which will make it easy."

Sean rolled his eyes. "Easy for *you*."

In a matter of a few minutes, Cooper had transferred Bitsy's image to Photoshop and created a simple flyer with all the pertinent contact information.

"Let's get this to FedEx to make copies." Sam stood and the others followed her lead.

Eli offered her a thumbs-up from across the room. "Use yellow paper," he mouthed. "It shows up better."

All those on flyer detail migrated to the driveway. "Whoa, not so fast," Jackie said when the four teenagers made a move to get in the same car. "We'll cover more ground if we divide up. Cooper and Sean, you take everything south of Main Street. Jamie and Annie are responsible for north of Main. Sam and I will hit the restaurants and marina east of Creekside."

They convoyed to FedEx where they printed two hundred copies of their Missing Bitsy flyer on bright yellow paper and purchased three rolls of duct tape. Once again they separated into groups. For the next two hours, they posted flyers to telephone poles and handed them out to dinner patrons coming and going from the restaurants on Main Street and along the waterfront. They spoke to shoppers at the hardware, liquor, and grocery stores, and to moviegoers at the nearby theater.

Jackie and Sam made their last stop of the evening at the Harris Teeter. After taping their remaining two flyers to the doors at both the main entrances, they went inside and purchased deli trays, four dozen fried wing dings, five bags of salad, and three roasted chickens.

Bill was waiting for them when they got back to Faith's, along with Moses and several of Mike's coworkers from the hospital. The local television news team was preparing to interview Mike and Faith for the eleven o'clock broadcast, and two agents had appeared from the FBI office in Columbia.

So far, they'd received no ransom calls from Chloe or tips from the Amber Alert. "She's gone into hiding," Moses said. "I imagine she's somewhere close by. She's making a point to Mike. We just need Chloe to tell us what that point is."

Thirty-Seven

SAM

ALL FAMILY MEMBERS and close friends spent the night at Command Central with the exception of Jackie and Bill who took a visibly fading Lovie back to the farm for some much-needed rest. The majority of those remaining caught a few winks here and there. Jamie, Cooper, and Sean managed a couple of hours crammed together in the queen-size bed in the guest room while Annie curled up on the floor next to Bitsy's bed. Sam spent much of the night trying to comfort her sister who vacillated between fits of anger, uncontrollable sobbing, and shivers of fear—never letting go of Bitsy's pink shoes. The only words that seemed to offer any solace came from Moses. He sat with Faith off to the side, murmuring words of encouragement only she could hear.

Her family's presence offered reassurance to Sam as well. Just being close to Eli gave her strength. Even though they barely spoke, they locked eyes across the room more than once, transmitting signals of support to one another. He'd been out looking for Bitsy for most of the night, and then came straight there once his shift ended.

Sam was dozing in one of the oversized chairs in the living room when her phone vibrated in her lap, a few minutes past seven the following morning. She took the call from Allen's doctor outside to the porch.

"I hate to disturb you so early in the morning, but Allen is asking to see his daughter." Dr. Garcia paused, breathing loudly into the phone. "There's never an easy way to say this. He doesn't have much time left."

Sam's mind raced as she considered the logistics of getting Annie to Charleston. "I have a business to run, Dr. Garcia, and I'm tied up with a family emergency of an entirely different sort. If I can juggle a few things, I might be able to get her there late this afternoon."

"It's impossible to predict these things, Ms. Sweeney. But my guess is that that might be too late."

"I understand, Doctor. I'll figure something out."

When she went back inside, she found Jackie and Lovie in the kitchen with a tray of Danishes and three four-pack carriers of coffee from the Island Bakery.

Lovie grew still at the sight of Sam's concerned face. "You look like you've seen a ghost. Has something happened?"

"Not to Bitsy, no. But I just got a call from Allen's doctor. They don't expect him to make it through the day." Sam turned to Jackie. "Can you take Annie to Charleston? I thought about closing Sweeney's because of what's happening with Bitsy. But the market is such a hubbub of local activity, I think it's best to keep the lines of communication open."

"That makes sense," Lovie said. "Someone might have

seen or heard something. The locals can always count on one of us being at the market."

"On the other hand, this thing with Allen is pretty important." Jackie stirred cream into one of the coffees and handed it to Sam. "I think you should be the one to take Annie to Charleston. Jamie may want to go with you as well. He may want to say goodbye to Allen."

"I ran the market fine by myself for years," Lovie said. "I can do it again today."

Ignoring her mother, Jackie said to Sam, "I can help out. I might not know how to handle the money, but I'm sure there's plenty I can do. And Cooper and Sean will pitch in. We need to do something constructive anyway besides hanging around here waiting for the phone to ring. I'm sure Faith will be glad to have us out of her way."

The tension drained from Sam's body. "If you're sure you don't mind. I'd really like to be the one to take the kids to Charleston."

Jackie squeezed Sam's shoulder. "I don't envy you, sis. This will be a difficult day for Annie."

"I hope this crazy bitch has brought Bitsy home by the time we get back." Sam inhaled a deep breath. "We should get on the road. Let me go wake up Jamie and Annie."

Initially, Jamie put up mild resistance to going to Charleston. "I don't want to see him again, Mom." But Sam convinced him he should be there to support Annie.

They stopped in at Sam's for a quick shower and change of clothes. Once they were on the highway to Charleston, Annie said, "Tell me again what the doctor said."

"He asked me to bring you to Charleston, that your father wanted to see you."

"Do you think maybe he's ready to perform the transplant?" Annie asked.

Keeping one hand on the steering wheel, Sam reached for the girl's hand with the other. "Annie, honey. Your father is not well enough for the transplant. You need to try and prepare yourself. He doesn't have much time left." Sam thumbed away the crocodile tear that spilled out of Annie's right eye and ran down her cheek. "I know how hard this is on you, how much you love your father. But I want you to know you are not alone. You are part of our family now. You have a place, here in Prospect with us."

Jamie leaned in between the seats. "That's right. No way am I letting my sister go, now that I've found you."

Annie smiled at them through her tears, then turned away and stared out the window for the rest of the drive.

When they arrived at MUSC, Annie hopped out in front of the cancer center and hurried up to see her father while Sam and Jamie went to park the Jeep. "I hope Allen doesn't ask to see me," Jamie said when they were in the garage elevator on the way back down. "Because I don't know what I'll say."

"The choice is yours, honey. But I don't want you to have any regrets." Sam looped her arm through her son's as they crossed the street and headed toward the cancer center.

"I don't care whether he's on his deathbed or not. Nothing he says will change the way I feel about him. I have no respect for him. He's a coward for abandoning us the way he did."

When they reached the revolving front door of the building, Sam stopped walking and turned to her son. "We need to remember that Annie's experience of her father was entirely different from our experience with Allen. Today is all about her. It won't be easy, but you need to try and put your feelings aside."

"Did you mean what you said about her coming to live with us?"

"Of course. The poor girl has no money and nowhere to go. I can't just put her out on the streets. I *have* grown to love her. She's a good kid. She deserves a chance."

"I feel the same way."

"And I see no sense in tarnishing her memories of her father by talking bad about him. He's the only family she's ever really known."

"That's fair," Jamie said after a brief silence.

They sat in the waiting room on Allen's floor, waiting for Annie to come out. When she finally did, her face was puffy and her nose red from crying. "Daddy wants to see you, Sam," she said, plopping down in the chair next to Jamie.

Reminding herself she was doing it for Annie, Sam reluctantly rose from her chair. Back in ICU, she approached Allen's bed with caution. As far as she was concerned, there was nothing left between them, but she suspected Allen had unfinished business concerning Annie. His appearance had diminished considerably in the past few days. The circles under his eyes were black and his skin was now the color of a field of wheat at harvest time. He eyed the chair beside the bed, but Sam was too nervous to sit.

"I realize I don't have any right to ask anything of you, Sam." He smiled a weak smile. "But I'd be awful grateful if you would keep an eye out for my daughter. She's a kid, all alone in the world. She doesn't deserve to suffer because of her father's sins."

Sam's bitterness toward Allen resurfaced. Damn straight

he didn't have any right to ask anything of her. Not only had he abandoned her to raise their son on her own but now he wanted her to take care of his daughter—the child he'd fathered by another woman, a woman he'd actually married. Her feelings toward Annie had nothing to do with it. She loved the girl. She'd take care of her regardless of who her father was.

"I'm one step ahead of you. I told Annie on the way here that she has a place with us. That is, if she wants it. She's a good girl, and we all love her."

A lone tear slid down his cheek. "I don't know how to thank you."

"I'm not doing it for you, Allen. I'm doing it for Annie."

"I guess I deserved that," he said, his expression resigned. "Annie told me that Jamie is here. Do you think he'll see me?"

"Honestly, I don't know. But I'll ask him." She started for the door, and then turned back around. Despite her feelings for him, her conscience wouldn't allow her to leave a dying man on a negative note. "You have nothing to worry about where Annie is concerned. You did a good job with her. She'll make her way in this world just fine. I promise, I'll see to it."

As it turned out, Jamie opted to see Allen. He didn't stay long and he didn't want to talk about it when he returned, but his drooping posture and runny nose indicated an emotion-filled encounter. Sad that his second time meeting his father would end up being his last.

Thirty-Eight
JACKIE

ALTHOUGH JACKIE HAD never admitted it to anyone, she'd always found the seafood business beneath her dignity. Much to her surprise, aside from the dark cloud of Bitsy's kidnapping looming over them, she enjoyed working with her mother at Sweeney's. Business was slow, typical of a Tuesday, and with Roberto in the kitchen, the twins were not needed.

Lovie shooed her grandsons out of the market. "Go. Catch something. Anything. Shrimp, crabs, fish. The two of you need to be out on the water on a nice day like today."

Cooper and Sean did not need to be told twice. They grabbed their buckets and cooler and bolted for the door.

"Thank you for that," Jackie said to Lovie once the boys were gone. "Those two are taking Bitsy's kidnapping hard, as are we all. But they need fresh air. They don't do well being cooped up."

Lovie assigned Jackie the job of keeping the showcases stocked. She showed her where to get replenishments and how to arrange the product on the trays and shelves.

Customers trickled in off and on for most of the day, many

of them acquaintances who didn't know Faith well enough to contact her directly but wanted to express their concern for Bitsy to someone in the family. While they appreciated the sentiments, Jackie and Lovie soon grew tired of hearing the townsfolk discuss the poor little girl who had already suffered so much at the hands of her father.

During a long spell with no customers, Jackie took it upon herself to rearrange the showroom—positioning the produce cart, wine racks, and dry goods display in a way that made better use of the space.

"I can't believe what a difference these few simple changes make," Lovie said, as she helped Jackie restack the bottles in the wine racks. "The showroom feels so much more open. You have a special knack, honey. I haven't given you much credit for your talents in the past, and I'm sorry for that."

Jackie beamed at the rare compliment from her mother. "Thank you, Mom. That means a lot coming from you."

"I owe you an apology for the other night. I was too hard on you. You've really come through for your family these past few days."

"I think you were just the right amount of hard on me. I needed to hear those things." Jackie blew dust off a bottle and slid it in the bottom rung of the rack. "I've been ignoring my family by chasing my own selfish goals. Cooper and Sean need me. I realize that now."

"You shouldn't give up on what you've worked so hard to achieve," Lovie said, handing her another bottle.

"I'm not. I'll have plenty of time for *me* when my nest is empty. It is the boys' senior year, and I want to enjoy these last months with them before all our lives change."

Bill stopped by the market midafternoon to see Jackie. "I

never would have believed it, if I wasn't seeing it with my own eyes. The distinguished interior designer is peddling seafood," he said, a playful smirk on his lips.

"She's been here for less than a day and already she's transformed the place," Lovie said.

Bill looked around the showroom. "I thought something was different. Somehow it seems bigger."

"Jackie waved her magic wand. Problem is, now I'm going to have to pay her triple what I pay Sam."

"For you, my services are free," Jackie said, planting a kiss on top of her mother's head.

Lovie walked out from behind the counter. "I'll leave you two lovebirds to talk. I need to discuss a new recipe with Roberto."

"But... What if a customer comes in? I don't know how to work this thing," Jackie said, running her hand atop the cash register.

"I'm sure you can figure it out," Lovie said, winking at Bill on her way to the back.

"I'm proud of you, Jack, for helping out your family." Bill leaned back against the counter. "Has there been any word from Faith? I've just come from making rounds at the hospital. The abduction is all anyone can talk about."

"So far, there have been no ransom calls or notes from Chloe. And very little response from the Amber Alert. The more time that passes, the more afraid we all become. Staying busy is all anyone can do. Except poor Faith. I don't know how she's coping."

"Bitsy was doing so well, poor kid. She'd just started talking again."

"I can't bring myself to think about what kind of torture she's having to endure and what kind of lasting repercussions the situation will have on her. We're lucky to have Moses standing by, not only for Faith and Bitsy but for Sam as well."

"Speaking of Sam, where is she?"

"She took Annie and Jamie to Charleston to see Allen. Sam got a call from his doctor this morning. The end is near."

Bill looked up in surprise. "That's too bad. I have to say I'm relieved for Jamie, though. At least now he doesn't have to make the difficult decision about having surgery."

"Thank goodness. I was concerned about the decision he might have made."

"Annie is going to need our support," Bill said, rubbing the back of his neck. "And not just financially, although I'm happy to help with her father's medical bills and funeral expenses. Hell, I'll even pay for her to go to college, if that's what she decides she wants."

Jackie reached for his hand and squeezed. "That's very generous of you. Thank you."

"And if she needs a place to stay, she can live with us."

She jerked her head back. "But... I thought. The other night, you said—"

"Having Annie live with us wouldn't be my first choice for all the reasons we talked about the other night. But I'm not going to turn her out on the street. We'll make it work, if it comes down to it."

She smiled warmly at him. "You're the best. You know that?"

He reached across the counter and ran his finger down her cheek. "I have a lot of making up to do."

"Keep it up. You're doing a good job." Jackie kissed her fingertips and brought them to his lips. "I'll talk to my sisters. I'm sure they feel the same way we do about taking Annie in."

"The most important thing is for her to know she has a family she can count on."

Thirty-Nine

FAITH

FAITH WAS GOING out of her mind with worry. She wanted to yank her hair out, rip the skin off her arms, claw at her eyes. She felt an urgent need to run—to look in every window and under every dock in search of her baby. But the police officers refused to let her leave the house.

"I should have told Bitsy to stay away from Chloe," she told Mike repeatedly. "Why didn't I warn her?"

"Because you didn't want to frighten her after all she's been through," he reassured her over and over again. "If anyone's to blame here, it's me. I should have told you sooner about Chloe. I should have reported her behavior to the hospital administrators." His list of should-haves was long. But, while Faith didn't blame Mike anymore than he blamed her, the guilt they both experienced prevented them from being able to offer one another much comfort. For the most part, they avoided each other, choosing to pace the floor at opposite ends of the house.

When her family left for work on Tuesday morning, Faith

was thankful to be alone with just Mike and the FBI agents in the house. She was tired of everyone hovering over her, catering to her every need except the one they couldn't fulfill. But as soon as they left, she wished them back again. The silence became unbearable, while the murmurs from the two FBI agents huddled together at the dining room table were worse than mosquitos swarming her head on a hot and sticky Lowcountry day.

A few minutes after noon, the ringing of Mike's cell phone shattered the silence. It rang once and then stopped. Thirty seconds later, Faith's phone rang once and then stopped. This pattern continued off and on for the rest of the afternoon. Even though the screen read "caller unknown," the FBI agents were able to trace the calls to four different numbers from four different disposable phones.

"That's our girl," the older of the two FBI agents said. "This is good news. She's engaging us. Now we need to find a way to draw her out."

They tried to catch her voice, but Chloe always managed to hang up before they answered the call. She never stayed on the phone long enough for the call to go into voice mail, but they changed their greetings anyway, begging Chloe to please release their daughter.

By the time her family returned a few minutes after six that evening, Faith's nerves were raw. The incessant ringing of the phone had driven her to the brink of madness. She was saddened for Annie's loss, but she was relieved to have a distraction.

"I'm so sorry about your daddy." She embraced Annie and held her tight rubbing her back while she sobbed.

Annie pulled away from her after a few minutes. "Here

I am slobbering all over you when you're the one who needs comforting. There's nothing more I can do for Daddy, but I'm not leaving this house until we find Bitsy. I refuse to lose another person I love."

Faith welcomed Annie's presence. They comforted each other in a way the others couldn't understand. The two settled into a quiet corner in the living room where they could discuss the possibilities of where Chloe might be hiding Bitsy.

"I'm surprised the Amber Alert didn't produce any leads," Annie said. "I guess that means she didn't go very far in her car."

"Which gives me hope that they are somewhere close by," Faith said.

"Have the police searched Chloe's house?"

Faith nodded. "They broke in this morning. There is no sign of Chloe or Bitsy anywhere."

"Is Chloe's stuff still there?" Annie asked.

"Yes, which the FBI takes as a sign she's planning to come back."

Neither Faith nor Annie considered themselves experts. They had the FBI agents and local police officers assigned to their case for that. But talking through the various possible scenarios offered Faith a glimmer of hope that her daughter might still be alive.

Later that night, Faith and Annie retreated to Bitsy's room where they stretched out side by side on the bed. Picking up where she and Bitsy had left off in *Charlotte's Web,* Annie read out loud to Faith until she fell into a deep sleep.

A few minutes past two the next morning, Faith sat bolt upright in bed. She nudged Annie, who was snoring softly beside her. "Wake up, Annie. I know where they are. I know where Chloe is holding Bitsy. It makes perfect sense." She smacked her forehead with her palm. "I'm so stupid. Why didn't I think of it sooner?"

Annie shook her head in an attempt to wake up. "What're you talking about? Why didn't you think of what sooner?"

"Chloe was at my wedding reception. She introduced herself to me that night. She looked different. Her hair was a different color or something." Faith kicked back the covers and hopped off the bed. "That's right. It's all coming back to me now. Mike told me she had dyed her hair brown and begun wearing those awful green contact lens." She paced back and forth at the foot of the bed. "But that night at the wedding, I specifically remember her talking about what a lucky girl I am to be marrying a doctor and working my way up from a 'trailer in the woods to a beautiful new house on the water.'"

Annie's doe eyes grew huge. "I can't believe she said that to you. And you'd never met her before?"

"Not before that night. I ignored her at the time. I've met a lot of callous people in my day. I just assumed she was one of them. And with all the excitement of the wedding, I didn't give her a second thought. But now it all makes sense. She had this whole thing planned from the start."

"Where is this trailer?"

"On the outskirts of town. I had it on the market for a while, but I didn't get any offers. I'm not surprised. No one wants to live in the woods in the middle of nowhere. And I can't say I blame them. If the town expands, the property might be worth something one day." Faith headed for the door. "We've gotta get out to the trailer. You go check to see if Eli or one of the other officers is still here while I wake up Mike."

Faith found Mike in their bedroom, lying flat on his back

staring up at the ceiling. "I know where Bitsy is," she said, rummaging in her handbag for her car keys. "I'm almost positive Chloe has taken her out to my trailer."

He sat up straight. "What gives you that idea?"

Car keys in hand, she waved him on. "I'll explain on the way."

A trail of cars—Eli's police cruiser, the FBI agent's unmarked sedan, and Faith's Buick—convoyed through town and onto the old highway that led to her property. At three in the morning, the roads were deserted and pitch-black with no moon to guide them. Eli parked his cruiser at the entrance to the dirt road that led to the trailer. He walked over to Faith's car and motioned for her to roll down the window. "We're going in on foot, so as not to alert Chloe of our presence. I want you to wait here." Faith started to object and he shot her a look. "I mean it, Faith. Your daughter's safety depends on you waiting in this car." He tapped on the roof of the SUV. "Let us do what we've been trained to do."

"Okay, fine. But keep me informed. I'm going out of my mind here, Eli."

"I'll text you updates as they happen." He pointed to the road in front of her. "Park over here on the shoulder, so you're out of the way."

She pulled over to the side of the road and killed the engine. "He has exactly ten minutes. If I don't hear from him by then, I'm going in."

Mike reached for her hand. "Be patient, honey. You heard Eli. Let them do their jobs."

Annie leaned over from the backseat and squeezed Faith's

shoulder. "The last thing Bitsy needs is for something to happen to her mom."

Faith settled deeper in the seat. "I know. You're right. But this waiting is killing me. What if I'm wrong? What if she's not in there?"

"Then we'll keep looking until we find her," Mike said. "But this is the best lead we've had."

"I don't know why I didn't think of it sooner." She sought Annie out in the rearview mirror. "Maybe our conversation earlier stirred something in my subconscious."

Annie held up her hands, her fingers crossed.

The first text arrived nine minutes later: "*We've detected movement in the house. Sit tight.*"

Faith read it out loud to Mike and Annie, and then pressed the phone to her chest. "I'm afraid to breathe."

"Hopefully it won't be too much longer." Mike stroked her matted hair. "Whatever happens, honey, whatever condition Bitsy comes home in, we will deal with it together."

"I'd like to help if you'll let me," Annie said in a sad tone.

Lost in her own turmoil, Faith had forgotten that this sweet teenage girl had watched her father die only hours ago. She turned around to face Annie. "We will need your help most of all. You're the one Bitsy will want to see first. You have a place with our family, in our home, Annie."

Faith was relieved when Mike nodded his head and winked at her. Although they'd talked about what would happen to Annie if her father passed away, they'd never discussed the possibility of her coming to live with them.

"Thank you," Annie said, her voice almost a whisper.

When ten more excruciating minutes passed without word from Eli, Faith said, "I'm going to see what's happening."

"Not alone, you're not," Mike said, and the three of them jumped out of the car.

Matching each other stride for stride, they hiked the long dirt driveway in silence, the shroud of darkness offering protection. When they rounded the last bend and the trailer came into sight, they ducked behind a woodpile to shield them from view. From their vantage point, they could see the two police officers crouched down on the front porch. They assumed the two FBI agents were around back. Another few minutes ticked by before a loud bang—the sound of the trailer's front door being kicked down—penetrated the silent night. They saw shadows of figures moving around inside, but it was impossible to tell if any of them was Bitsy.

Although it seemed much longer, it was probably only a couple of minutes before Chloe appeared on the front stoop, her wrists handcuffed behind her as one of the FBI agents propelled her forward. Faith's body relaxed with relief when Eli emerged from the trailer with Bitsy in his arms, her hands gripping his neck and her legs wrapped tightly around his waist.

Faith rushed to Eli's side. "Mama!" Bitsy cried out when she saw her. "You're here."

Faith took Bitsy from Eli and held her tight. "Are you okay?" She kissed all the parts of her daughter's body she could get her lips on—hair, face, neck, hands, and bare dirty feet.

"I was scared being in the trailer. I had bad dreams about Daddy. But I had Dolly." She held up her doll. "And Chloe was nice to me. We watched SpongeBob and ate lots of pizza."

When Annie and Mike joined them, Bitsy leapt from her mother's arms into Annie's. "I knew you would come for me! I just knew it."

Forty

FAITH

FAITH AND MIKE didn't return home with the girls until nearly five thirty when the room began to turn pink with the first morning rays. Bitsy insisted that Annie sleep with her in her bed, and the two went out like flashes of light. But Faith and Mike were wound too tight to think about sleeping.

Coffee mugs in hand, they watched the sunrise from the porch, while discussing their family's future. Around seven, Faith sent a group text to her family, which included Moses, notifying them of Bitsy's safe return. "We might as well make breakfast," Mike said, rising from his rocker. "It's only a matter of time before everyone arrives. We'll let the girls sleep as long as they can."

They made large platters of scrambled eggs, french toast, sausage, and bacon. Faith set out the last of the pastries from the Island Bakery and used the juicer Moses had given them as a wedding present to make two pitchers of orange juice.

First came Jackie and Lovie with Sam and Jamie on their heels. Then Cooper and Sean stopped by in their boat on their way out fishing. Even Roberto popped in to pick up Jamie on his way to open the market. Bitsy was too busy basking in the attention to touch the food on her plate. Watching her daughter, Faith remained cautiously optimistic that the child had survived the ordeal unscathed.

They all gathered around the table, kids at one end and adults at the other, as they'd done two days ago at Mack's funeral. Cooper and Sean gobbled down their breakfast before excusing themselves in order to take advantage of the changing tides.

Mike pushed back from the table. "What say, Bitsy, are you up for working on your playhouse?"

"Yeah!" Bitsy hopped to her feet and performed a victory dance in her chair.

"If we work real hard, we might get a couple of walls up today." Mike stood with his back to Bitsy's chair. "Climb on and we'll go take inventory to see what we need from the hardware store."

Bitsy jumped on his back and he took off like a galloping pony.

Jackie took a sip of her coffee and set her mug down. "Annie, honey, my sisters and I, and Lovie of course, would like to talk to you about your plans for the future."

Annie's face filled with fear as she slowly nodded her head.

"But before we get to the future,"—Sam turned to Annie who was sitting next to her—"have you given any thought to burying your father?"

Annie shrugged. "Don't they bury people like us, people without any money, in a poor person's field?"

Sam smiled. "It's called a potter's field, but we can do better than that for your father." She brushed a strand of stringy hair out of Annie's face. "We all know how much your dad meant to you. Did he ever talk about his burial preferences?"

A look of sadness settled on her face. "He mentioned once or twice that he'd like to be cremated and his ashes spread across the water. He said the ocean was the only place he'd ever truly been happy. We have a few friends in Florida, but nobody that would come this far for his funeral."

"Then that's what we'll do," Jackie said with a decisive nod. "With your permission, I'll have Bill call MUSC and make the arrangements."

Annie was too choked up to manage more than a mumbled, "Thanks."

"You're a special person, sweetheart," Jackie said. "You've come to mean a lot to each of us in a very short period of time. If you'll have us, we'd like for you to consider us your adopted family."

Annie stared down at her plate, swiping at her eyes with the back of her hand. "I'd like that very much," she said.

"Great!" Jackie clapped her hands. "That's settled, then. All we need to do now is figure out the living arrangements, which we don't have to decide today. You have plenty of time to think about it. You can continue living in the guest cottage, if you'd like, although I'm not sure that's the best choice."

Annie looked up, surprised. "But... I thought... Cooper and Sean said their grandmamma might be moving into the guest cottage."

"We've tossed around the idea, but we haven't decided anything." Lovie glared at Jackie, although Faith knew by the tone of her mother's voice that she was teasing. "My daughter seems to think I'm not up to living alone. If you'd like to move into my townhouse with me, we could have a grand old time."

Annie's face lit up. "Think of all the new recipes we could create."

"You're welcome to live with us," Sam chimed in. "Jamie and I would be thrilled to have you."

"Jamie will be going back to school soon." Annie smiled, a mischievous twinkle in her eye. "Having a teenager living in your house might cramp your style, since it's only a matter of time before you and Eli get back together."

"A-men!" Lovie said and they all laughed.

"Then it's settled," Faith said, grinning from ear to ear. "You'll come live with us. Mike and I talked about it this morning. Having you here will make our family complete. And nothing would make Bitsy happier."

"Do you really mean it?" Annie's face brightened. "Because I would love to live here with you. I know it doesn't make much sense—I'm sixteen and she's eight—but Bitsy is like my best friend."

"The two of you need each other," Faith said. "I've known that since the night of the wedding. You're lucky to have one another."

"You'll have a built-in babysitter," Annie continued. "You and Mike can go on date nights, and I can take care of Bitsy after school if you need to work. I can help with the laundry and the cooking and the housework."

Faith brought her fingers to her lips to hide her smile. "I'm not hiring a housekeeper, Annie. Although I will certainly appreciate help with the chores. Your life has not been easy until now. But that's going to change." She gestured to her sisters and her mother. "We all want you to have a normal life. Be a teenager while you have the chance. Make friends. Go on dates with boys. Play sports."

"Go to college," Jackie added.

Annie gulped. "College?"

"Bill and I will pay for your college, if that's what you decide you want to do."

Annie placed her hand over her heart. "This is like a dream come true."

"We'll fix up the guest room any way you want it," Faith said.

"Can I move in right away?" Annie asked, on the edge of her seat.

"Of course."

She rose from the table. "I can't wait to tell Bits. I mean, if that's okay."

Faith waved her on. "Of course. Go tell her. She's gonna be thrilled. We'll listen out for her squeals."

The Sweeney women got up from the table at once and began clearing the breakfast dishes. "That girl is an enigma," Lovie said. "One minute she's like a six-year-old child, innocent and unsure of herself, and the next minute she's the streetwise young woman she's learned to be to survive these past years."

"She certainly has Sam pegged," Jackie said. "Like the rest of us, she knows what a huge mistake you'll be making if you let Eli go."

Faith bobbed her head enthusiastically, and Lovie added, "A-men again!"

"What is this, some sort of intervention?" Turning her back on them, Sam went to the sink and began rinsing dishes. "Now that you have Annie's life all sorted out, you have to start interfering in mine?"

"As a matter of fact, yes." Jackie joined her at the sink. "We didn't plan an intervention, but one is certainly in order." She took a plate from Sam and placed it in the dishwasher. "Not only is Eli one of the most handsome men I've ever had the pleasure of setting my eyes on, but he is sweet and thoughtful and supportive."

"What he has done for this family goes above and beyond the call of duty," Faith said, covering the leftover bowl of fruit with plastic wrap. "I want you to know he never left our side the whole time Bitsy was missing, not even to go home and shower."

Lovie deposited two handfuls of dirty silverware on the counter beside Sam. "Eli loves you, honey, so much. It is evident by the way he lights up when you enter the room."

"He's leaving Prospect because he can't be in the same town with you if you're not together," Jackie said. "He loves this place. One word from you, and he'll stay."

"My feelings for Eli aren't in question. I love him more than I ever thought I could love a man." Sam squirted liquid soap in a pot and began to scrub with vengeance. "I've learned a lot about myself this week. I want to be with Eli. That's not the issue. But I'm afraid. Of a lot of things. Of change. Of letting myself be vulnerable to another person. Of losing the special bond I have with my son. I can't help the way I feel."

"Tell him that, then" Jackie said, waving a dishtowel in the air. "Not only will Eli understand, he'll give you the space *and* the support you need to get over your fears."

Taking her by the arm, Lovie spun Sam around until they were eye to eye. "Eli deserves your honesty, sweetheart. It's time you stopped playing games with that man's emotions."

Forty-One

SAM

A N HOUR LATER, Sam was stopped at the light at the intersection of Main and Creekside on her way to work when blue lights appeared in her rearview mirror. She turned on her blinker and pulled into the marina parking lot.

When the police cruiser pulled in behind her, Sam was relieved to see Eli get out of the car.

Arriving at her open window, he tipped his hat at her. "Morning, ma'am. If you don't mind stepping out of the car."

"Did I do something wrong, Officer?"

"Yes, ma'am," he said in a gruff voice. "You failed to come to a complete stop when you exited the driveway two miles back."

Sam stepped out of the car. "But there is no stop sign in my sister's driveway, Officer."

"I'm going to have to issue you a citation anyway." He removed his notepad from his shirt pocket and, walking backward to the rear of her jeep, jotted down her license plate number.

Placing her hands together in prayer formation, she said, "Please, Officer. I can make it worth your while if you'll give me a warning instead. I have an exemplary driving record. I promise it won't happen again."

Eli stopped writing and looked up at her. "Are you offering me a bribe, ma'am?"

"You name it," Sam said. "I won't be able to afford my insurance premium if you give me a ticket."

He closed the space between them. "I might consider letting you off the hook if you'll agree to have dinner with me tonight."

She slumped back against the Jeep. "I would love to have dinner with you tonight, Officer, but only if we can agree to take things slow. A very wise woman recently advised me not to play games with your emotions."

"That wise woman wouldn't by any chance be Lovie Sweeney?"

Sam smiled. "The one and only."

"In that case, I think you should listen to her."

Wrapping her arms around his neck, Sam drew his face closer to hers until their lips met. As the hurt and uncertainty between them dissipated, sparks ignited and erupted into a flame. By the side of the road at the busiest intersection in Prospect, they came together in a passionate embrace, kissing for all the townsfolk to see, with toots of horns from passersby egging them on. When she finally pulled away from him, over his shoulder, she saw Jamie standing at the front window of the market offering her a thumbs-up.

"It appears as though we have an audience," she said.

Eli followed her gaze. "Who? Jamie? He's been expecting this."

Sam scrunched up her face. "Why do you say that?"

"I told him I was planning to stalk you until you agreed to take me back."

Sam stepped away from him. "I said I'd have dinner with you. I don't remember agreeing to take you back."

He ran his finger down her cheek. "It's only a matter of time. You can't live without me anymore than I can live without you."

"Does this mean you're not moving to Columbia?"

"I don't want to go." He traced her lips with his finger. "But I need a wink and a nod from you to stay."

Sam winked her eye and nodded her head. "But that's all I can give you right now, Eli. I admit that things look a lot clearer to me today than they did a week ago. But I'm still scared to death. Yes, I want to be with you. More than anything in this world. But…"

His face fell. "You don't hear wedding bells in our future."

"Is the forever commitment really necessary for expressing our love for one another?" she asked, her head cocked to one side.

"That's what I wanted to talk to you about over dinner, but I might as well say it now. I made a mistake. I got caught up in the excitement of the wedding, of seeing Faith and Mike so happy together. I didn't stop to think about how much pressure I was putting on you, about how resistant you are to change. Things were great between us before the wedding. I realize now that getting married isn't all that important to me. Don't misunderstand me. If you wanted to get married, I'd walk you straight to the altar. But no, I don't need a forever commitment as long as I have you in my life."

"What about your job in Columbia? You can't just pass up a promotion."

"Actually, Chief Andrews offered me an even better promotion to stay." He pointed at the nameplate pinned to his chest. "You may call me Lieutenant, milady."

"Eli!" She offered him a fist bump. "That's wonderful!"

"What's wonderful is that I'm next in line for detective."

"Detective? Wow! That's what you've always wanted. Congratulations."

"And I don't have to move from the town I love to get it." He leaned back against the Jeep beside her. "That's not to say I haven't outgrown my tiny apartment here. I'm in the market for a small cottage on the water. When I find it, maybe I'll invite you over to spend the night."

"I'd like that." She moved close to him, laying her head on his shoulder. "We can watch the sunrise over the water together."

He kissed the top of her head. "And, if you're a good girl, after that, I'll make you some waffles."

White Gazpacho

3 medium cucumbers, peeled seeded, chopped
3 cups chicken broth
3 cups sour cream OR 2 cups sour cream, 1 cup yogurt
3 tablespoons or sweetened rice vinegar or apple cider vinegar
2 teaspoons salt, or to taste
2 Garlic cloves, crushed

Condiments
4 medium tomatoes, peeled, seeded, and chopped
3/4 cup chopped almonds, toasted
1/2 cup sliced scallions
1/4 cup chopped fresh parsley

Put cucumber in food processor with a little chicken broth. Pour into mixing bowl add remaining broth, sour cream, vinegar, salt and garlic. Stir just enough to mix. Chill thoroughly at least 2-3 hours. Before serving, stir again and pour into chilled bowls, sprinkle condiments on top.

If you enjoyed the book and have a moment to spare, please consider posting a short review on Amazon and Goodreads to share your thoughts with others...

Please visit my website at ashleyfarley.net for more information about my characters and upcoming releases. You will also have an opportunity to sign up for my newsletter. For a limited time, just for signing up, I'm offering a free e-story that dovetails into the Sweeney Sisters Series.

A Note to Readers

EVERYTHING I'VE LEARNED during my writing journey came together for me in *Her Sister's Shoes*. After exploring the brother/sister bond in *Saving Ben*, a study of three middle-aged sisters was a nice change of pace. I was thrilled, and pleasantly surprised, when *Her Sister's Shoes* began to fly of the e-bookshelves at Amazon, Barnes and Noble, and iTunes. I was even more excited when I began receiving wonderful emails from you, my faithful readers, sharing what you enjoyed about the novel and which sister you identified with the most. You saw the Sweeney sisters as I hoped you might—flawed women facing real-life issues as they struggle to balance career and home. I returned briefly to the brother/sister bond in *Merry Mary* and *Breaking the Story*, with Scottie Darden, an impulsive photojournalist whose brother, Will, saves her from herself when she gets into trouble. Which she often does. I'm not finished with Scottie and Will, but for the time being, my heart is deep in the Lowcountry with the Sweeney family.

While I love Richmond, Virginia, my home for the past twenty years, I miss the easy-going ways of the folks who reside in the Lowcountry. Writing about these quirky characters and their unique way of life is the next best thing to experiencing them on a daily basis. I love the beauty of the area—the marshlands and moss-draped trees—and the southern accents and local cuisine. I have become so immersed in the lives of these three special ladies that I dream about them at night, think about them during the day, and plot ways for them to keep you entertained.

I love hearing from you. Feel free to shoot me an email at ashleyhfarley@gmail.com or stop by my website at ashleyfarley.net for more information about my characters and upcoming releases. For a limited time, I'm offering a free e-story, *Heading Home,* for those who sign up for my newsletter. *Heading Home* dovetails between *Lowcountry Stranger* and my third installment of the Sweeney Sisters Series, which is scheduled for release in fall 2016.

Acknowledgments

I am blessed to have so many supportive people in my life, my friends and family who offer the encouragement I need to continue the pursuit of my writing career. On the top of my list, I would like to thank my husband, Ted, not only for believing in me, but for being my biggest fan and never letting me give up. I am forever indebted to my beta readers—Mamie Farley, Alison Fauls, and Cheryl Fockler—for the valuable constructive feedback, helping me with cover design, and promoting my work. I wouldn't survive a day in the world of publishing without my trusted editor, Patricia Peters, who challenges me to dig deeper and helps me to make my work stronger without changing my voice.

A special thanks to Damon Freeman and his crew at Damonza.com for their creativity in designing stunning covers and interiors, and for their patience in dealing with my fickleness and occasional temper tantrums.

Thank you to my family and friends for your continued support. I'm so very grateful to each and every one of you. To my mother, Joanne, my Lovie, for whom this novel is dedicated. Thank you, Mom, for being you. Thanks to Karen Stephens for answering my endless questions regarding real estate. To Carter Foster, caterer extraordinaire, for her cooking tips, including the White Gazpacho recipe at the end of the last chapter. And to Catherine Kresken for scouting out restaurants and hotels in Charleston. I appreciate the folks at the Yellow Umbrella in Richmond who continue to offer great service and inspiration for Captain Sweeney's Seafood. And to all my close friends and exercise buddies, you know who you are, thank you for making my days brighter and supporting my work. Most importantly, to my children, Cameron and Ned, who provide inspiration for me every single day.